A scheme of simple petty theft runs far worse than anyone imagined in **Michael Armstrong**'s "Following the Quarters."

Mike Doogan's "Gambling on Death" becomes a deadly game when the atomic bomb tests of the 1960s yield a far more dangerous and unexpected weapon.

In **S. J. Rozan**'s "Birds of Paradise" unusual clues alight for a private eye investigating a reverend and his shady motives for preaching salvation.

And more stories of wild men, wild women, and *Wild Crimes*

WILD CRIMES

Stories of Mystery in the Wild

Edited by
Dana Stabenow

A SIGNET BOOK

SIGNET
Published by New American Library, a division of
Penguin Group (USA) Inc., 375 Hudson Street,
New York, New York 10014, U.S.A.
Penguin Books Ltd, 80 Strand,
London WC2R 0RL, England
Penguin Books Australia Ltd, 250 Camberwell Road,
Camberwell, Victoria 3124, Australia
Penguin Books Canada Ltd, 10 Alcorn Avenue,
Toronto, Ontario, Canada M4V 3B2
Penguin Books (NZ), cnr Airborne and Rosedale Roads,
Albany, Auckland 1310, New Zealand

Penguin Books Ltd, Registered Offices:
80 Strand, London WC2R 0RL, England

First published by Signet, an imprint of New American Library,
a division of Penguin Group (USA) Inc.

First Printing, September 2004
10 9 8 7 6 5 4 3 2 1

Contents

v

INTRODUCTION
Dana Stabenow

So I edited this anthology of short crime fiction called *The Mysterious North,* which was subsequently published by Signet in October 2002. Three of the stories have already been reprinted, one of them three times, and one of them, Mike Doogan's "War Can Be Murder," won the 2003 Robert L. Fish award for best mystery story.

Really, quite enough to rest on my laurels, and I would have, except that James Sarafin, whose story "The Word for Breaking August Sky," which had won the Fish award in 1996 and which I had reprinted in *The Mysterious North,* had written another story. It's a sequel to "August Sky" and one that I think is even more wonderful, and I simply couldn't bear not seeing it in print, too.

So I suggested we, well, do it again. Signet said, well, okay.

This time, I told my writers, I wanted wild, but it didn't have to be set in Alaska. I wanted them to go where the wild things are, where it's wild and fair and wild in the streets with the call of the wild ringing in their ears. (Okay, I'll stop.) I wanted, I told them, a story of suspense set in the wild.

Let's see what Webster's has to say about wild, shall we?

wild: 1. living in a state of nature; not tamed or domesticated, also "uncivilized, barbarous," "of unrestrained violence or intensity," "characterized by violent feelings or excitement," "unruly or lawless . . ."

And then there are the wilds, in the plural:

wilds: "an uncultivated, uninhabited region or tract; wilderness . . ."

So "wild" could be a strip club in Anchorage called the Alaska Bush Company, as one smart-ass who shall remain nameless but whose initials are Mike Doogan suggested. It could be the Wild Wild West, or it could be the wilds of the Canadian/American border during Prohibition, or it could be a story with a bear, or a wolf, or a really big rat if you were writing about an urban wilderness.

As I rav'd and grew more fierce and wild at every word (I lied), I told them I didn't care where the story was set, I didn't even care if there was a murder. Good, tight, suspenseful writing in rhythms measureless and wild that kept the reader in wild ecstasy seemed not so wild a dream.

Wonderful writers that they are, they responded with wild enthusiasm. In Michael Armstrong's "Following the Quarters" PI Nick Hughes and young Simeon Atanasuq stumble into a scheme that turns out to be a little more than petty theft. Margaret Coel's

"The Man Who Thought He Was a Deer" turns poaching to murder in present-day Leadville, Colorado. Mike Doogan's "Gambling on Death" plunks us down on Amchitka during the atomic bomb tests of the late sixties, where it turns out the bomb isn't the only working weapon on the island.

Loren Estleman places "The Bog" literally in our own backyard. In "The Salt Pond" Laurie R. King has turned the hoary old best revenge tale on its ear, and in Papua New Guinea, no less. Skye K. Moody's "These Crowded Woods" gives a whole new meaning to the legend of the troll under the bridge.

In Brad Reynolds's "Bad-Hearted" two Yupiq schoolgirls get more than they bargained for when they trade elder Idisore Pete *agutaq* and moose meat for stories of the old days. S. J. Rozan's "Birds-of-Paradise" proves that the righteous will triumph, given a lesson strictly for the birds.

In "The Quiet Cold," his second tale of Nuyaqpalik, the Yupiq village on the edge of the Bering Sea, Jim Sarafin exacts less than divine but much deserved retribution on a bootlegger. In John Straley's "My Heart Went Boom," Sitka detective Cecil Younger stops death from taking a walk-on part in the fifth-grade play. As for me, I think "Wreck Rights" might have been inspired by reading *Jamaica Inn* when I was too young, but private investigator Kate Shugak and state trooper Jim Chopin don't let that stop them.

Everyone anted up nicely, with each author adding new definitions to the meaning of "wild." We are not Caesar's, but we are wild for to hold, though we seem tame.

Enjoy, then, this walk on the wild side.

FOLLOWING THE QUARTERS

Michael Armstrong

The drive up the Della Spit into town didn't take Nick long, not even in his old beater Toyota pickup that could barely top 50 mph, only long enough, he thought, to contemplate explaining to his old girlfriend Martha how and why it happened that Simeon, Martha's ward and nephew, had been popped on a petty theft charge at oh-sucking-dark hundred on a wet Alaska fall morning. Nick didn't quite understand it himself. Stealing quarters from a newspaper box?

Nick drove across the little finger of land between the Spit and Della's Lake, over the causeway, and up into town, right past the old McDonald's now turned into a Thai restaurant. Nick always smiled when he drove past that resurrected Mickey D's, although it made him wonder what Simeon would make of the jailhouse food that Taco Bell served for breakfast. Simeon had always been a Happy Meals fan and might have been the only Delloid to mourn its demise.

One more block, a left at Della's only four-way stop, then a right off of Pioneer Avenue and he was at the cop shop: jail, Alaska State Trooper and Della Police headquarters, right next to the fire hall. One-stop public safety, in the thick of town. Nick could see a few trucks and cruisers in the parking lot, including ol' Roger Dodger's tricked-out cherry red '75 Ford pickup, license plate LOCKED.

Nick had to buzz the door leading into the foyer, usually open but not after hours. Roger himself met him, a guy with a thin mustache, a thick brush cut, and Buddy Holly glasses. He had a linebacker's wide shoulders and the torso and legs to support it, but a smile that disarmed even meth-head biker drunks, although Nick liked to think it was easy to have a disarming smile with a body like that. Nick had heard that in all Roger's ten years at the jail he had laid hands on only one perp, and that, as the word had it, wasn't because the perp acted up; it was just a serial rapist who had it coming.

"Hey, Nick," Roger said. "Thanks for coming down. Simeon's getting a little goofy on me."

"You think?"

"I mean, goofier than usual. Certain breeds of human don't belong in jail."

Nick nodded at what Roger didn't say. Simeon didn't like confined spaces, but then his brain was more jail than any person should endure. Concrete walls couldn't harm him more than nine months floating in an alcohol-drenched womb already had. Martha liked to say that a fetal-alcohol kid might as well have been born in jail.

"I'll make bail." Nick didn't think he had the 250

dollars in his checking account and sort of hoped that no one would have to cash his check before Nick got Simeon before a judge. "Simeon really get caught pilfering quarters from a newspaper box?"

"They call 'em 'racks,' " Roger said. "I used to do distribution for the *Peninsula Clarion* out of Kenai. Yeah, that's what the arresting officer put down." He buzzed open the door to the back. "Not that Gumbo knows shit," he said quietly.

Roger led Nick past the squad room and dispatch, back toward the jail officers' desks and their view of the two small blocks of cells, women's on the right, men's on the left. Nick could see Simeon in the nearest cell, back to them and facing the wall. He held his knees tightly against his chest and rocked slowly back and forth, back and forth, Pinky, his Beanie Baby stuffed flamingo tucked under one arm.

"Hey, Simeon," Roger said. "Got a visitor."

Simeon kept rocking.

"Simeon?" Nick asked. "Hey, pal, it's me."

Simeon's head jerked up, and he spun around, standing in what was for him an elegant movement.

"Hughesy Woozey!" he yelled.

Nick smiled. Simeon had taken to making up rhyming names, and was glad to see he'd convinced him not to use "Nicky Dicky."

"Yeah, it's Woozey. You want to get out?"

"You got my phone call? Aunt Martha called you?"

"No, you called me, remember?"

"Oh yeah. You have to make pail, right?"

"Bail. I have the money." He handed Roger a check, already filled out, and then begin filling out some forms Roger handed him. Roger nodded, took the form, hung a clipboard on a hook, then dialed into the phone and asked Lorraine in dispatch to buzz Simeon out. He opened up a filing cabinet and got out Simeon's personal effects: a still-damp jacket and Simeon's duct-taped attaché case.

Simeon ran toward Nick, all 155 pounds of him, and gave Nick a running hug. Nick knew to roll with the hug and did this little sideways dance to keep from being bowled over. But he hugged him back just as hard.

"The office-sir said I stole, Nick. I didn't steal. I was putting quarters in the rack, not taking them out." Simeon puffed up a little. "It was my *job*, and Tom said I could keep some of them, that's all."

Roger shrugged. "The rack wasn't scratched or anything. It's in Gumbo's report, but he says Simeon did have a bag of quarters, and you have to wonder why someone's putting quarters in a newspaper rack at three-thirty a.m."

"To buy a paper?" Nick asked.

"I was putting the quarters in just like Tom told me," Simeon said. "I wasn't buying papers. I'm not supposed to."

Roger shrugged, and Nick raised his hands. Even when Simeon made sense, he didn't make sense.

"Just be sure Simeon's in court at one p.m. this afternoon," Roger said. "Lawyer Andy ought to be there around eleven to meet his clients, if you want him to defend Simeon."

"I'll call Simeon's aunt—his guardian—and she'll probably get someone down from Anchorage. You ever meet Martha? She's connected to all the players in the criminal-justice system, starting with bottom feeders like me."

Roger laughed. "See you guys later. Simeon, I'm sorry I had to lock you up."

Simeon nodded. "It's OK, Roger. I'm sorry I peed in your sink." He picked up his attaché case. "Woozy, can you take me home?"

It took a while to get Simeon settled down and rested, and by the time he did, Nick couldn't get back to sleep. He supposed he should have taken Simeon back to his group home over above and behind the Thai McDonald's, on the north side of the lake, but it seemed simpler just to take care of him until court. It sort of bothered him that Simeon could slip out of the group home in the early morning, too.

Nick dreaded calling Martha, not because of the time—it was six a.m., but she ought to be up—but because of what she'd say. He could play out the conversation in his mind: Why didn't he bird-dog the group home better, why didn't he visit Simeon more. Why didn't he?

As he thought about calling Martha, he picked up the .45 Colt Commander he kept as a paperweight on his desk, right next to the phone. Nick took guns seriously, especially this one, since he'd shot and killed a man with the Colt years ago—which was why he'd filed off the firing pin and turned a nine-hundred-dollar custom handgun into a worthless pile of steel. Old habits died hard, though, and while handling it he slid back the chamber to check that a round hadn't snuck in there even though long ago he threw out every box of ammo he ever owned. Nick sighed, put down the gun, and took up the phone.

Martha answered on the second ring, sounding more alert than someone had a right to before nine a.m. He'd always hated that in her. After explaining to her that Simeon had gotten arrested, that he'd made bail, and yes, he was sleeping safely in Nick's Suckass Spit Shack, Martha paused and didn't say anything. Nick cringed.

"Nick," she said quietly, "I thought I told you to keep a fucking eye on Simeon."

"He's in a group home with two adult live-in housekeepers," Nick said. "They keep an eye on him, for at least fifteen dollars an hour." He knew; he had actually once thought of doing the job.

"Which is why he was out on the streets at three-thirty a.m. pilfering newspaper boxes?"

"Racks," he said. "Not stealing: putting quarters in." Nick paused; it still sounded goofy. "OK, I don't know what the hell he was doing, and you're right, he shouldn't have been out. You want me to call the group home?"

"No," she said. "I'll do it. I know the director at MentalHeal. Simeon's OK?"

"As if it never happened." Which, Nick knew, was more or less what went on in Simeon's mind: not much association between memories. He was perfectly amoral, because he couldn't make the distinction between cause and effect.

"I can fly down there in time for court if you want me to, Nick—bring a lawyer, dip into Simeon's trust fund." Martha had pushed for a big lawsuit against the liquor store chain that sold Simeon's mom her booze when she was pregnant; they'd settled, and Simeon was set for life, so to speak.

"If you want. I'll talk to Lawyer Andy, who does most of the criminal law in town. He could probably at least get the hearing postponed."

"Do that." Nick heard her sigh. "I'll come down. It would be good to see Simeon again. And Della." Nick waited. "OK, and you, goddamn it, Nick."

"Eleven thirty plane?"

"Yeah. Be at the airport. Oh, one other thing. I suppose it's obvious . . ."

Nick tried to think what could be so obvious, then realized. "The paper. Right. They would know if the box was pilfered."

"No pilfering, no crime."

He looked at the clock on his cheap microwave. He'd call the paper when they opened. Or maybe he'd just stop by.

Simeon came out of the back room, the converted closet that Nick had remodeled into Simeon's guest room for when he did sleepovers, and came into the cramped kitchen. One of the things Nick liked about Simeon was that he didn't talk much in the morning, just sat down with his chocolate milk and Frosted Flakes and ate. Simeon ate slowly, but Nick didn't mind; they had some time to kill. A third cup of coffee later, Nick got Simeon dressed and ready to visit the *Della News*. He'd thought of calling in a favor and having one of his old "let's just be friends" girlfriends come over and watch Simeon. Then he considered the value of visiting the *Della News* with an FAS kid going wonky and thought, Hey, there could be a tactical advantage in that.

Nick got Simeon buckled into the Toyota, and they headed over to the *Della News*. The *News* office was barely a block off Ocean Drive, but in all his years Nick never had a reason to swing by there. Ever since the little local paper had been bought by some multimedia national chain and moved across town to the south side of the lake he hadn't any real reason to visit its offices. The paper came out. He bought a copy and read it. Sometimes he phoned in a classified ad or e-mailed a letter to the editor. That was it.

The *Della News* office seemed modest enough, a single-story building sprawling on the edge of the lake. As he drove up to the place, he noticed things that made it stand out, like the recent neo-Victorian paint job, the intricate landscaping, or the little sculpture garden. Most of the cars in the paved lot looked like they'd been washed and waxed that morning, and something you'd waste money keeping clean: two Benz M30 SUVs, a Jeep Grand Cherokee, a Land Rover, even a Porsche SUV. As Nick drove in he passed a big red Chevy Suburban with DELLA NEWS painted in gold lettering on the side. It looked like a big-city paper truck scaled down to Della size.

Nick and Simeon walked in the public entrance and a man and a woman looked up at them as they came in. Eye candy, Nick thought, taken by the startling attractiveness of the two. People in Della rarely looked that good. The guy wore his hair in sort of a neo-punk style, short on the sides and then tousled into blond-tipped spikes. He had gorgeous green eyes, Nick had to admit, and a toned body that did justice to the tight pullover sweater he wore. The woman looked just as hot, with immaculate blond-streaked red hair, tasteful makeup, and a silk corset top with pink and blue roses that was as bizarre as it was archaic.

They didn't seem busy, just sitting there reading magazines or cruising the Web. They both had Mac G-4s that looked new out of the box, with twenty-one-inch flat screens. The carpet looked new, the paint new, and the display of art even newer. Nick recognized a Deland Anderson painting on one wall, a piece he had drooled over around permanent fund dividend time but couldn't quite see spending $4,500 on. Simeon stood before the painting, analyzing it like a New York art critic, bouncing up and down on his sneakers, what Nick liked to call Simeon's "steady-ready-go" stance.

"I'd like to see Mr. Tyler," Nick said. He set on the counter his business card, the one with the .45 Colt Commander logo on it right above the words HUGHES SECURITY SERVICES. He noticed a stack of glossy brochures that read ADVERTISING RATES, and snagged a copy.

"Is this regarding a legal matter?" the guy asked.

Nick shook his head. "Not yet, but you never know."

"I'll get Billy," the woman said.

A man followed her back out a moment later, walked up to him, and stuck out his hand. Nick recognized Tyler then, a guy he'd dealt with on a complicated little legal matter involving a domestic dispute. Nick nodded and kept his hands in his pockets.

"Billy Tyler," he said, letting his hand drop and dusting a bit of fluff off his slacks. "Publisher, business manager, the guy who rolls quarters." He said the last one as a little joke.

"This is my associate, Mr. Simeon Atanasuq," Nick said.

"What can I do for you gentlemen?" Tyler asked.

Nick looked at Tyler, noticed the neat khaki pants, the casual leather shoes, the Tencel shirt, the tasteful leather watch band. The look said Hollywood casual, expensive but comfortable, and if Nick had to guess, this was the guy who drove the Porsche SUV.

Tyler led them down a hall into his office, a huge suite with a knock-'em-dead view of the lake and a Cessna 185 on floats moored at a dock. Nick noted the coloring of the plane and realized it was the same as the *Della News* Suburban: red with gold lettering. The walls had more expensive art—some Nancy Yakis, a Toby Tyler, a Lynn Naden—and a shelf of bound copies of the *Della News*. Tyler sat in a leather executive chair behind a custom wood desk, a Mac G-4 on his desk and another on the credenza to the side. Nick and Simeon sat in two chairs in front of Tyler's desk.

"My assistant said this might regard a legal matter?" Nick nodded. "I'm a bit touchy about these things, as you can guess. I need to warn you that I might have to put you off while I call corporate in Atlanta."

"Sure. Let me lay out the situation and see where we can go, OK?"

"Any way I can help." He stared at Nick, and Nick thought, *Yeah, sure.*

"Simeon is one of my clients. He's an FAS kid I

watch out for as a favor to his aunt and guardian. Simeon got arrested last night for allegedly pilfering one of your racks."

"Ah." Tyler looked down at a pink message slip. "That would explain the phone call from Officer Gumbo."

"Officer Bower said he caught Simeon taking quarters out of the rack box by the Thai McDonald's. Simeon is alleged to have had a bag of quarters on his person." Nick shook his head: He hated it when he reverted to cop speak. "Just out of curiosity, and to avoid an arraignment this afternoon, I was kinda sorta wondering if you would by chance know if that box was pilfered?"

"I didn't pilfer it," Simeon said. "I was putting quarters in it."

Tyler glanced at Simeon, raised his eyebrows, then picked up the phone and punched in some numbers. "Our driver, Joe, is doing his biweekly pickup of the racks. I'm sure he did the Thai Mickey D's this morning. Ah, Joe. Hey, look, you done the McDonald's rack yet? You did? Cool. Can you bring the receipts by here? Say in five? *Bueno.*" Tyler hung up. "He's on his way from the Spit. Joe just checked the rack."

Nick eased back into his chair. He knew that, had passed the red *News* Suburban on his way in, had seen it pull out of the McDonald's parking lot. Before coming to the *Della News*, Nick and Simeon had driven back to the scene of the crime. Nick had watched Joe open and close the box, empty out the quarters, restock it, and leave. Then Nick took some digital-camera shots of the rack, making sure to get a closeup on the coin mechanism.

"Coffee? Espresso? I can have Liz make one while we wait."

"That would be great."

"Chocolate milk, please," Simeon said.

Tyler buzzed on the eye candy, and a minute later, she came in with a red-and-gold tray, three cappuccino mugs, and some of those dainty Pepperidge Farm cookies. Simeon gulped down his milk and grabbed a handful of cookies, stuffing them into his mouth in one gulp. Nick and Tyler stared each other down over their lattes, and just about when they had gotten to the eye twitching stage of a testosterone duel, Joe came in.

"What's up, Billy?" he asked.

Nick stood for Joe, because Joe was one big person, and he realized as Joe came in that he knew Joe, had seen him around town a lot, usually racing a souped-up Jap speed cycle. The red leathers and that long bleached-blond braid down his back were hard to miss.

Tyler explained the situation. Joe glanced over at Nick and Simeon, then flipped through his paperwork and handed him a yellow receipt. "I didn't count the quarters. That's Tom's thing," he said, glancing over at Nick. Tom, Nick thought. Right, the guy who handled the quarters. "But everything looked copacetic. A big bag of quarters, a few papers left."

"Would it be possible to count the quarters? I mean, right now? I'd appreciate it." He looked at Tyler, who nodded at Joe.

Joe reached into a canvas satchel, like a plumber's bag, and pawed through some plastic Ziploc bags until he found one bag in particular. He pulled out a white receipt, the original of the yellow copy, Nick guessed, and poured out a pile of quarters on Tyler's desk. Together they sorted the coins into piles of four, then counted them. Joe wrote some numbers down on the white copy and pushed it over to Tyler. He looked at it, handed it to Nick.

Nick examined the receipt. It showed that 170 papers had been delivered to the box the last Thursday, five remained, and that $41.25 in change—165 sales at a quarter each—had been collected. "Doesn't look like anything's amiss here," Nick said.

"No one tampered with our rack," Joe said. "No newspapers or money are missing." He smiled at Nick. "No one fucks with my racks, not in this town."

"I bet," Nick said.

"I'll have Joe be extra careful on his other rounds," Tyler said. "I mean, in case maybe Officer Gumbo got his retards and racks confused."

" 'Challenged,' " Nick said. "Not retard." He glanced over at Simeon. "Mr. Atanasuq is developmentally disabled, intellectually challenged."

"Oh, that is so politically correct," Tyler said. "So if there isn't anything else?"

"Uh, would it be possible for you to write up a quick statement summarizing what we just discussed? And maybe get me a copy of that receipt? I mean, just to dot our i's?"

Tyler buzzed the eye candy again, and this time the cute guy came in, passed by Joe so close he almost brushed him aside, took the receipt, photocopied it, brought it back, then left. Joe looked at the guy as he went out, and Nick noted the leering stare.

"I can give the police a call, or maybe the judge," Tyler said. "There's really no crime here."

"I'd appreciate that."

"Anything else? Maybe a free subscription?" Billy asked.

"One other thing: Simeon said some guy named Tom told him to pump quarters into the rack. Said he could keep a cut of the quarters."

Simeon perked up at the sound of his name. "Yeah, that's right. I was s'posed to put quarters in all the racks at the Mickey D's, at the grocery store, at the post office, until I filled them up and Tom said I could keep all the quarters left over." Simeon swung his feet back and forth under the chair. "Officer Gumbo took my quarters. I had some left, and they're mine."

Tyler ignored him. "Tom? Our circulation director? Now, why would he do that?"

"That's what I'm curious about," Nick said.

"Seems to me you've already satisfied your curiosity."

"You might be right. I just hate these nagging little questions."

"I'm in the business of answering questions, Mr. Hughes," Tyler said. "And I've learned that sometimes you can go a question too far, if you know what I mean."

Nick didn't; it seemed to him there were questions and then there were questions, but never too many questions—only never enough answers. He just stared back at Tyler. "Thanks for your time," he said.

"Phil will show you out. If there's anything else?"

Nick looked at Tyler's hands, at the way Tyler

rubbed them back and forth. He wanted to ask, "Broken your hand on any walls lately?" thinking of that time Tyler had thrown a punch at his ex-wife, who had hired Nick to watch her, and Nick had caught the punch by grabbing Tyler's wrists and directing the blow into a wall. Nick had thought he aimed between studs, but it was two-by-sixes on twenty-four-inch centers, and he got it wrong.

"Nah, nothing else," Nick said, and he and Simeon went out.

Out in the parking lot, Nick looked at his watch, realized that Martha would be heading to the Anchorage airport soon to fly down to Della. He called her from his cell phone, and when she didn't pick up within two rings, wondered if he had missed her. But she answered on the fourth ring, a little out of breath.

"Nick?" she said. Of course, she had caller ID, Nick remembered. She would. "Hey, I was heading out the door to the airport."

"I took care of Simeon's problem." Nick stood by his truck, looking up at the fancy *Della News* building. Simeon had already climbed in and fumbled around fastening his seat belt. He told Martha about his meeting with Tyler.

"Nice work, Hughesy," she said. "So I don't have to bring in the suits?"

"It wouldn't hurt to have them follow up with the Della cops and the court, but yeah, I think we're OK at this end."

"I could still come down."

Nick thought about it; he'd like to see Martha

again, and he knew Simeon would be thrilled. He could sense by the question, though, that Martha had other plans. "Nah, we're cool. You're coming down for Halloween, though? You know how Simeon's group home loves to decorate for Halloween."

"Sure. If you don't need me . . . ?"

"I can wait a few weeks."

"Thanks. I'm really jammed at work. I'll have one of these big-city Anchorage lawyers make a few calls. Any expenses I need to cover, other than the usual retainer?"

Nick smiled at that; the "usual retainer" was dinner out on Martha the next time she came to town. "No . . . Wait." He thought of the 250-dollar bail check. "Could you cover the bail check?"

"I'll wire the money." She paused. "Nick, thanks again. I didn't mean to yell at you earlier. It really eases my mind that you're down there in Della for Simeon."

Nick glanced over at Simeon, still fumbling with his seat belt. He sighed. "Hey, glad to help. Look, I'd better get Simeon back to his group home."

"See you at Halloween."

"Trick or treat. Wear the cat suit." She laughed and hung up.

It took the better part of the day to verify that the charges against Simeon had been dropped, that Martha had wired money to his checking account (though it turned out Nick's bail check hadn't been cashed anyway), and to get Simeon settled in at the group home. The director of MentalHeal, the mental health organization that supervised the group homes for developmentally disabled adults, met Nick personally when he dropped off Simeon. Normally she was terse and impolite, as if receiving state and federal money to care for disadvantaged adults was too great a chore. Nick figured Martha must have chewed her a new asshole, because the director was all over herself apologizing for their lax security, the poor supervision of their residents, and so on. Nick let her bow and scrape and then made sure Simeon was back home among his buddies, safe.

Back at his Suckass Spit Shack later that night, the day's drama behind him, Nick got to thinking about why the hell Simeon had been putting quarters into the downtown racks of the *Della News*. He'd never doubted that Simeon told the truth; Simeon could misunderstand things, could talk of details that for some reason stuck in his odd brain, and he could craft amazing fantasies. Lying involved a skill he hadn't quite mastered, so when Simeon explained that some guy named Tom hired him to put quarters into the red-and-gold boxes of a small-town newspaper owned by a big multimedia national chain, weird as it might seem, Nick took it as the truth. He didn't question that Simeon had done it. What he didn't understand was why.

Nick sat at the cluttered table in his kitchen, looking across the Spit Road toward Kachemak Bay, watching the sun set and a gentle surf splash against the shore. He flipped through the *Della News*, a big fat forty-eight-page tabloid-size paper, not really reading it so much as looking at it. He had never been really fond of it, not like some old-timers spoke of the paper. More than half the paper consisted of ads, lots of national ads, not a lot locally. The editorial content had maybe a half-dozen stories, much of it filler columns like The Boat Beat or On the Town, with lots of syndicated columns, food recipes, home-improvement columns, astrology guides, puzzles, and the like. The half-dozen writers on staff wrote competent stories on the usual silly politics of Della, but the reporters wrote with little style or flash. Everybody read the *Della News* because no other paper in Alaska covered the town, and besides, at a quarter a copy, it was dirt cheap.

Nick looked at the rate sheet he'd snagged at the *Della News* office. Back in college Nick worked selling ads for the school paper, had actually been pretty damn good at it, and remembered how papers calculated ad rates. Ads sold by the column inch, so many dollars an inch down, multiplied by the number of columns across. The *Della News* had six columns across, sixteen inches down, which would make each page ninety-six inches of ad or copy. He took out a ruler and began measuring and adding ads, wrote the numbers down on the back of an overdue electric bill envelope.

Nick took out a calculator, added up the inches, then multiplied by the basic ad rate. He saw that classified ads had a rate by the ad, that legal ads had another rate, but didn't separate them out, just worked on figuring out the average take per paper. He tapped in the numbers, looked at the result, did it again. The number seemed too low. That edition happened to have a postal report, and it listed the average print run broken down by subscriber and rack and counter sales, something like six thousand total. Figure a quarter a sale, the paper took in fifteen hundred dollars a week in sales. Well, advertising was the game, he knew, but still, that seemed a pissant amount for a weekly newspaper. He kept adding numbers, guessed at the salaries of the fourteen people on staff—editors, reporters, assistants, graphic artists, drivers, all of 'em—and realized that what the *Della News* took in barely paid for salaries. On top of that they had to pay printing costs, utilities, taxes, overhead. No way the *Della News* made enough money to pay its nut, not with the expensive art and employees who could afford fancy cars and nice clothes. Nick knew enough newspaper writers over the years, had seen enough papers, to know they made crap.

So where the hell did they get the money? Nick thought about the question, thought about why he asked it, and he understood.

From the quarters. It all came from the quarters.

Nick took a nap after dinner, watched a little TV, and when nine o'clock rolled around put on his prowling clothes—basic black and his surplus Soviet night-vision goggles—and fired up the old Toyota. On the way out of town he made sure to drive down some muddy roads and thoroughly cover the beater pickup truck, make it nice and anonymous.

Parked just outside of Della, on a side road with a clear view of the highway, he waited for the red-and-gold *Della News* Suburban to come down the road from Kenai. He knew the paper got printed up there at a sister publication of the *Della News*. Nick had done the math: six thousand forty-eight-page papers ought to squeeze the springs of a standard Chevrolet Suburban, but when the truck whizzed by, it rode high on its springs. Of course: If the *Della News* sold six thousand papers in Della, that meant every man, woman, and child bought a copy.

Nick eased behind the Suburban, followed it as Joe made his rounds. With that long blond braid, Joe stood out in the night. Nick parked well away from Joe when he stopped at a newspaper rack, far enough that Joe wouldn't see his truck, near enough that he could see through the night-vision goggles that Joe didn't put all that many papers in each rack, maybe a bundle or two. Nick stopped at one of the racks, the one right outside a Pioneer Avenue hotel, put in a quarter, took out a paper, and counted the stack: twenty-five papers. Not one hundred or two hundred, just twenty-five. He tried a few more racks, even at high-traffic places like the post office, and found a similar amount.

Nick followed Joe in the Suburban to the Thai McDonald's, watched him get out, load up the box, then drive away. Nick bought another paper, counted the papers that Joe had just delivered: 25, not 160. OK, maybe Joe changed the delivery amount, but that didn't make sense. Nick walked back to his truck, turned on the dome light, and glanced at the paper, with a big special fall-shopping insert. That wouldn't be an edition you'd skimp on delivering.

A shiny car pulled into the Thai Mickey D's parking lot, and Nick turned off the dome light. The car stopped under one of the high-mast lights that used to glow down on the McDonald's, the bulb now burned out. Nick raised the night-vision goggles, saw two people talking in the car, a Mercedes 330 SUV, he realized. The door opened and a slight man got out, a heavy daypack making him stoop forward. Something about the man seemed familiar—

"Shit," Nick said. "Simeon." He started the pickup, hit the gas, and drove up to the driver's side of the Mercedes, flicking on his high beams at the last moment. The driver raised his hands at the glare.

Nick jumped out, ran in front of the pickup and around to the SUV. He'd angled the pickup so that if the driver tried to open the door, the pickup trapped him. Nick yanked the door open and pulled out the driver, a slightly overweight man with slicked-back graying hair. He slammed the guy against the SUV's door, pulled the guy's right hand around and twisted it, so the only way he could move was into the door.

"Simeon!" he yelled. "Get in the truck!" Simeon just stood there, staring at Nick, confused and doing what he did when he got confused, which was nothing.

"Who the hell are you?" the guy shouted.

"Who the hell are *you*? And what are you doing messing with my pal Simeon?"

"Tom," the guy said, wincing as Nick yanked harder on his arm. "Tom Jenks. I'm the circulation director for the *Della News*."

"Tom . . ." Nick pointed a big four-cell Maglite in the guy's face. "Yeah, the guy who pays developmentally disabled people in bags of quarters to pump the *News* racks. Now, why the hell do you do that?"

Simeon came out of his daze then, moved closer to Nick's truck. "Hughesy," he said. "Hey, it's OK.

Tom was just paying me my quarters cause Officer Dumbo took them."

"See?" Tom said. "It's OK. I wouldn't hurt your friend. You can let me go."

Nick turned his arm harder, so Tom had to wrench his body around to keep his arm from breaking. "You didn't answer my question. Why pump the boxes with quarters?"

"You don't get it, do you?" Tom said. "We're laundering money. Think about it. Who would want to launder money in this turd of a little town?"

"The Mob."

"We say 'the Outfit' these days," Tom said. "Yeah, people who make money illegally and need to make it legit."

Nick thought about it, realized how it could work. You took the dirty money, all bills and cash, of course, and moved it through something that took in a lot of coins, like arcades or laundromats. The feds watched places like that since they were such obvious ways to change money, so the coin-ops had to be clean. You could launder the money through other enterprises that took in coins, though—like newspapers. Pay some mentally challenged people, the homeless, drifters, people who wouldn't talk, get them to put a lot of quarters in the racks and the money would appear clean, and if any of the quarter pumpers got caught, you'd have a cover. Show a lot of expenses, send the profits south, and that's how dirty money got washed. It explained a lot, starting with why a big media corporation run from Georgia would even buy an end-of-the-road Alaska weekly newspaper.

"It's up to you," Tom said, "but if you ask me, I think you should let me go. Take the retard home and count quarters together."

"That would be a real good idea," a guy said from behind Nick. Joe grabbed Nick's biceps, lifted him up, and shoved him against the pickup. Nick bent his knees as he hit the truck, taking the blow on a hip.

Tom stood up, rolled his shoulders a bit, then came up to Nick and threw a roundhouse punch at Nick's jaw. Nick saw it coming and turned his head with the blow to take as much of it as he could. Still hurt like a sonofabitch, though. But the momentum caused Joe to step back and pull Nick away from the truck, giving Nick just enough room to step forward, reach up and grab Joe's left hand with both of his hands, turn, kneel down, and use the motion to break out of Joe's grip and come behind him. Nick intended only to run away, around to the driver's side of his truck, shove Simeon in and get the hell out of there.

Except that he saw Joe's long white-blond braid hanging down his back, and it tempted him. Joe kinda pissed him off, and he needed to hurt Joe hard enough that Joe wouldn't mess with him. Nick grabbed the end of the braid, swung it around Joe's neck, and with one hand choked Joe with his own hair and with the other hand pulled on the base of the braid so that Joe had to bend backward. One quick snap and Nick could break Joe's neck.

"Easy, easy," Tom said. "You seem like a reasonable guy. . . . Joe, just who the hell is this guy anyway?"

"Hughes," Nick said. "Nick Hughes."

"So, Hughes, on the one hand you don't want to mess with the Outfit because we could kill you, or hurt you really bad, or hurt Simeon really bad. Only, that's so twentieth century, all that violence. I'm more inclined to bribe you to shut you up. Need a new truck? Maybe an infusion of cash? Get you a job with the *Della News,* nice salary with benefits. That's how we bought off everyone else there."

"I'm kind of a fan of the old ways," someone else said.

Nick looked up, saw Tyler, Billy Tyler, standing behind Simeon. Tyler held what looked like a Colt Commander, his Colt Commander, he realized, the one with the special bluing and the fossil ivory handle. Bastard must have broken in to the Suckass Spit Shack, where Nick left it on the desk by his phone. Nick never took it anywhere, never used it, after long ago realizing that guns created more problems than they solved. He kept it around only for sentimental purposes.

"I'll really scramble this retard's brains," Tyler said. "Then take a piece out of you."

"I'm not a retard," Simeon said quietly. Nick saw Simeon tense up, then relax. He smiled to himself. Simeon didn't have the patience to learn the art well, but he learned a few things. Nick knew Simeon really hated to be called a retard, and Nick knew that if you wanted to get Simeon mad, mad enough to step out of the complacency of his damaged mind, that would do it.

Nick saw the four men there: Tom relaxed and leaning against the Benz, Joe struggling to breathe,

Simeon shuffling around with the Colt at his head, Tyler holding the gun and trying to figure out what to do next.

Then the lights came on.

It seemed, Nick would think later, as if the flashes came from everywhere, and he'd later find out that the Feds only tossed in three flash-bang grenades. Nick blinked his eyes and felt Joe go slack on him, realized he held the cut end of Joe's braid in his hand and saw Joe turn and raise the knife toward him, or something toward him; he didn't quite understand what Joe had done until he saw the knife and knew that to get away from Nick, Joe had flipped open a knife and sliced away his own hair.

Even in the noise and confusion, Nick saw that he could step away from the knife and avoid the blow, and reached up to do so when he heard the shot and saw Joe's hand quiver from the shock of the bullet ripping through Joe's arm, saw the knife fall free and Joe fall to the ground. Nick dropped down, too, but not before he heard a click as Tyler pulled the trigger.

Simeon would later tell him that when the flashes went off, he dropped down, letting the weight of all the quarters in the daypack pull him down. A good thing, too, Nick found out, because when Tyler pulled the trigger, the FBI sharpshooter who shot off Joe's arm put a second round right through Tyler's head. No one really needed to see that.

When the shooting stopped and Nick got his vision back, he saw men in jumpsuits rush forward and grab Joe and Tom. Other men hustled him away to the edge of the parking lot where the Feds had staged and they dragged Simeon to safety. They

handed him off to some troopers and Della cops
backing up the Feds, although from the looks of the
men in the jumpsuits, they didn't need much backing up.

Roger led Nick and Simeon over to an EMT and a
crash truck, and the EMT checked them out, made
sure the blood on Simeon belonged to Tyler. Roger
handed Nick a cup of coffee. He'd have preferred a
beer—hell, a shot of tequila—but the coffee felt
comforting.

"You OK, Simeon, Nick?" Roger asked.

Simeon blinked his eyes. "Roger Dodger! Do I
have to make pail again?"

"No, you're not going to jail, guy," Roger said.
"You're cool."

"Where the hell did the Feds come from?" Nick
asked.

"Anchorage. Seattle. They've been on the case for
half a year." He pointed at a Fed in a sharp black
suit, and Nick realized it was Phil, the eye candy at
the *News*. "Undercover, too." Phil walked over to
them, introduced himself as Agent Gray.

"So why'd you come in balls busting now?" Nick
asked. "The *Della News* is one big money-laundering
scheme, right?"

Phil looked at Simeon. "Mr. Atanasuq's arrest
cinched it," he said. "We've been following the
money—following the quarters." He held out his
hand, a normal-looking quarter in it, then shined a
flashlight with a purple glow to it. "Ultraviolet light
and paint. We suspected a Laundromat up in Kenai
was how the money got processed, but we didn't
know where it went. So we put quarters painted with

ultraviolet paint in the machines, tailed the drivers who came in to pick up the quarters. The trail led to Della and got cold, until some of these quarters showed up in the bag when Officer Bower arrested Mr. Atanasuq. Then we followed the two of you."

Nick looked over at Tyler's body, uncovered at the police scene. One of the *Della News* reporters had shown up and took a shot of the body with a tele-photo lens. Must have been weird, Nick thought later when he saw the front-page photo the next week, taking a photograph of the corpse of the guy who signed your paychecks.

"He used my gun," Nick said, looking at Tyler. "I filed the pin off of it fifteen years ago."

Agent Gray shrugged. "Our sharpshooter didn't know that."

"No," said Nick. "No, he didn't."

Nick looked around at the chaos, at the cops, the troopers, the federal agents, at the crowd of his neighbors and friends awakened by gunshots and si-rens. Simeon smiled at him, that innocent, nearly mindless smile. Roger had gotten him a cup of cocoa, with marshmallows like Simeon liked, and the vio-lence didn't even touch him. The EMTs had cleaned the blood off of Simeon's face, but splatters still dot-ted Simeon's jacket, splatters of blood and other stuff.

The sun rose over the mountains at the head of Della's Lake, a good crisp early-fall morning. The FBI had taken Simeon's backpack, and they still crowded around Nick's truck. Nick put an arm around Simeon and they began walking away.

"Want to get some breakfast?" Nick asked.

"At Mickey D's?"

"No, it's closed, remember? How about we walk up to the Bear Claw and put away an omelet?"

"Can I get a Happy Meal there?"

"Maybe," Nick said, not wanting to explain what Simeon couldn't quite understand. "Maybe."

THE MAN WHO THOUGHT HE WAS A DEER

Margaret Coel

She was so pretty.

Her coat was like gold, and sleek. Not the matted, dull coat of the other yearlings. He had been watching over her since the day she was born a year ago June, in the meadow up the mountain. Spindly legs and a little white rump that floated through the wild grasses. She'd moved with such grace and confidence that he'd started crying, despite himself. And he'd made her a promise: "No harm will come to you, pretty one. I'll look after you."

It was his job. Dennis Michael Lockett was his name, but that was in the human world, before he'd become a deer. And not just one of the herd roaming the wilderness of Mount Massive. He was the chief. He took care of the herd. Even the bucks—including the old one-horn that lost half a rack last rutting season—bowed to him. Literally bowed. Bent their front legs and swung their racks up and down. Oh, they understood he'd come into the wilderness to save them from the cruelty of humans. Men tramping up the mountain with guns to harvest the dear. Harvest! Even the word was cruel.

A rifle shot sounded in the distance. Pretty didn't move, but Dennis caught sight of the tremor running along her flank and down her legs. She was waiting for him in the trees up above, head crooked back, brown, patient eyes beckoning him forward. He adjusted his rifle in the sling that he'd buckled over his orange jacket and started climbing. A snowy sky poked through the tops of the spruce trees. He had to duck past the branches covered with last night's snow, his breath floating ahead in gray puffs. He picked his way through the ice-crusted undergrowth so that the scrunching noise wouldn't alarm her.

Maybe she'd let him touch her this time. Pat her back, scratch her ears a little, let her know everything was gonna be fine. He bet she'd like that.

He was close enough to make out the drops of moisture on her coat. Just as he reached for her, she bolted, swinging her head and running for the meadow beyond the trees. She ran like a dancer, high on her toes, gliding around the branches. The pleasure in watching her almost eclipsed the stab of disappointment he'd felt when she turned away.

Another rifle shot cracked the air. Dennis held his breath, trying to gauge the distance by the reverberations. Close. His heart felt as heavy as lead. The hunter was coming for his herd. And Pretty—where was she? In the meadow? There were no trees in the meadow, no protection.

Dennis started running up the slope, crashing through the branches that tore at his jacket and scratched his face. He darted out of the trees and into the meadow. The wild grasses rose out of the ground like stalks of ice. Looming overhead were the barren, snow-dusted peaks of Mount Massive. Pretty stood about thirty feet away, her little head lifted toward the dark figure crouched in the outcropping at the far edge of the meadow. The hunter's orange hat bobbed over the boulders.

Dennis sprinted toward Pretty, waving his arms overhead so that the hunter would see him—an orange streak through the meadow.

"Mine! Mine!" he shouted. "Don't shoot."

The rifle shot almost knocked him off his feet. He staggered sideways before regaining his balance. Then he waved his orange cap toward the boulders, shouting and crying, "No! No!"

But it was too late. Pretty was down, her golden body sunk into the grass. He could see the depression, like a grave. He stumbled forward, then dropped on his hands and knees and crawled to her. She lay on her side, left leg twitching, brown eyes—so sad now—staring at him. He watched her heart thump against the shiny coat a couple times, and then she was still, her eyes frozen and dull. He ran his hand over her flank. Her coat was so soft, it made him weep.

After a moment, he wiped at the moisture on his cheeks with his jacket sleeve and pushed himself to his feet. The killer was crouched in front of the boulders, shoulders and head jutting toward the meadow, as though he couldn't understand why another hunter had claimed his kill. The fluorescent orange jacket and orange cowboy hat shimmered in the flat, gray light.

Dennis reached back, unsnapped the sling, and pulled out his rifle, not taking his eyes off the killer. He brought the orange vest into the crosshairs before his finger squeezed the icy metal trigger.

Holy shit! Mickey Hoffman dove backward and clambered into the boulders. The bullet had whooshed past him like a rocket. His shoulder was burning. He took off his glove and dipped his fingers into the warm stickiness of his own blood. Then he pressed himself against the rough granite surface, unable to stop shaking.

The crack of another shot reverberated around him, bouncing off the trees and boulders. Just his luck to run into some crazy coot. How'd he know another hunter was stalking that little deer? He hadn't seen the guy until he came bounding out of the trees, yelling and hollering. Wonder the deer didn't take off. But she was his kill. So the other hunter was pissed off, so what? He was willing to share the meat.

"Hold on," Mickey shouted. "Let's parley."

The guy fired off another shot. Pieces of granite, sharp as needles, exploded in Mickey's face. What the hell? His heart knocked against his ribs. He had to get out of here before the crazy coot killed him.

There was another shot, then another. He started crawling through the boulders. His truck was in the trees about twenty feet away. He'd have to make a run for it, but the coot would pick him off for sure.

Crouching low, he worked his way out of his jacket, then took off his cowboy hat and rolled them together, fiddling with the jacket snaps until he had a floppy basketball, which he threw as hard as he could across the boulders, away from the trees. He sprinted for the truck. The sound of the rifle shot shook the ground under his boots.

He threw his rifle into the cab and, wincing with the pain in his shoulder, jumped in after it. He stomped on the accelerator and headed into a narrow tunnel of trees before turning away from the meadow. The truck bounced over the scraggly brush and up onto the dirt road, tires squealing, rear end slipping on the hard, icy ground. The campsite was five miles away. He hadn't spotted any other vehicles parked in the area. Chances were good the crazy coot was on foot.

Mickey drove with one hand and clamped the other over his shoulder. The blood oozed through his fingers.

He drew in a long breath. He was safe.

Dennis clambered over the boulders and stared at the pickup bouncing down the mountain, belching black smoke from the tailpipe. The mixture of grief and anger that boiled inside him was so strong he had to hold on to the edge of a boulder to steady himself. Distracting the hunter was the oldest trick in the book, and he'd fallen for it. Even the old bucks knew the trick, but Pretty—she hadn't been on the earth long enough to know how to survive. He should have protected her.

He knew where the killer was going. All them

killers stayed at Halfmoon Campsite. Five miles down the winding, narrow dirt road. Two miles, the way the crow flies. He could run down the mountain like a deer. He'd be waiting when the killer pulled in.

Deputy Sheriff Shelly Maginnis knocked on the front door of the two-story Victorian house on West Seventh Street in Leadville. Strips of brown wood showed through the faded yellow paint on the facade. The once-blue trim around the windows was almost white. She glanced around. Black clouds drifted down the slopes of Mount Massive west of town. There was a cold bite in the air. It would snow again today. It always snowed in October in deer hunting season.

She knocked again, wondering what was taking Mrs. Lockett so long to respond. The woman had called the sheriff's department thirty minutes ago. Sheriff Nichols himself had spoken with her, then planted himself in the doorway and surveyed the empty desks in the outer office. The other two deputies were already out on calls. She was the only one free.

"Maginnis," he'd shouted. "Get over to Marybelle Lockett's place. See what the hell's going on with Dennis. Don't know why his mother don't put that boy in an institution. Gonna be the death of her, if he don't kill somebody else first." He'd paused at that, then disappeared back into his office.

Shelly didn't mind taking the call. She'd known Dennis Lockett all her life. Went to school with him, until Dennis dropped out of Leadville High somewhere around tenth grade. Sure, he was an oddball, but who wasn't these days? She'd have a talk with Mrs. Lockett, then talk with Dennis and see what was bothering him. In any case, it felt good to get out of the office. She'd been cooped up indoors with paperwork for two weeks while the other deputies had taken the calls. It wasn't just that she was the only woman: She refused to believe that had anything to do with it. She was the greenhorn, that was all. She still had a lot to learn.

She pounded on the door and pressed her face against the oblong block of beveled glass to one side. The blurred figure of Mrs. Lockett emerged from the kitchen in back and headed into the living room. A second passed before the door creaked open. The woman wasn't much older than fifty, Shelly guessed, but she looked ancient, with deep furrows in her brow and eyes red rimmed from crying. Her gray hair was pinned back, except for a strand that had worked loose and fallen over her cheek.

She said, "You gotta help my boy."

Shelly followed the woman into the tidy living room with an Oriental rug spread over the wood floor and crocheted doilies on the high-backed Victorian chairs. The air was close and stale, like the air in a museum.

"What's going on?" Shelly waited until the woman dropped into one of the chairs before she sat down across from her.

"Every time hunting season comes around," the woman began, "Dennis gets himself into a tizzy. No telling what he might get up to. You gotta bring him home, Shelly, where I can look after him."

"Where is he?"

"Staying in that old prospector's cabin on Emerald Lake."

Shelly could picture the place. Kids in Leadville grew up hiking in the mountains around town. They knew all the prospectors' cabins and abandoned mine shafts and wagon roads left behind from the time when silver and gold had flowed out of the mountains like molten rivers.

"Haven't seen my boy in two weeks now," Mrs. Lockett went on. "I been taking his food up to the cabin every couple days, but he ain't there. Oh, I know what he's up to." She was ringing her hands in her lap. "He's out with the deer herd."

"Hunting?" Shelly heard the surprise in her voice. Dennis was always a sensitive kid, the perfect target for the other boys to bully. She couldn't imagine Dennis hunting.

The woman leaned so far forward, Shelly thought for an instant that she would tumble out of her chair. "My boy don't go hunting deer. He *is* a deer."

"What!"

"I'm trying to tell you, Shelly, that Dennis thinks he's a deer. He's got himself a human body, but inside, he says, he's a deer. He says it's his job to protect the rest of the herd up on Mount Massive 'cause he's got advantages. He knows all about people. So he wears an orange hunting jacket and cap and goes out with the herd, thinking the hunters'll see him and won't shoot."

"Dennis'll get himself shot by accident."

The woman flinched, and Shelly regretted having blurted out the thought. She would have to learn to keep her thoughts to herself.

Mrs. Lockett drew herself upright, as if she were drawing on some invisible reserve of strength. "I guess he's safe enough with his orange on," she said. "It's them hunters I'm worried about. They come after Dennis's herd, he's likely gonna shoot 'em. You gotta find him before he kills somebody."

Shelly got to her feet. She could see the campers and pickups that had been crawling through town all week, rifles locked in frames across the rear windows. Dozens of hunters heading into the mountains to harvest deer. And waiting for them was a crazy man with a rifle.

"I'll see what I can do," she managed.

She'd started for the door when the older woman propelled herself out of her chair. "Wait a minute," she said, heading toward the kitchen.

After a moment, she returned and handed Shelly a bulky brown bag. "Will you take this here food up to my boy?" she said. "Some bread, vegetables, fruits, nuts. Deer don't eat meat, you know."

"Deer don't eat meat?" Shelly repeated the words out loud as she drove south through town on Highway 24. Hard to tell who was crazier, Mrs. Lockett or Dennis. At any rate, Dennis was the one with the rifle, and she was going to have to find him before he killed somebody.

She was halfway to Emerald Lake on the two-lane road that wound around the base of Mount Massive—too far out of town, she hoped, for the sheriff to call her back—before she picked up the radio and called the office. When she had Sheriff Nichols on the line, she told him what Mrs. Lockett had said.

"Soon's they get in, I'll send Ellis or Moore after Dennis," the sheriff said.

"I'm twenty minutes from the cabin." Shelly steeled herself for the reply.

"Damn it, Shelly. The man's dangerous."

"I've known Dennis for years." A man who thought he was a deer? She didn't know him at all. "I'll be okay," she heard herself saying.

"Stay in contact. Oh, and Shelly, you got orange with you?"

Shelly glanced around at the supply kit in the back. "Yeah."

"You put it on, hear?"

Shelly drove the Bronco up what passed for a road, the engine screaming in low gear, tires crawling over the rocks and slipping on the ice. Last night's snow glistened on the branches of the spruce and alpine fir that clawed at the sides of the Bronco. The rock-strewn slopes and shadows of the forest rose on both sides of the road. She had a sense of the mountain itself closing in upon her.

She'd come around a wide bend when she spotted the logs piled across the road ahead. Dennis. He didn't want hunters in the wilderness. She shook her head at the futility: He couldn't block all the roads.

Shelly parked with the front bumper up close to the logs and got out. The snow blowing off the trees felt like ice pelting her face, and the wind pressed her uniform against her skin. Shivering, she pulled on the orange vest over her jacket, glad for the extra layer of clothing. Then she put on the orange cap.

A rifle shot cracked the cold air, followed by another and another. She stared at her own rifle locked in the frame inside the Bronco, debating whether to take it. She had her revolver; she was suddenly conscious of the weight of the gun on her hip. But a revolver in the mountains with the far distances . . .

She unclipped the rifle from the frame, grabbed the bag of food, and headed up the road. The ground was hard with the cold and snow; the pine needles crackled under her boots. After about a half mile, the road veered to the right. She turned left into the forest and started climbing the steep slope. The air was filled with the odors of dense under-growth and fallen, rotted trees. As she ducked past the branches, snow showered down on her. Icy flakes stuck inside her collar and dripped down her back.

She was breathing hard when she reached the top of the slope. Beyond the tree line, the lake lay quiet and gray under the heavy sky. In the clearing, close to the shore, was the cabin, a lopsided wreck of old logs topped with a rusted tin roof. The place proba-bly hadn't changed much since the day the prospec-tor had walked away a hundred years ago.

"Dennis!" Shelly called. She stayed back in the trees, her eyes searching the cabin and the clearing. No sign of anyone.

Hoisting the rifle, she hurried across the clearing to the cabin and pushed open the door. A column of gray light fell over the bunk against the far wall. In the center was a chair and a table made of a plank on two upright logs. A dark jacket hung off a hook on the log wall, and next to the jacket was a rack of guns. The top space was empty.

Shelly set the bag of food on the plank table and

went back outside. Silence, except for the wind in the trees and the distant crack of a rifle. She looked around, half expecting to spot Dennis lurking about somewhere. She could make out the faint mark of her own boot prints in the snow, and beyond the cabin, leading back into the trees, another set of boot prints, as clear as if Dennis had left her a map.

She fingered the radio in her belt, debating whether to check in with the office, then decided to wait. Dennis had probably heard her approaching and was hiding nearby. She wouldn't have any trouble finding him.

She started following the boot prints. For the most part, they moved in a straight line through the trees, but here and there, they doubled back, then shot ahead again, as if Dennis wasn't sure where he wanted to go. Shelly crouched low, not taking her eyes from the trail. It was easy to get disoriented in the mountains; it happened to hunters all the time, and it was the sheriff's deputies who had to go out and find them.

She could see the boot prints running ahead into a meadow. And there were other prints now: small bisected marks of deer hooves. The meadow was a good hunting place, she thought. Close to the lake, plenty of wild grass. And the hunters had a clear shot from the trees and rock outcroppings around the periphery.

Shelly stopped at the edge of the trees. She could hear her heart thudding in her ears. The meadow was almost a perfect circle, quiet and peaceful, layered with ice that glinted like glass. On the opposite side was an outcropping of granite boulders, and rising over the meadow, the brown, snow-washed shoulders of Mount Massive. The meadow was no place for a human being in hunting season; no place for a man who thought he was a deer.

When she was certain there was no movement around the periphery, Shelly started forward, glad for the orange vest and the too-big orange cap that flopped over her ears.

"Dennis! Where are you?" she shouted. The grass was trampled, as if he'd been running, hitting the earth hard, but he was nowhere in sight.

Then she saw the brown hump. She moved closer. Somebody had harvested a deer: a young doe, probably a yearling, stretched on its side, thin legs frozen in the air, brown eyes staring into nothingness. Odd, she thought. Hunters didn't walk away from the kill. They cleaned the carcass and took the meat.

Dennis had found the animal, probably knelt down, judging by the depressions in the grass. And there was something else: the glint of a gray metal cartridge. She scooped it up and rolled it around her palm. A rifle cartridge. She spotted two more cartridges, which she dropped into her vest pocket with the first. Then she started following the tracks across the meadow, glancing about as she walked. Her skin felt prickly; the rifle a dead weight in her hand.

She reached the outcropping on the far side and made her way around the boulders, losing Dennis's trail, then picking it up again in the snow. There were other boot prints; hard to tell which belonged to Dennis and which belonged to . . . a hunter? As she came out on the far edge of the outcropping, she spotted the blood-spattered boulder.

"What the hell happened up here?" she said out loud, startled by the sound of her voice in the quiet. She clambered back up onto a boulder and peered around the area. A vehicle had been parked in the trees. She could see the depression made by the tires.

A picture was moving in her mind, like an old film, jumpy and black-spotted, cutting off and starting up again. You had to pay attention to make sense out of it, but it was all there, in front of her. Dennis had found the doe in the meadow and had shot at the hunter. The cartridges were from Dennis's rifle. The hunter had been hit, but he'd gotten to his truck and driven away.

And—the film rolling to the climax now—Dennis had gone after him. Which meant he knew where the hunter was headed: Halfmoon Campsite, where most of the hunters in the Mount Massive wilderness stayed.

The hunter was wounded, she reminded herself. If he had any sense, he'd drive straight down to town and find a doctor. But she knew hunters, knew the type. He'd want to collect his camping gear. He'd figure he had plenty of time. He had a vehicle and Dennis was on foot. But Dennis knew every inch of the mountain. He'd head straight downslope, and when the hunter drove into the campground, Dennis would be waiting.

Shelly grabbed her radio and pressed the cold plastic against her face. "Deputy Maginnis here," she shouted into the mouthpiece.

"Where the hell are you?" The sheriff's voice crackled back at her.

She gave her position and told him what she'd learned. "I'm on my way to Halfmoon," she said.

"Negative. Get back . . ."

Shelly cut him off. She stared at the inert plastic in her hand, then clipped it on to her belt. It clanked next to her handcuffs. Mrs. Lockett's voice sounded in her head, as sharp as if the woman were next to her: *You gotta find him before he kills somebody.*

The rifle shot jolted the truck, sending it swerving across the campground. Mickey fought the steering wheel for control and tapped on the brake, finally bringing the truck to a stop next to the fire pit. Another shot crashed through the windshield.

Mickey rammed down the door handle and slid onto the ground, hunkering close to the front tire. He peered around. There was an orange flash in the trees on the north edge of the camp. He spit out the wad of acid that had welled up in his mouth. How the hell that crazy coot get there so fast?

Mickey gripped his wounded shoulder—it was numb now and stiff—his eyes following the orange in the trees. Should've gone straight down to Leadville, he told himself. Now he was facing off with a nutcase, nobody else in shouting distance.

Okay. He drew in a long breath; the cold air burned in his chest. He'd faced worse in Nam, gooks in front and gooks in back firing away at him. He'd taken a couple slugs in the gut that made the shoulder graze look like a splinter. He was a survivor.

"Come and get me, you bastard," he shouted at the orange weaving back and forth.

"Why'd you kill Pretty?"

Hello, looney tunes! The guy's voice was as high-pitched as a girl's, and real shaky, like he was scared shitless. Scared killers. In Nam, they were the most dangerous.

"She ain't dead, you fool," Mickey shouted. "Look over there on the right. She done followed you."

A half second was all he needed. The orange jacket hesitated, then swerved to the right. Mickey reached up, grabbed his rifle out of the front seat, and ran into the trees on the left.

The orange vest had turned around. Mickey saw the rifle come up. Another shot fractured the air between them. A cloud of dust and snow swirled around the front of the truck, and one of the wheels sank into the ground.

"That's right," Mickey said under his breath. "You think you got me pinned by the truck. Come on, bastard. Come on."

The coot stepped out of the trees, hesitated, then started walking at a diagonal from Mickey, the rifle trained on the truck.

Mickey lifted his own rifle and sighted in the orange vest.

The rifle shots thudded through the trees.

Shelly was running full out down the slope, gripping her rifle in both hands, crashing through the branches and scrub brush. She could see Dennis standing in the middle of the campsite, arms raised into the sky, eyes wide with surprise, like those of a deer suddenly aware he was in the hunter's crosshairs.

A rifle lay at his boots.

She stopped running. Her chest felt like it was going to explode. Someone else—a man—was crouched in the clump of trees directly below, a rifle pointed at Dennis.

"Drop the gun!" Shelly shouted. "Sheriff's officers!" She reached down for a dead branch and threw it as hard as she could to the man's left, desperate to make it seem that there were others, that she wasn't alone.

"We got you covered," she yelled, working her way down the slope.

The man didn't move. His rifle was still on Dennis.

Shelly lifted her own rifle and fired into the air. She scrambled backward with the recoil.

"Set the gun on the ground," she yelled. She was about fifteen feet behind the man. He knew—she could see it in the drop of his shoulders—that she was close enough to blast a hole in his back. He set the gun down.

"Kick the guns to the side, both of you. Do it now!"

The man stuck out his boot and gave the rifle a shove.

"Harder!"

He shoved the rifle again. It was more than an arm's length away.

Dennis was reaching down. "Don't touch the gun!" she shouted. "Kick it away."

"Shelly! That you?"

"Do like I say, Dennis, or we're gonna have to shoot you." Her heart was hammering. There was no *we*.

Dennis prodded the rifle with his boot, then sent it skimming over the ground. "He's a killer, Shelly."

Shelly walked down and picked up the other hunter's gun. She could see the blood-matted spot on the shoulder of the tan jacket. Stepping back, she shoved the gun into the scrub brush.

"I got a right to defend myself," the man said. "Guy's crazy. Shot me up at the meadow."

"Shut up and get down on your stomach," Shelly said, trying to keep her own fear out of her voice. "Face into the dirt." She waited while the man flattened himself around the brush and rocks. Who would believe it? she was thinking. She'd run to the campsite to save some hunter, and now it looked like she'd saved Dennis. She had no idea who the hunter was, but she knew Dennis. She had to take a chance on what she knew.

"Get over here, Dennis," she shouted.

He started walking up the slope, his hands shaking at his sides, as if they'd come unstuck from his arms.

"He killed Pretty." It sounded like a whimper.

"I know."

"I was just gonna punish him."

"You can't take the law into your own hands, Dennis. You know that."

"I got a license to kill that damn deer." There was a hard resolve in the hunter's voice. He was dangerous.

"Scoot yourself over to the truck," Shelly said.

"You alone, ain't you, lady?"

"I got this." Shelly fired the rifle again. "Do like I say, or the next shot's for you."

The man started pulling himself forward on one elbow, dragging his wounded shoulder, digging the toes of his boots into the ground. His stomach bumped over the rocks. Finally he lay still next to the truck.

Shelly unhooked the handcuffs from her belt and tossed them to Dennis. "Get a cuff on his left wrist," she said.

Dennis stared at the cuffs as if they were fireworks about to explode in his face.

"Do it, Dennis."

He started shuffling toward the truck, and Shelly moved closer to the man stomach down on the ground. "One wrong move, cowboy," she said, "and you're a dead man."

Dennis leaned over and clamped on the handcuff.

Shelly said, "Raise your left arm alongside the truck, cowboy."

He started to turn on his wounded shoulder, winced, and dropped his forehead on the ground. Slowly, his left arm started scrabbling up the side of the truck. "You're gonna pay for this." He spit out the words. "I gotta get to the hospital."

"Okay, Dennis," Shelly said. "Cuff him to the door handle."

Dennis looked around, like a deer about to bolt.

"You can do it, Dennis."

Dennis stood frozen in place.

"Come on." Shelly motioned him with the rifle. "I don't wanna have to shoot both of you."

"For crissake!" the hunter shouted. He raised himself up on his knees and snapped the other cuff to the door handle. "You happy now? Get this nutcase's rifle before he kills you and me both."

The hunter was right. Dennis's eyes were sliding toward the rifle about fifteen feet away.

"On the ground, Dennis," she said.

"I ain't gonna hurt you, Shelly." Dennis did a half

turn toward the gun. She could sense his muscles coiled for the sprint.

"I know that. Your mother sent me up to find you."

"Huh?" He swung toward her.

"Sit over there." She nodded toward a large rock and held her breath. If he went to the rock, she could get between him and his rifle. "Your mother's real worried about you."

Dennis rolled his head around, as if he expected his mother to walk out of the trees. "She don't understand."

"I understand. You're a deer now."

The man handcuffed to the truck let out a loud guffaw. "What is this, Disneyland?"

Dennis looked as if his legs had started to melt beneath him. He stumbled backward, grabbed for the rock, and dropped down.

"How'd you know?" he said.

"Your mother said something about it." Shelly moved sideways to the rifle. She picked it up, then walked over to the trees and pushed the gun into the shadows, out of sight.

Still keeping her own rifle on Dennis, she fumbled for the radio and called the sheriff.

The sheriff's voice burst through the static. "Damn it, Maginnis. What's going on?"

"I'm at Halfmoon," she said. "I've got Dennis and another guy covered. They're both disarmed. Could use some backup about now."

"Ellis and Moore are on the way. You gonna be able to hang on?"

"Looks like it." Yes, she could hang on, she was

thinking. Everything under control. She heard the sound of her own breathing—slow and regular.

She shut off the radio and smiled at Dennis.

"Tell me about Pretty," she said.

GAMBLING ON DEATH
Mike Doogan

Speedy Dave hated mornings. He hated opening his
eyes. He saw things. Not just the fake wood walls of
his room in the barracks trailer. Not just the empty
jug of Canadian Club, a new one every morning, that
sat next to his little traveling alarm clock on the built-
in nightstand. Things. Creepy things. People, mostly.
Sometimes it was the doughboys he'd seen when he
was one himself, seventeen years old and scared shitless. They'd frozen overnight after being blown up
by Kraut artillery in their dugout. Sometimes it was
an operator named Terry Grady who had his head
torn off when a crane cable snapped and came strik-
ing back into the cab like a huge, hungry snake.
Sometimes it was somebody who was still alive,
really, somebody from the shower room or the mess
hall dead in some god-awful way. Speedy Dave lay
in bed, listening to the noises of the camp coming
awake and getting up his nerve. He had to open his
eyes. He needed to keep this job for just three more

months and he'd get his pension. He raised himself up on an elbow and forced his eyelids apart.

It was one of the still-alive ones this time, a desk jockey Speedy Dave had seen around. The desk jockey had the handle of a knife sticking out of his chest and old blood that stained his shirt and the blanket on the bunk where he lay. Speedy Dave shut his eyes again, squeezing the lids tight, and counted to ten. That made them go away sometimes. But when he opened his eyes again, the desk jockey was still there. It was going to be one of those mornings. Speedy Dave got out of bed, careful not to look at the desk jockey again, and put on a bathrobe that didn't hide his thin, wrinkled calves. He grabbed his shaving kit and walked down the hall to the shower room. He'd take a long shower, and the desk jockey would be gone when he got back.

The desk jockey wasn't gone. Speedy Dave put on almost-clean underwear, blue Dickies pants and shirt, wool socks, and Red Wing work boots. He took his Carhartt jacket off one hook and his yellow hard hat off the other and walked over to the mess hall. The room was alive with the sounds of men getting ready to go on shift: talking, ordering breakfast, scraping plates, banging coffee cups. Speedy Dave grabbed a tray and got into line. He hated to eat, too, but he knew he'd feel worse if he didn't. He asked one of the cooks for a couple of fried eggs, got some black coffee out of the urn, and went and sat down. When he poked his fork into the eggs the yolk ran out and looked like the blood on the desk jockey's shirt. He looked around the mess hall and saw the trooper sitting a couple of tables away. *If I go tell the trooper,*

Speedy Dave thought, *maybe that'll make the desk jockey go away.*

Stan Grivach saw Speedy Dave get up and walk his way. He knew Speedy Dave in the same way he knew every one of the 157 men in base camp, just well enough to know who to watch out for. His mental file on Speedy Dave read: old, alky, harmless. *Working a remote construction site like this wasn't all that much different from working a road town,* Grivach thought, *except there were no women here.* That was good, too. Men and alcohol were almost always trouble, and women just made everything worse.

"I—I—I got a problem," Speedy Dave said. Old booze rose from Speedy Dave and wrapped itself around Grivach like a mist. *This is going to be good,* he thought.

"I seen something. In my room. A dead guy."

"This a real dead guy?" Grivach asked. "Or an out-of-the-bottle dead guy?"

Speedy Dave didn't say anything for a while.

"Okay," he said. "That other time . . ."

"Other two times," Grivach said.

"Other two times," Speedy Dave said, "there weren't any dead guys. And I don't know, maybe there isn't this time, neither. But it couldn't hurt for you to look."

Grivach didn't say anything.

"Please," Speedy Dave said.

"Okay," Grivach said. "After I finish breakfast."

"Thanks," Speedy Dave said, and went back to his eggs and coffee.

Grivach sat there for a while, picking up oatmeal in his spoon and dropping it back into his bowl. He'd gained twenty pounds since coming to Amchitka a year ago. He could barely get into his blues. So he'd stopped eating bacon and eggs for breakfast and started eating oatmeal. Or rather, playing with oatmeal. He dropped the spoon, dug a Camel out of his pocket, tamped it on his thumbnail, and lit it with a Zippo. Coffee and cigarettes, there was a healthy breakfast.

Nothing but paperwork this morning, he thought. Might as well start by looking at the alky's dead man.

A stiff wind blew rain into his face when he walked out of the mess hall. *Another glorious spring day in the Aleutians in the year of Our Lord 1966,* he thought. They said the wind out here, the big wind, the williwaw, could knock a man off his feet. Grivach hadn't seen anything like that, but he'd seen a lot like this. Gray. Wet. Blowing. No wonder guys got rock fever, drank too much, got into fights, and had their asses shipped back to town on the next plane. What else was there to do out here? On Amchitka Island, you were as close to Tokyo as Anchorage and more than a thousand miles from either one. Well, he supposed if you were going to set off atomic bombs, this was the place to do it. Nobody'd miss this island if the scientists screwed up and blew it to hell.

Grivach could have driven his blue crew-cab pickup with the magnetic Alaska State Trooper insignia on the side, but he decided he needed the exercise. All around him were the camp buildings, a few big ones left over from World War II, and a couple of barge loads of Atco trailers clipped together in various configurations: barracks here, offices there. Farther up the road were some prefab plywood warehouses; farther than that was the airport with its war-era hangar and control tower. You'll love Amchitka, his boss had told him. A woman behind every tree and not a tree on the island. That was just fine with Grivach.

He walked into the unit with the alky's room in it. He could see the bull cook working his way down the hall with a vacuum cleaner. Everybody else was already at work. Once he shooed the ghost, or whatever the hell it was, out of the alky's room, he'd walk over to his office and start filling out the forms for the last couple of brawlers he'd bundled off the island. He stopped at the alky's room and took his master key out of his pocket. But the knob turned under his hand. *The alky must not have much to steal,* he thought. He was still thinking about the alky, about how he must have been a regular person once, as he entered the room. Once of the beds was a mess. He looked at the other bed.

"Holy shit," he said out loud. "The old bastard wasn't seeing things after all."

"No chance the old fellow did it, I suppose," Norton said to Stan Grivach. Norton was the camp manager, as tall as Grivach but a lot thinner. He looked like a bishop, but word was he'd been a colonel in the army before retiring and going to work for the prime contractor. The prime was a company out of Las Vegas started by an ex-general and an ex-admiral. They had a lot of ins with the Department of Defense and a lot of ex-military workers. That was

okay with Grivach. He'd been in the army himself.
Made sergeant, too. Twice.

"They call him Speedy Dave because nobody's
faster to the liquor store at the end of a shift," Grivach said. "His routine is to buy a bottle, have three
or four drinks in his room, go eat something, then
go back and finish the bottle. Knock off at five, pass
out by nine. Liquor-store clerk and line cooks say he
followed his usual pattern last night. Knife wasn't
his. He didn't know the deceased. The deceased had
twenty-five years and fifty pounds on him. Nothing's
impossible, but him being the killer's pretty un-
likely."

Norton sat there looking sour. Grivach could tell
he was one of the ones who really missed people
having to salute him.

"We'll have to have the FBI in, then," Norton said.
Grivach snorted. Norton ignored him and went on.
"This is a federal installation, and Eliot had a Q clearance. There's no way we're keeping the FBI out of
this."

Great, Grivach thought. *The Feebies. Probably Atomic
Energy Commission security. DOD security. Hell, maybe
the National Guard.*

"Besides," Norton said, "you aren't exactly out
here for your investigative abilities."

Grivach briefly considered leaping over the desk
and strangling the shit out of Norton. But the uppity
prick had a point. Grivach was there to catch sneak
thieves, break up fights, and put the screw-ups on
the outgoing plane. He was just official muscle,
really, the state of Alaska's donation to a smooth-
running camp, not Sherlock fucking Holmes.

"With this weather, there's no telling when the next plane gets in," Grivach said. "So if it's all the same to you, I'll keep gathering evidence. For the FBI. Why don't you tell me what you know about this Eliot?"

Grivach had already taken pictures of the corpse, then carefully removed the knife and sealed it in plastic. Not that he had any hopes for fingerprints. He'd been in the Troopers sixteen years and never seen fingerprints catch anybody. He'd put the corpse's personal effects in another bag. Then he and the medic had wrapped the body up in the blanket from the bunk and put it into one of the cardboard coffins they'd shipped in for just such an occasion. They got the bull cook to find a cart and wheeled the body over and stuck it into the walk-in freezer, right next to that night's steaks. He'd asked the medic for a guesstimate on the time of death, but the medic couldn't put it any closer than Speedy Dave's timetable: sometime between nine p.m. and six a.m. When today's shift ended, he'd be able to ask the rest of the men in Speedy Dave's unit if they'd heard anything.

"I'm not certain I should tell you anything," Norton said. "You're not cleared for his work, and the personnel files are private."

"Okay by me," Grivach said. "You want to run a camp where everybody's looking over their shoulder all the time, that's fine. Don't see how much work'll get done, but that's not my lookout."

Norton said nothing. *He really could use a good strangling,* Grivach thought.

"Look," Grivach said, "I don't want to know the

particulars of his job." He heard a wheedling note in his voice and hated himself for it. "And the deceased can't expect much privacy anymore. So why don't you tell me what you can, I'll go around looking like I'm investigating, and everybody'll feel better."

That seemed to satisfy Norton.

"What I can tell you about his work is that he was in procurement, classified procurement. As for his personnel file . . ." Norton opened a file that had been laying on his desk. *Son of a bitch*, Grivach thought, *he was going to tell me all along.*

". . . his name was Samuel Morison Eliot. He was forty-one. He'd put in his twenty in the army, reaching the grade of master sergeant, joined the company after retiring three years ago. Assigned to Amchitka two years ago. Good health, no wife, no children, father dead, mother remarried . . ."

"Does it say anything in there about bad habits?" Grivach asked. "Old grudges? Enemies?"

"Just that he liked to gamble," Norton said. "A lot of the men do. That's one of the reasons they like working for a Las Vegas–based company."

Gambling was illegal in Alaska, but Grivach knew better than to think none was going on. As long as it didn't cause problems, he turned a blind eye.

"Was the background check thorough?" Grivach asked. "He didn't show up three years ago from Minsk or Pinsk with a paper life?"

"Do you mean, was he a spy?" Norton said. "I assure you, Corporal, our background investigations are very thorough. Very thorough."

"How about here?" Grivach asked. "In the camp? Who were his friends? What did they do for fun?"

Norton gave him the sort of smile an officer gives to a particularly stupid question from a noncom.

"I could hardly be expected to know that," Norton said. "But feel free to inquire in the procurement office. I'll telephone and let them know you will be asking questions. Nonclassified questions, of course."

The head of procurement, a pinch-shouldered, pasty-faced bird named Sims, heard Grivach out and said, "Go see the Mexican."

The Mexican turned out to be a shipping clerk named Garcia.

"That effing Sims," Garcia said when Grivach introduced himself. "I'm no Mexican. My people are Spaniards who got to America in the sixteenth century. Before the pilgrims. With Ponce de Leon, to discover the Fountain of Youth."

"My people are Hunkies who came over this century to discover steel mills," Grivach said. "Now that we've swapped family trees, why don't you tell me about your good friend Eliot?"

Garcia was past fifty but fighting it. He had a lot of suspiciously black hair, even, white teeth, and a million-dollar suntan. *One of those guys who can't pass a mirror without looking*, Grivach thought. Well, Eliot had been good-looking, too, until somebody'd stuck that knife in his chest.

"We weren't such good friends," Garcia said. "I never met the man until I came to the island."

"Sims said, and everybody else in that office agreed, you and Eliot and a guy they called Big Chief were as thick as thieves," Grivach said.

Garcia showed him the even, white teeth.

"We got along," he said. "We have similar interests."

"What are those?" Grivach asked.

"Art," Garcia said. "Literature. The symphony. About what you'd expect on a construction site."

"You're a snotty bastard, aren't you?" Grivach said. "Maybe you can tell me what Eliot was doing over in a subcontractor's barracks last night."

"I'm afraid I can't," Garcia said. "I have no idea."

"Then maybe you can tell me where you were last night."

"I had a couple of drinks in the bar, dinner in the mess hall, watched the movie, turned in about midnight, and slept the sleep of the just. You can ask the Chief. He's my roomie."

The Big Chief, actually a housing clerk named Paul Standinghorse, was every bit as unhelpful.

Yes, he knew Eliot and Garcia.

Yes, they were friends.

What did they do together?

"We work. We eat. We drink. We bullshit."

What did they talk about?

"You kiddin'? What does anybody talk about in a place like this? Sex, money, and machines."

Yes, he and Garcia were roommates. Yes, they were both in their room around midnight. No, he didn't know who killed Eliot or why anybody would want to kill Eliot.

When he was finished getting nothing out of Standinghorse, Grivach cooled his heels until Norton could find thirty seconds to give him permission to search the dead man's room.

The rooms were all set up for two people, but if

you had enough pull or enough bad habits you could live alone. They were ten by ten with two beds, a shared desk/nightstand between them with a window above it and a couple of closets with a few drawers in them at the foot of the beds. Cheap paneling, cheap carpet, and a reading light above each bed. All the comforts of home, if home was a medium-security prison.

The dead man's room was not much different from the alky's, or Grivach's for that matter, except somebody'd torn it apart. Clothing and papers were scattered around, and the drawer of the nightstand had been forced open. It was empty. Grivach raked through the debris without finding anything interesting, then locked the place up. Maybe the Feebies could use some crime-scene practice.

When Grivach got back to the procurement office, Sims was giving a thick form the fisheye.

"Somebody forget to fill in the goldenrod copy?" he said.

"Everyone makes fun of the paperwork," Sims said. "But without the paperwork, an installation like this would be total chaos." He seemed to like the sound of that, so he said it again. "Total chaos."

"I'm sure you're right," Grivach said. "I need to search the deceased's desk."

"I don't think that will be possible," Sims said. "The desk may contain classified material."

"Then Uncle Sam will have to depend on you to be sure that I don't memorize the details of any classified paper-clip purchases," Grivach said. "Somebody tore apart Eliot's room, and I'm going through his desk while it's still in one piece."

"I really don't think this is at all appropriate," Sims said. "How will I explain it to the manager?"

"Tell him I had a gun," Grivach said.

Sims fussed around while Grivach went through the government-surplus metal desk, whisking forms and files away like they contained the codes to launch SAC bombers. The bottom right-hand drawer was locked.

"Got a key?" Grivach asked.

"Why would I have a key?" Sims asked in a tone that made Grivach certain he had one.

"I was just hoping," Grivach said. "Eliot's key is with his personal effects, and I don't feel like walking all the way back to my office. So if you don't have a key, I'm afraid I'll have to shoot the lock off."

Sims bustled off and returned with a ring of desk keys. The third one fit. Inside the drawer was a black metal box, locked. Grivach raised an eyebrow at Sims, who shook his head. Grivach took a letter opener from the middle drawer of the desk, jammed it into the keyhole, and twisted hard. The top popped open. Inside the box was a small key with a long barrel and a thick sheaf of letters held together with a red rubber band. Grivach gave them a once-over. The letters were from different women in Las Vegas. Each was heavily perfumed. The first one contained sexual details so explicit that Grivach found himself blushing. Beneath the letters was a picture of the dead man, Garcia, and Standinghorse. Eliot and Standinghorse had their arms around chorus girls, while Garcia had his draped over the shoulder of a stunning twentyish brunette in an evening dress.

"None of this looks classified," Grivach said. "So I think I'll just take it along as evidence."

"Shouldn't we write down what you found so there's a record?" Sims asked.

Grivach snorted and left.

Back in his office, Grivach called Anchorage to give them the bad news. While he waited for the connection, he looked through the things he'd taken off the body. A wallet, some change, half a pack of Marlboros, a gold lighter, a wristwatch with a gold band, a few keys on a ring. He held the keys up closer to his eyes. Eliot seemed to have two room keys. He put them together. Not quite the same.

The telephone rang. The voice on the other end belonged to his boss, a lieutenant named Dankworth. Grivach told him about the body and sketched in what he'd found so far.

"I'll be up to my wallet in Feebies the next day the weather's good enough to let a plane land," he said.

"That's fine," Dankworth said. "They've got the two-way wrist radios. Let them do the work. You're not there to catch spies."

"Not likely to be spies, Loot," Grivach said. "We're in a lull between tests, so there's nothing particularly classified out here, except maybe for the prime's profit margin. Besides, how'd a spy get here? Swim in from a submarine?"

"Not your problem," Dankworth said. "Just let the FB and I do their job and don't go making any trouble."

Grivach couldn't think of anything to say to that, so he kept quiet.

"Martha called," Dankworth said at last.

"That can't be good," Grivach said. "What did she want?"

"She wanted to know why she didn't get a check this month," Dankworth said.

"There isn't any check," Grivach said. "It's all direct deposit. I told her that a dozen times. Told you, too, Loot."

"I know. I know," Dankworth said. "I explained it all to her. I'm not sure she understood, though. Sounded like she'd been drinking."

"No surprise there," Grivach said.

Neither one of them said anything for a while.

"Guess it's a good thing you didn't have kids," Dankworth said at last, his voice soft.

"Yeah," Grivach said. "I guess so."

When Grivach looked out his bedroom window the next morning he saw the island's first sunshine in four months. He said several bad words in a row. The Feebies would be in on the afternoon plane for sure.

When he saw Speedy Dave in the mess hall, he walked over to him and snarled: "If you see one more dead body, I'm shooting you."

Then he sat down to drink his coffee and play with his oatmeal, reviewing the take from his questioning of the other men who lived in Speedy Dave's barracks wing. The unit was half-empty, so there were only five of them: a twitchy loner named Murphy and two sets of roommates named Cal, Hal, Mal, and Sal, or something like that. The roommates all wore work clothes that looked like they'd been ironed. None of them had heard anything or seen anything out of the ordinary. No, nothing. And none of them knew the dead man.

"What can you tell me about Speedy Dave?" Grivach had asked Cal and Hal.

"Well," Cal—or maybe it was Hal—said, "he snores horribly, just horribly. And sometimes he shouts at night."

"Shouts what?" Grivach asked.

"He shouts things like 'Look out' and 'Oh my God,'" Hal—or maybe it was Cal—said.

So all Grivach had gotten out of his questioning was that Speedy Dave had the yips. That, and the distinct impression that none of the men was telling him everything.

He gave up on breakfast and drove to his office, where he spent the morning doing paperwork and getting it ready for shipment into Anchorage. At noon, he drove back to the mess hall and got himself a couple of sandwiches and an RC cola and ate lunch in the office. He read the letters he'd found in Eliot's lockbox while he ate. They were from five different women, each of whom had written extensively about the sex they'd had, and hoped to have, with Eliot. Grivach had a hard time believing some of the descriptions.

"Nobody would ever write a letter like that to me," he said aloud as he put down the last one. "Not even Martha."

Especially not Martha, he thought.

The letters didn't seem to be evidence of anything but Eliot's skill in the sack. Even if they were, there wasn't really any way to find the women. There were no envelopes and four of the women had signed their letters with first names only. The fifth had simply used an initial, H. Aside from the fact that they all seemed to live in Las Vegas and three of them mentioned husbands, there wasn't much to go on. Well, if they had to find the women, the Feebies could just interview every female in Nevada.

Grivach put the letters down, picked up his paperwork, put on his Smoky Bear hat, and drove to the airport. The big Reeve Constellation bobbed and weaved onto the runway and roared past, its four engines popping and cracking, the props cutting through the air like four big circular saws. When it taxied to a stop at the terminal, Grivach helped roll the stairway to its door, then stood back waiting for the Feebies.

There were four of them, three hard-eyed kids in their twenties and an older guy named Goodwin with a graying crew cut and a handshake that could crack walnuts. Grivach handed his paperwork to a stewardess he knew and asked her to give it to the duty trooper at the Anchorage airport. Then he helped the Feebies throw their bags into the back of his pickup.

"I've got to go watch them put the body on the airplane," he said to Goodwin.

"Good," the FBI man said. "We've made arrangements to have the body transshipped in Anchorage and sent straight to our lab in Virginia. The murder weapon going along?"

Grivach nodded. "Taking this pretty seriously, aren't you?" he said.

"Atomic secrets. Spies. Communists," Goodwin said.

Grivach couldn't tell if he was serious or not, but the three younger agents all nodded. They seemed downright happy at the prospect of spies and Communists. Oh, well. They were probably great at hand-to-hand combat and could shoot the eyes out of a mosquito at four hundred yards.

Leaving the other agents at the pickup, Goodwin and Grivach walked over to where two men were wrestling the coffin off a forklift and into the belly of the airplane. When that was done and the cargo bay closed, a line of men began filing from the terminal toward the Connie.

"Who are these people?" Goodwin asked.

"Going on R and R," Grivach said. "Most of them get a couple of weeks off every six months."

"I'm afraid they are going to have to wait," Goodwin said. He pulled his identification from his pocket, held it over his head, and walked over to intercept the head of the line. The line stopped and the men in it crowded around him.

"I'm Agent Thomas Goodwin of the Federal Bureau of Investigation," he said in a loud voice. "My men and I are here to investigate a homicide, and nobody is leaving this island until the investigation is finished or until he's cleared to go by me."

"That's bullshit!" someone yelled. His voice was followed by others. "I've got plans!" "Plans, hell, I've got a contract!" "Contract, hell, I've got to get laid!"

Grivach pushed his way gently through the crowd and stood at the agent's side. He picked out the faces of several men he knew, including Garcia. They all looked thoroughly pissed off.

"Sorry, fellas, that's the way it is," he said. "And

all standing around bitching about it is going to get you is older."

"We could walk right over you and get on the airplane," a guy named Young, who worked at the power plant, said. Young was big, one of the few men on the island who could look Grivach in the eye flat-footed, and he had a mouth to match.

"You could try," Grivach said, staring into Young's eyes, "and the best that you'd get out of it is a couple of years for assaulting an officer."

Young dropped his gaze. The men dispersed, grumbling and lobbing curses at Goodwin. The agent walked into the terminal and repeated his order to the airport manager. Then he and Grivach got into the crew-cab with the other agents and drove to Grivach's office. They left the three younger agents there and went to see the camp manager. Norton kept them waiting for ten minutes, and when they finally entered his office, his security chief was there, too.

"I thought Simmons should be here so that we could go over the ground rules," Norton said after they'd all shaken hands and taken seats.

"Okay," Goodwin said. "Here are the ground rules. You give me complete cooperation. My men go where they want and talk to whomever they want whenever I want them to."

"That's not exactly what I meant, Agent Goodwin," Norton said. "We are doing important work and the schedule can't be disrupted. In addition, there are secure areas that cannot be compromised."

"I forgot one of the ground rules," Goodwin said. "Anyone who obstructs the investigation in any way will be arrested and sent back to Anchorage in handcuffs." He looked straight at Norton. "And I mean anyone."

There was silence in the room.

"Now, before you start burning up the telephone lines and trying to stir up the Pentagon and God knows who else," Goodwin said, reaching into his coat pocket, "you should read this." He handed Norton a letter.

The camp manager unfolded it and read. "I guess that settles any other questions there might be," Norton said.

Goodwin took the letter from him, refolded it, and put it back into his pocket. All Grivach could see was a gold seal at the top of the page. Goodwin got to his feet.

"Trooper Grivach was kind enough to drive us here," he said. "But we'll need vehicles. And maybe Simmons here could show a couple of my agents how to get to the science complex. We'll also need office space, preferably next to the trooper office. And a place to bunk."

"You'll have full cooperation," Norton said. It sounded to Grivach like every word had to be surgically removed from the camp manager's throat.

"I hate all this my-dick's-bigger-than-yours nonsense," Goodwin told Grivach as they were driving back to the trooper's office. "But with guys like this Norton, it's unavoidable."

When they reached his office, Grivach sat in the chair behind the desk, Goodwin sat in the chair in front of it, and the other agents perched wherever they could. Then Grivach told the whole story, beginning with the alky coming up to him in the mess hall.

"I'd like to see that key you found," Goodwin said when he finished. Grivach handed it to him. The agent looked at it.

"Safety-deposit box?" he said.

Grivach shrugged.

Goodwin handed the key to one of the other agents.

"Get on the phone to the Anchorage field office," he said. "Give them a description of the key and this number on the barrel. Ask them to check the banks. Then call the Las Vegas field office and do the same. If they find the right bank, have them get a warrant and get into that safety-deposit box."

The agent looked around the room. Grivach sighed and got up, signaling the agent to take his chair.

"Why don't I take a couple of your men and collect some transportation?" he said to Goodwin. "I'll get your room assignments and drop off your bags, too."

And later maybe I can clean your weapons and polish your shoes, he thought as he left the room.

Grivach didn't see much of the FBI agents for the next week. Goodwin and one of his helpers went every day to the science complex, while the other two retraced Eliot's life on the island, reinterviewing everyone Grivach had talked to plus everyone else they could corner. It got to be a joke among the workers.

"You ain't shit," he heard one man tell another at breakfast. "You been interviewed only once. I been talked to twice."

"That's because the blond one thinks you're cute," the other man said, to the laughter of everyone within earshot.

Grivach spent his time trying to keep the men from braining each other. The ones who were losing their R and R were the worst. On the third day, he had to step between two of them in the line at mail call.

"Just because I can't ship your asses off the island doesn't mean there's going to be any fighting," he told them. "I've got a cell over in the office that you can sit in until this is over. Then I'll ship you out."

"This ain't fair," one of the men said. "I didn't even know Eliot, or whatever the fucker's name was. How come I'm stuck here instead of back home?"

"Now, you all know about fair," Grivach said to the men who had crowded around in hopes of seeing a fight. "Fair is a place where men in overalls throw cow chips for distance. So you boys just behave yourselves, and you'll be home giving the old woman what for soon enough."

The men didn't appear to believe that, and Grivach didn't blame them. The investigation didn't seem to be going anywhere. Toward dinnertime of the seventh day, Goodwin stuck his head in Grivach's office. He looked like he'd been dragged through a knothole.

"You wouldn't have something to drink in here, would you?" the agent asked.

Grivach got a bottle of bourbon out of his bottom drawer and poured some into a pair of coffee mugs. Goodwin sat, took a pull at his mug, and sucked air in through his nose.

"Doesn't need a chaser," he said. "Nothing can catch it."

They sat sipping their drinks.

"Scientists," Goodwin said at last. "Ask one how

old he is, and he starts reciting the periodic table of elements."

"Not getting anywhere?" Grivach said.

Goodwin grimaced.

"We interviewed the scientists because we figure that if this is espionage, one or more of them must be involved," he said. "Eliot might have had a decent security clearance, but the really classified material didn't even come through his office. I conducted the interviews because they're a bunch of prima donnas, and if one of them gets in a snit, my bosses are going to hear from the AEC.

"But we didn't get anything. Nobody knew Eliot or had ever seen him with any of the other scientists. They didn't even know there'd been a murder. You could stage World War III on this island and they wouldn't know unless it showed up on their instruments.

"So I was thinking that this might just be a plain vanilla construction camp killing when, two days ago, the Las Vegas field office called. Eliot's key fit a safety-deposit box in a bank there, and inside was almost a hundred thousand dollars, most of it in small bills. Where the hell does a clerk get a hundred thousand dollars in cash?"

Goodwin shook his head.

"Washington's convinced he got it from the Russians. But there's not a hint of Russians in Eliot's past. I don't think he ever even ate in a Russian restaurant. And none of the hush-hush surveillance apparatus showed any Russian submarines or anything else near this island before the murder or since. You can imagine the difficulty we had getting that information. Anyway, every single person on the island, you included, has been double-checked for subversive activities. Outside of a fellow who turned out to be wanted in connection with a murder in Missouri, and a couple of college kids working here this summer who went to a Vietnam protest, there's nothing."

He drank the last of the bourbon and set his mug down on Grivach's desk. Grivach raised the bottle. Goodwin shook his head.

"So you think it's not spying?" Grivach said.

"I think that whole thing is a snipe hunt," Goodwin said. "But my agents haven't gotten anything in the rest of the camp, either. The only reason I'm sure there was a murder is the autopsy report, which says Eliot had eaten pork chops for dinner, had consumed a moderate amount of alcohol, and died because someone stabbed him in the heart with a kitchen knife."

"Fingerprints?" Grivach said.

Both men laughed.

"About the only thing I've detected so far is that tonight is steak night," Goodwin said. "What do you say we go eat three or four each?"

They talked about other things at dinner. They were both baseball fans, although Grivach favored the Indians while Goodwin was a Red Sox supporter. They both liked to fish. Neither one of them thought much of LBJ or any other politician. The agent had a wife and kids at home and pictures of all of them.

"You have a family?" Goodwin asked.

"I have a wife, sort of," Grivach said.

The agent raised an eyebrow.

"We're separated," Grivach said. "It's complicated."

When they'd finished their pie and coffee, Goodwin announced that he was headed for bed.

"Maybe I'll have a brainstorm in the morning," he said. "If not, I'm going to at least release the men who are overdue for R and R. We'll spend another week or so investigating, but if that goes the way I think it will, we'll turn the investigation over to the local authorities."

He grinned.

"I guess that's you."

Grivach walked over to check on things in the bar. That was a normal part of his nightly rounds because it was the most likely place for sudden violence. *Men and booze,* Grivach thought. Women and booze, for that matter. When he'd first gotten to the island he'd questioned why they allowed booze. But every contractor's rep said they wouldn't be able to keep a crew on the island without it.

"I'd sooner serve 'em bad food," one of the reps said, and that was that.

The bar was, as usual, doing a booming business, and Young, the power-plant operator, was sitting at a table full of men doing most of the booming.

"Goddamn fedral guvmint," he told his audience, waving his arms around. "They can't keep me here inde—indef—indefnitely. I got rights."

Grivach ambled over to his table.

"A little early to be this drunk, isn't it?" he said pleasantly. "Maybe you should go back to your room and get some sleep."

Young lurched to his feet and belched booze fumes into Grivach's face.

"What do you know?" he shouted. "Kissin' up to them FBIs. You don't know shit!" He smiled a sly smile. "Dumbass cop," he said. "You don't even know 'bout the 357 Club."

"The 357 Club?" Grivach said, keeping his voice light. "What's that, a gun Club?"

"Gun club," Young said. "That's right, gun club. Dumbass cop."

"That's enough," Grivach said. "You can go to your room or to the cell. Your choice."

"How 'bout I choice kickin' your ass?" Young said, and threw a looping right hand that looked to Grivach like it would take a week to land. He stepped inside the punch, put his left forearm under Young's chin, and bum-rushed him until he slammed into a wall.

"Knock it off," Grivach said, "before I get mad."

About that time a left that he hadn't noticed hit him above the right ear. Young was drunk and off balance, but he was a big man and the punch hurt.

"That's it," Grivach said, stepping back. He whipped his nightstick off his left hip and jammed it into the other man's stomach, then jumped aside as Young spewed steak dinner and vodka tonics across the room. Men scrambled to get out of the way.

"Shit," the bartender called. "Stop that. I gotta clean that mess up."

Young slid slowly down the wall. Grivach reached down and got his hands on the front of Young's shirt.

He bunched up his back muscles and jerked the drunk to his feet.

"Any more trouble and I'll coldcock you," he said. "Now, come on. You're sleeping it off in the cell tonight."

He half led, half carried Young to his truck and drove to the office. He laid the other man on the cell's bunk, turning him so that if he vomited again he wouldn't drown himself. Then he sat down at his desk and started thinking.

The next morning at breakfast, Grivach ordered bacon and eggs, then sat down next to Speedy Dave.

"Tell me about the 357 Club," he said.

"What 357 Club?" Speedy Dave said. "I don't know nuthin' about no 357 Club."

Grivach put a forkful of egg into his mouth, following it with a piece of bacon. He chewed for a while and swallowed.

"Wrong answer," he said. "You don't want your ass fired off this island, you better start talking."

Speedy Dave's eyes darted this way and that, like he was looking for a way out.

"They said they'd hurt me if'n I said anything," he said at last.

"I suppose they did," Grivach said. "Not to mention buying you a bottle every night to keep you quiet."

He ate another piece of bacon. Damn, he liked bacon. Maybe he'd give up the oatmeal and start going to the gym instead. Maybe he should quit this chicken job and move to Tahiti. *I wonder if they've got bacon in Tahiti,* he thought.

"But here's the thing, Dave," he said, draping a big arm around the old man's shoulders. "The time to be worrying about them is past. Now it's time to be worrying about me."

The old man looked this way and that, this way and that.

"God," he said. "I hate mornings."

Then, in a low and halting voice, he started talking.

When he'd finished eating, and Speedy Dave had finished talking, Grivach drove back to his office. Young was sitting up on the bunk with his head in his hands. Grivach unlocked the cell door.

"Up and out," Grivach said. "If you hustle you can still punch in on time."

Young looked at him.

"You ain't shipping me out?" he asked.

"Nope," Grivach said. "Today's your lucky day. By being a complete asshole, I think you helped me solve this murder."

Young got up and stumbled toward the door.

"But if you pull anything like that again," he told the departing man's back, "I'll ship you home in a body cast."

He walked over to Goodwin's office.

"Might not be quite time to let the R and R guys go home," he told the agent.

"Why? Do you know something?" the agent asked. "I've already cleared them to leave."

"Get the keys Eliot had on him and come with me," Grivach said.

He and Goodwin drove to the barracks where Eliot's body had been found. On the way, Grivach asked, "The guy wanted in Missouri, is his name Murphy?"

"Yes," Goodwin said. "How did you know that?"

Grivach just grinned.

Inside the barracks, Grivach walked to the second door on the left and tried the keys. The second one opened the door. The two men stepped in and Grivach switched on the lights.

They were in a big room full of gambling equipment. There were a couple of six-sided felt-covered poker tables, a craps table, a blackjack layout, even a roulette wheel. A dozen chip holders were lined up on a table on one wall.

"This looks like a casino," Goodwin said.

"Welcome to the 357 Club," Grivach said.

"The 357 Club?" Goodwin said.

Grivach walked over to one of the poker tables and sat down. He pushed a chair out with his foot and motioned to Goodwin, who joined him.

"Every one of these housing trailers is set up more or less the same way," Grivach said. "Each trailer has a letter designation, and each room has a number. There are eight rooms to a trailer, and the numbers start with one from the left-hand side. Room two is across the hall from one, room three is next door to one, room four is across from three and so on. So we are sitting in what would ordinarily be rooms three, five, and seven. The 357 Club."

Goodwin nodded.

"Somebody went to a lot of trouble to set this up," he said. "And to keep it quiet." He slapped his palm on one of the mats that covered the walls and gestured at the blackout curtains covering the windows.

"That's not the half of it," Grivach said. "The same somebody—somebodies, I think—installed just the right people in the other rooms, people who would give the place the lived-in look without making trouble: a guy hiding out from the law in room two, an old alcoholic in four, and two pairs of guys who want to play hide the salami without anybody knowing in six and eight."

"And in one?" the agent asked.

Grivach shrugged.

"I'd guess it's the casino's supply room," he said. "I could go break down the door, but I'm feeling lazy."

"And you didn't know this was here?" Goodwin said.

Grivach gave him a rueful grin.

"Yeah. Great police work, huh?" he said. "But I was trying to not know about gambling. There's plenty of pressure here and not many outlets, and nobody holds a gun to your head and makes you play poker. I figured there were card games here, dice, bets on this and that. I didn't figure on anything this elaborate."

Neither man said anything for a moment.

I guess this shoots any chance I had of joining the Feebies, Grivach thought. *Not a big deal, though. I look like a horse's ass in a suit.*

"This would certainly explain the money in the safety-deposit box," Goodwin said.

Grivach nodded.

"You think Eliot was involved in this, then," Goodwin said.

Goodwin sat there looking at the roulette wheel for a minute.

"Eliot was in procurement, so he could order this paraphernalia," the agent said. "Then he'd need somebody in shipping to get it here and somebody in housing to secure the space."

Grivach nodded.

"Garcia and Standinghorse," he said. "I figure they just greased everybody else involved: the Teamsters who hauled the stuff over, the bull cook, whoever."

Goodwin got up, walked over, and gave the roulette wheel a spin. The noise it made reminded Grivach of when he was a kid and used to clothespin playing cards to his bike wheels.

"You think this has something to do with the murder?" the agent said.

Grivach got up and went over to look at the wheel. It had stopped on the number seventeen. He gave it another spin and stood there listening to the sound. *If I'd known what I was in for*, he thought, *I'd never have gotten off that bike.*

"Yeah, I do," he said when the wheel stopped on twenty-two. "I'm just not sure what. Some gambler might have gotten tired of losing and stabbed Eliot. But I think the reason is something to do with the three club owners."

Goodwin nodded.

"Seems likely," he said. "You've had more time to think about this than I have, so what do you think we should do next?"

Grivach started for the door.

"Well, I'd guess Standinghorse is the most vulnerable, since I bet his records show people living here," he said. "So why don't we grab him, take him over to my office, and sweat him?"

"And Garcia?" Goodwin asked, turning out the light and closing the door.

"We've got a few hours until the plane's due," Grivach said. "Let's let him think he's getting away."

Sweating Paul Standinghorse didn't prove easy. He sat there looking proud and defiant, answering questions with a shrug or a grunt.

"Goddamn it, we've got you," Goodwin said after about forty-five minutes. "You've got fictitious people assigned to those rooms, and you've been changing the names during the past two years. You're good for gambling, misappropriation of government property, and probably tax evasion."

Standinghorse answered that with a shrug and a grunt.

"We know you and Eliot and Garcia were in on it, so you could easily get a piece of a murder charge, too," the agent said.

That seemed to get Standinghorse's attention. Either that, or his nose itched.

"Okay, you don't want to talk about any of that, talk about this," Grivach said, putting the picture from Eliot's lockbox down in front of him.

"It's a picture," Standinghorse said with a smirk.

"Those agents you got with you, the young guys," Grivach said, "they know anything about torture?"

Goodwin laughed.

"I don't think so," he said, "but they could balance your checkbook in less than ten minutes."

That made Grivach laugh. Then he turned back to the Indian.

"The men in that picture are you, Eliot, and Garcia, right?" he said.

"Right," Standinghorse said.

"Who are the women?" Grivach asked.

"Don't remember their names," Standinghorse said. "Two of 'ems just good-time girls me and Eliot were with. The other one's Garcia's wife. He called her Cia, but she's really got one of them long Spanish names."

Grivach went over to his desk and sat down. Goodwin started in on the Indian again, but Grivach shut their voices out. After several minutes, he called to Goodwin, "You still got Garcia's personnel file?"

"I'll go get it," the agent said. Grivach and Standinghorse sat there looking at each other. The agent returned and handed Grivach the file. He opened it, read for a moment, and put it down on the desk.

"Okay, Standinghorse," he said. "I know who killed Eliot and I know why. This is your last chance to come clean. If you don't tell us what we want to know, we'll charge you with accessory to murder. You'll be an old, old man before you get out of prison."

Standinghorse stared at Grivach for a long moment. Then he blew air out his lips and seemed to deflate.

"Okay," he said. "What you want to know?"

"The night Eliot was killed, you said both you and Garcia were in your room," Grivach said. "That true?"

"No," Standinghorse said. "We always had two guys at the club when it was open. That night it was Eliot and Garcia."

He had to struggle to get the words out. Grivach could tell he really didn't like talking to cops.

"Why'd you say Eliot was with you?"

"He told me he didn't have anything to do with the killing," Standinghorse said. "And telling would have meant the end of the club and probably jail, just like now."

When Standinghorse was done answering questions, Grivach locked him in the cell. Then he and Goodwin went into the agent's office to confer. After several minutes, Goodwin said, "Well, we know who did it and why, but we don't have an ounce of proof."

"No, we don't," Grivach said. "But why don't you send your agents to the airport to arrest Garcia, cuff him, and stick him in an empty room to stew? I think I've got something to use on him."

"What's that?" Goodwin asked.

"The truth," Grivach said.

Garcia was sitting in the station manager's office, hands cuffed in front of him. Grivach came in and sat down beside him.

"What the fuck's going on?" Garcia asked in a loud voice. "Am I arrested? What for? And why the handcuffs? Where would I run?"

Grivach just sat there until Garcia ran out of questions. Then he sat there some more. When he opened his mouth at last, he said, "I know."

That set Garcia off again.

"You don't know nothing," he shouted. "There's nothing to know. I haven't done nothing."

Grivach let him run down again.

"I know what you did," he said. "And I know why."

He tapped his head.

"I don't just know why here."

He tapped his chest.

"I know why here."

Garcia was studying him now, silent and wary. Grivach started talking again.

"I was stationed out in Bethel, ten, twelve years ago," he said. "Going on thirty and thinking about settling down. I met a woman there named Martha. She was younger than me, young and beautiful. One thing led to another. When I was transferred out, we got married and she came with me."

Grivach paused. *Garcia looks like a fox I found caught in a trap once,* he thought. *That fox watched every move I made until I brained him with a birch branch.*

"When you're the only trooper for hundreds of miles, you're not home a lot," he said. "She got lonely. She missed her family and friends. I was too dumb and too caught up in the job to see she needed me around. She hung in there, making a home and doing good works, even in these little road towns where being a Native is considered one step above being a dog."

He stopped there and thought, *This is more than I'd planned to tell him.* But he was in it now, in the story. He had Garcia's attention, and he couldn't stop.

"But when I was transferred to Anchorage, that was too much," he said. "The town was just too big. I think it scared her. So she found friends in a couple of bars. She'd come home drunk at all hours and we'd fight, and she'd sober up and promise not to do it again, and we'd make up until the next time.

"Then, two years ago," he said and paused. "Jesus, two years ago this week, I got a call from a guy I know in the Anchorage Police who said he'd picked her up drunk with a construction worker in a no-tell motel on the east side. Said they were making so much noise the manager'd called. You have to make a lot of noise to get the manager of one of those places to call the police.

"I went and got her. The construction worker was gone, which was lucky for him. I think I might have killed her then, but my job was to enforce the law, not break it.

"So I had the records lost, got her sobered up, and shipped her back to Bethel. Every payday I send her money. Her family says she's better, but she's still drinking. For a while she'd call me up drunk and ask me why I'd abandoned her. That's her word, 'abandoned.' So when this job came open last year, I took it. Stretches the paycheck, and I'm not so easy to get on the telephone."

He looked up into Garcia's eyes and saw the look he was sure had been in his own eyes that day two years before: pain and anger and humiliation and something else. *Guilt, I suppose,* he thought.

"Sometimes I think that if I hadn't blundered in there, she might have had a good life," Grivach said. "Other times, I think she was no damn good. But mostly I think there's just something about women that makes men helpless and crazy."

Grivach stopped talking then and waited. Garcia looked at him and opened his mouth to speak, but nothing came out. A tear leaked from the corner of his left eye and ran down his cheek.

"You—you—you do know, don't you?" he said. "How did you find out? About Eliot, I mean?"

"Letters," Grivach said. "He had letters from women, locked in a box in the bottom drawer of his desk. You can guess what's in them. One set was signed with an H. You call your wife Cia, but her real name's Hortencia, isn't it? That's what it says in your file."

Garcia started crying then, whooping and gasping, the tears running down his face. He cried so hard Grivach was afraid he'd break something. When he stopped, Grivach said, "How did you find out?"

"That fucking Eliot, he told me," Garcia said. "Can you believe it? We were having an argument about the money. We've had this club running a little more than eighteen months, and it's been a real money-maker. The first time, we all three went on R and R together, spent some of it and put the rest in a safety-deposit box. But we had to close down, and we figured we'd make more money if we took separate R and R. Eliot went out first, then Standinghorse, then me. We'd spend some money and put the rest in the box. Everybody had a key, and everybody knew how much money'd been put in.

"But when the Indian went to the box this time, it was a little light. He told me, and we asked Eliot. He said he didn't know what we were talking about.

"We let it go. But then, last month, Eliot and me were having a few drinks after we closed the club and I got on him about it again, and you know what he said? He said, 'I spent it on that wife of yours.'

"I called him a fucking liar and said she'd never take up with a limp-dick whitey like him. That made him mad, and he told me a couple things about her. There's only one way he could have known them."

Garcia was silent, as if listening to Eliot's words again.

"Why didn't you kill him then?" Grivach said.

"I got my honor, don't I?" Garcia said, sounding indignant. "Sure, he had to die, but so did she. She's the one gave me the horns. So I waited until the night before I was supposed to go on R and R. I figured I could kill him, stash the body, and get on the plane. Then there was a chance I could get to Vegas, deal with Hortencia, the slut, get the money, and head for the border."

He paused again.

"Can I get some water?" he asked.

Grivach went to the door and asked for water. When it came, he held the glass for Garcia as he drank. When the glass was empty, he set it down on the desk.

"What happened?" he asked.

"I stole the knife from the kitchen one night and waited," Garcia said. "I planned to kill Eliot in the club and hide his body in the supply room. I liked thinking about that. Then the night before I was supposed to go on R and R rolled around and I thought, It's now or never.

"But I guess I wasn't as good a killer as I thought. I let him see the knife too early, and he ran out the door and into that old wino's room. I got him there all right; one stab and he was done.

"But before I could move the body, the wino rose up out of the other bed yelling: 'Oh my god! Oh my God! Oh my God!' I thought somebody'd be coming to check on the screaming, so I ran. I figured you'd come and get me the next day. Why didn't you?"

"Speedy Dave wasn't really awake," Grivach said. "He just has the yips. So he didn't see you. His neighbors are used to the noise, so nobody came to check."

Garcia gave a big sigh.

"So I could have gotten away with it?" he asked. "I could have killed the slut, too?"

"I don't know, could you have?" Grivach asked.

The two men looked at each other. Time passed.

"I don't know," Garcia said finally, shaking his head. "I just don't know."

Then he started crying again.

The Reeve plane made it back in the next day, and Garcia and Standinghorse left the island in handcuffs, accompanied by the FBI agents.

"Next time," Goodwin said, shaking Grivach's hand, "we'll just leave the crime-solving to you."

Grivach went back to his office to type up his report and Garcia's confession. In the late afternoon, he drove to the little Quonset-hut gym and threw some iron around. *Man, this is boring,* he thought, *but it's better than giving up bacon.*

His phone rang the next morning. It was Dankworth.

"We got this Garcia fella in custody," he said. "The Feebies done kept the other one. That agent, Goodwin, had good things to say about you. Said he's going to write a nice letter for your file."

"That can't hurt," Grivach said. "I'll be sending the paperwork in on the next plane."

"A fella like you ought to be a sergeant," Dankworth said. "There's an exam in a couple of months.

You got lots of time to study out there. And in the fall Jimmy Winston, the sergeant at the Bethel post, is retiring. You know people in Bethel, don't you?"

"I'll think about it, Loot," Grivach said. He hung up the phone, got out a cigarette, and lit it. He got up and looked out the office's little window. The rain was falling in sheets, the sheets blown almost sideways by the wind.

I might just do that, he thought. *It'd be a gamble, but life's a gamble.* Garcia took a gamble, and on most construction sites he might have gotten away with it. Most construction sites aren't worried about spies. And most construction sites don't have a cop. Especially a cop with a guilty conscience of his own.

THE BOG

Loren D. Estleman

Watching Hufnagel take the strychnine, I felt a twinge of remorse.

Certainly not for Hufnagel, or for the fact that the primo cocaine he thought he was ingesting contained enough mole poison to ensure the pristine character of every lawn in suburban Michigan. He'd bought that fate five years before, when he plagiarized one of my best ideas and pissed it away on a desktop novel that languished in Borders and died on the remaindering table, forever beyond the reach of a writer who knew best how to make use of the subject matter. I'd have taken him out then, but there'd have been scant satisfaction in an act performed in the heat of first wrath. The thing needed time to plan, to refine, to make friendly overtures, to overcome through patience and grim sincerity the natural suspicions of a thief whose victim has elected not only to forgive him, but to include him in his circle of intimates. The *center* of the circle.

The best con men, they say, con themselves first. It was necessary to remind myself of how close we were before the betrayal, in effect to erase all surface memory of the incident and re-create emotions formed in an innocence I no longer possessed. Fortunately, good writers and method actors have that ability in common, and if I may say so, I succeeded as thoroughly as an Olivier, a James Dean. There had even been times, dining and drinking with the man I despised above all others, when I felt as close to him as a brother, and when thoughts of the despicable theft occurred unbidden, managed without much effort to convince myself it had all been a mistake, a laughable coincidence, and that since he had failed so miserably to profit from it, that the thing was of no great consequence. But an actor or a writer who is unable to separate himself from his self-delusion when not actually performing is a tiresome creature. A good con man never loses sight of the prize. In my mind, Hufnagel was as dead as the idea he had appropriated and defiled with his hackery. It was a corpse I sat beside at ball games. It was a cadaver I invited to my home in the country. All that remained was to put the concept into practice.

No, it wasn't Hufnagel who made me contrite, and I had lived with the plan too long to feel guilty for my deception. I grieved for the loss of another idea. It was as good as or better than the one he'd stolen, there was an Edgar in it at least if I used it in fiction, and once I'd used it in fact, it would be lost to me forever. While writers make their best work public, murderers bury theirs. It's a near thing for an artist or an entertainer to seek success through obscurity.

But a twinge was all it was. Ideas aren't hard to come by, unless you're deficient enough creatively to have to filch them from others. I didn't lament the one he'd made away with as much as the making away. The hard part had been winning his trust and convincing him that I shared in his vice. I drink in moderation, smoke not at all, and had been pompous on the point that I'd never taken an illegal substance, not even so much as a single puff of marijuana back when Mary Jane was the girl voted Most Popular at every undergraduate party. In order to get strychnine into my enemy's system, I was forced to present myself as a liar and a hypocrite. It was humiliating to do so before Hufnagel, my personal Antichrist, and to suffer the sight of his blubbery, condescending grin when at last he'd accepted it as truth. *So you're no better than me after all*, it said, complete with his indifference to elementary grammar.

No matter. It was a corpse's grin.

I'm nothing if not a thorough researcher. I had no trouble persuading him to believe that the Ziploc bag I produced contained the purest cocaine the coastal village of Cannaveieiras exported, obtained through special anonymous sources for roughly the same amount I'd paid down on my mortgage. His only response, aside from actually licking his lips when he saw the flaky white powder, was to comment that my books must finally be in the black. I barely noticed the jibe. I placed a shaving mirror on the coffee table, picked up a razor blade, and separated the sample I'd poured on the glass into parallel lines, as neatly as if I'd been practicing it for years instead of hours.

I wasn't a good host. I helped myself first, to remove any lingering doubt on his part. It was unnecessary. He was so intent on his own approaching pleasure he didn't notice that what I inhaled into my right nostril through the dollar bill I'd rolled up was empty air from an unoccupied part of the mirror. Impatient as he was, he didn't bother to count the remaining lines and notice that there were still as many as we'd started with. I'd expected that. There is no underestimating the greed of a plagiarist, nor his insensibility to the consequences of his actions. He seized the bill, bent to the line nearest him where he sat on the sofa, and made an appropriately porcine noise sucking it up into his nasal cavity, into his empty brain.

When you hate a man, truly detest him enough to see him punished, strychnine's the thing. It doesn't take long for symptoms to appear—ten to twenty minutes on an empty stomach, much less time when the poison's taken directly into the exposed capillaries inside the nose—but I suppose any time spent in violent convulsion is an eternity for the victim. Puzzling a little over the immediate sensation—a disappointment apparently, given the buildup—he reached up a hand to massage his stiff neck. When he moved it around to probe at his face, stiffening as well, I got up from the sofa. I did this as much to remove myself from the range of his flailing arms and legs as to observe the rest.

The rest was satisfying. He crashed to the floor, knocking the coffee table askew and scattering its contents, rolled over onto his back, and arched his stomach toward the ceiling, keeping his head and feet on the floor. (One of the accepted positions for Lamaze and convulsions.) His entire body was quivering like a drawn bow. Spittle frothed at the corners of his mouth, which drew farther and farther apart in a rictus that was not at all similar to the superior leer he'd given me only minutes before. His face looked slimy; he sweated through his sports shirt; he made a gurgling noise in his throat that may have been an attempt to speak (cry for help? express his disappointment with the good people of Cannaveieiras?). He released the contents of his bladder.

Enough detail. I'm not a sadist. Soon enough he was dead, and I got to work.

The beauty part of the plan wasn't the murder; that was pedestrian. It was the disposal of the body. That was where most amateurs fouled up, for not thinking things through. Either they chopped up the remains and parted them out, thereby multiplying the chances of discovery, or they buried them in a flower bed or something on their own property or—just as bad—tossed them in the trunk of a car and drove to some secluded spot, risking a police pull-over on the way for a cracked taillight or failure to signal a turn or just because the cop was bored and wanted someone to talk to, and even if they succeeded and got back home undetected and removed all traces of the body from the trunk, some crime-lab geek going over the body collected traces of the trunk from the body, which was a guaranteed conviction. You couldn't count on the corpse not being found, not completely, and you had to prepare for the possibility that you would be suspected and scrutinized.

With the advance from a three-book contract, I'd

bought a house on a hundred acres in the country. It was mostly wilderness: hills good for hiking and not much else, patches of woods and swamp. A lot of empty acreage, perfect for keeping the neighbors at bay and a writer in solitude. At the back, it bordered on a farm belonging to an old recluse named Lundergaard, whose wife had left him forty years ago, after which he'd retired from the world, working his field for his own subsistence and entertaining no visitors. In the ten years I'd lived there I had yet to lay eyes on him. We shared a dense stand of cedars and impassable swamp, with only a strand of rusted barbed wire to mark the property line, strung straight through the middle of the bog.

The dear old bog.

I'd gotten my bright idea the first time I saw that brackish green stretch of no-man's-land, and had kept it in reserve while I worked on other projects, never dreaming at the start that I would employ it anywhere other than in a novel or a short story. The bog was covered by a spongy layer of decayed vegetation, only inches thick, but resilient enough for a man to stand on if he was careful not to tear the fabric with the corner of a heel. How deep went the pool of muck and wriggler-infested water beneath it I couldn't guess, but when I tested it by piercing the loam with an eight-foot pole of dead stripling, it never touched bottom and slid out of sight when I let go of the end. Nor was there any way of telling its age. For all I knew, there were bones of woolly mammoths and saber-toothed tigers down there, still waiting to be exhumed after a couple of thousand centuries, on top of sixty million years' worth of dinosaur. There was no reason to believe that a newer and much smaller skeleton shouldn't remain there as long.

But I wasn't counting on even that. That was the beauty part.

It was a long walk from my house to the bog, much of it uphill. It was tempting to consider throwing Hufnagel into the back of the four-wheel truck in the garage, drive as far as the cedars, and carry him the last hundred yards to his final resting place. But that meant tire tracks, simplifying things for the boys from Homicide. I put on dark clothes against the chance of being spotted by a late-night hiker, hoisted my guest into a fireman's carry across my shoulders (he was stiff already, the strychnine having advanced the process of rigor mortis), and set out through the back door.

Forty-five wheezing, sweaty, mosquito-bitten minutes later, I came to the edge of the bog, which by moonlight glistened like fresh tar. The woods were alive with chattering raccoons, inquiring owls, and lead-footed squirrels, whose hopping gait through dry leaves sounded exactly like a SWAT team in full charge; I was shaking, and not just from fatigue. It's one thing to stand among sunshine-dappled trunks planning to dispose of a body, quite another to stand supporting the weight of that body in striped shadows squirming with nocturnal predators and one's own demons. I wanted to put Hufnagel down and rest. I didn't. I shifted the burden a little to relieve one set of screaming muscles and stepped onto the squishy surface of the bog.

For a panicky moment I wondered if that thin layer

of long-dead flora would support my weight and Hufnagel's combined; I had a fleeting, vivid vision of the two of us plunging through icy, bottomless offal, my nose and throat and lungs choking with muck and algae, then blackness—Hufnagel and I joined for eternity along with all the other fossils. But the surface held. Foul-smelling water bubbled up around the thick soles of my boots, forced through the porous moss and lichen and corrupted plant flesh by my weight, but the loam didn't part. I took another tentative step, then another. It was like walking on a waterbed. I plunged ahead, growing more confident with each yard. I came to the wire that separated my property from Lundergaard's. I improved my grip on Hufnagel's arms and legs and high-stepped over it.

Trespassing.

With a murdered corpse, yet.

That was the big idea.

I wasn't arrogant enough to assume I was the only one capable of looking beyond the bog to its possibilities. Any homicide detective with enough head to keep his hat from settling on his shoulders would obtain a warrant to excavate that part of the property, find the elusive bottom, and drag it for a corpse.

But a warrant was only good as far as the strand of barbed wire. Beyond it was my neighbor's land, and without probable cause to suspect him of complicity (no danger there; I'd never met the man or knew anyone who had), the police were barred from searching it. They probably wouldn't even consider it. Premeditated murderers are far too wary to bury the evidence on adjoining property. The risk of the neighbors selling out and the new owners developing the land and turning up the body with a power shovel was too great. Much better to dig the hole in one's own real estate and never move. A lifetime of self-imposed house arrest was a small price to pay to avoid discovery.

My case was different.

I had an accomplice.

His name was Uncle Sam.

The bog was registered with the county clerk as wetlands, and the Environmental Protection Agency in Washington prohibits draining and developing wetlands, which endangers the wildlife that depends upon the habitat. An act of Congress would be required to change the law, and since Congress acts about as swiftly as the brontosauri that were dozing beneath my feet, I could have buried the corpse on my side, sold the property to a developer the next day, and gone to live wherever I pleased, secure in the knowledge that no bulldozer or backhoe would ever profane the bog's natural beauty and incidentally fork up Hufnagel.

Poor Hufnagel. The cokehead plagiarist never stood a chance against me and the federal government.

For once in my life I'd kept my mouth shut about an idea. I was afraid I'd talk it to death and never write it. It occurred to me, as I trudged far enough onto Lundergaard's to prevent the remains from drifting back onto my side (and also to observe a reasonable margin of error on the part of the surveyors), that if I'd taken the same precaution elsewhere, Hufnagel would never have had the opportunity to take advantage of my trust and I wouldn't be forced to throw away a good plot situation on a real-life murder. But at least there was no one to educate the police. It would've been a joke on me if I'd told the little thief and there was an unfinished manuscript on his desk outlining my plans for his removal, just waiting for the police to read.

Finally I stopped and lowered my burden to the ground, if the rippling sheet of compost I was standing on could be called that. I stretched, crackling my bones and lighting up all the pain points in my muscles, then took the garden trowel out of my hip pocket, squatted on my haunches, stuck the pointed end through the loam, and cut a slit three-feet long. I dropped the trowel through the slit, having no more use for it, then slid Hufnagel by his collar to the edge, encountering no resistance at all from the smooth moist surface of the bog. I got his feet in first; the rest was leverage. A little tip, and Hufnagel slid out of my life as quickly as the eight-foot pole I'd used to try to plumb the depth of his grave.

The job was finished. I'd thrown away the rest of the poison in a city Dumpster, keeping only the amount I'd needed to dispose of my pest problem, flushed the residue down the toilet, and washed the hand mirror. The cheap bastard didn't own a car, preferring to ride a bus to the nearest crossroads and walk the rest of the way. I thoroughly enjoyed the stroll back to the house. It was a mild night. I had no corpse to weigh me down, and the squirrels didn't frighten me. They were just rodents, after all. A bit of strychnine, and poof! No more squirrels. That gave me an idea for a story. I had Hufnagel to thank for it, which balanced things out and filled me with happy remembrances of our friendship.

The detective's name was Congreave.

He was a sergeant, and from the dirty gray in his shabby comb-over and broken blood vessels in his cheeks, that would be his rank when he retired. He showed me his badge, and I sat him on the sofa where Hufnagel had tooted his last toot, and he told me that Mr. Hufnagel had been missing for two weeks. An acquaintance had heard the missing party mention an appointment to visit me on the twenty-eighth, which if true made me the last person who had had any contact with him before he vanished. I said it was true. We'd had a drink or two and some enjoyable conversation, but I couldn't have been the last person to see him because we'd parted early in the evening so he could catch the last bus home.

"He missed it," Congreave said. "At least, the driver doesn't remember him boarding, and he knew Mr. Hufnagel well enough to talk to. He was a frequent passenger."

"Yes, old Huf was high on public transportation."

The sergeant's eyes got a little less dull. "Don't you mean he is?"

I smiled.

"Did I say was? I must've caught it from you. You referred to him in the past tense."

He grunted. "Did he say anything about going away somewhere? He missed an important meeting with his publisher. Something about writing a movie tie-in."

Same old Hufnagel. Handed the chance to put his

name on someone else's plot, he was inspiration itself.

I said he hadn't mentioned taking any trips. Congreave asked many more questions, wrote my answers in a grubby little notebook with a well-nibbled stub of pencil, thanked me, and left.

Three days later he was back, more animated this time. He'd spoken with some people who remembered my grudge against Hufnagel. I told him that was water under the bridge, but he asked me if I'd consent to a search of my house and property. I refused indignantly. I'd given that inevitable question a lot of thought and decided that being too cooperative was as bad as obstructing justice, at least from a detective's suspicious point of view. He said that was my privilege and that he'd be back.

He got me out of bed the next day at dawn, with a squad of officers and crime-scene investigators and a paper covered with archaic printing, signed by a judge. They went through the house from the attic to the basement, then went out to join the team that was probing the bushes looking for freshly turned soil. Late in the afternoon the backhoe arrived. An officer stayed behind to keep an eye on me while the rest gathered around the excavation site. I gave Congreave credit for recognizing the bog's potential much earlier than I'd predicted, based on the impression he made. I offered to put on a pot of coffee, but the officer declined. I put it on anyway. The sergeant might appreciate it when he came back empty-handed.

But there was no disappointment on his face when he showed up just before dusk. His eyes were bright

and he was smiling. "You can change your story any-
time you like," he told me. "I'd pick now. It could
be the difference between twenty years and life."

I felt weak suddenly and started to sit down, but
the sofa reminded me how clever I'd been, warned
me not to fall for any tricks. I remained standing.
Something made a purring noise, and Congreave
pulled a cell phone out of his inside breast pocket.
He listened, then said, "Human. I'm sure of it.
When? 'Kay." He beeped off. "What'd you use, some
kind of acid?"

He was looking at me. "What?"

"Doesn't matter. Medical examiner's on his way.
He'll know what you used to strip the meat off
that corpse."

"Meat?" Some writer. My vocabulary had been reduced to single-syllable words.

"I guess I should be grateful," he said. "Bones are
a lot less messy than your average eighteen-day-old
corpse."

That confused me. In my mind I'd rehearsed every
conceivable method of interrogation, and this one
hadn't figured. I wondered if the bog contained some
kind of scavenger that picked skeletons clean of flesh,
and if despite my precautions the remains had
drifted back across the property line. Maybe the police had cheated, extended the excavation onto Lundergaard's. That was infuriating. Didn't we all have
to obey the law?

Two hours later, we were joined by a scrawny
middle-aged character, bespectacled and bald,
dressed incongruously in a wrinkled tweed suit and
rubber hip boots. He took off his glasses and rubbed

his eyes. "Damn arc lights are going to give me cataracts. What's your victim's name?"

"Harvey Hufnagel," Congreave said.

"Well, unless her father wanted a boy, this isn't her."

"Her?"

"Remains are female."

"No mistake?"

"Pelvises don't lie."

Congreave scowled at me. "What are you, a mass murderer? How many more you got buried back there?"

I kept my mouth shut. I wasn't sure English would come out.

"You might want to stop talking before you give this gentleman grounds for a slander suit," the medical examiner said.

"You saying she died of natural causes?"

"No, I'm pretty sure that hole in her skull came from a bullet. But this gentleman couldn't have been five years old when it happened. Those bones haven't had skin on them in thirty or forty years."

"Bullshit."

"Cross my heart."

"I've lived here ten years," I said. "I spent my whole life before that in Seattle."

Very soon I was alone. The medical examiner was polite enough to say good night.

The sergeant wasn't entirely without manners. Two days later he knocked at my door and asked if he could come in. I was still sufficiently rattled from our last meeting to feel cold dread when I saw his face, but that evaporated when we sat down and he began to speak.

"I've made my share of mistakes, but when I'm wrong, I say it," he said. "You know your neighbor, Mr. Lundergaard?"

"I know of him. We haven't met."

"No surprise. He's a real hermit. He's going to be tough to crack, because he's been alone so long he's gotten out of the habit of talking to anyone. But he'll crack. Those bones we found on your property used to be Mrs. Lundergaard. Her dentist is retired, but he still had her records, so the ID's positive. She and her husband had an argument, apparently. He shot her and threw her in the bog. Told everyone she'd left him. He came over on your side to dump the body so a search warrant at his address wouldn't turn her up. Pretty clever for an old Dutchman."

Clever for anyone, I thought testily. But I was feeling charitable toward Congreave, so I kept the edge out of my voice. "What about Hufnagel?"

"Still open. FBI's tracking a serial killer who picks up pedestrians on country roads, cuts their throats, and ditches them at industrial sites. They think he came through Michigan last month. Maybe Hufnagel ran into him on his way to the bus stop from here. Bad luck."

"Rotten." I shook my head sadly. I wanted to do a somersault.

He rose. "Anyway, sorry we gave you a hard time. We've got to be thorough."

"I understand. It's the same in my work."

"I almost forgot you're a writer. Not much of a story in Lundergaard, I'm afraid. He's sewed up tight, once we find the gun he used. He didn't dump it with his wife, so we're getting a warrant to search the bog on his side of the line. I'll be surprised if we don't turn up something useful."

THE SALT POND
Laurie R. King

All kinds of human flotsam washed up in Highland New Guinea in the early 1980s, riding the tides of God, or gold, or glory. Missionaries sought to bring heathen sheep into the fold; the first scouts of multinational corporations came to gouge riches from the earth, or to shake it from pockets. And then there were us misfits, seeking adventure, academic treasure, or simply escape into the earth's last wild frontier.

And wild it was: When the tiny prop plane with the Air Niugini markings on it left me on the runway at Mt. Hagen, I might as well have been on Mars.

Part of the disorientation, no doubt, was simple jet lag. In the previous day and a half I had crossed the States, the Pacific, and half of Australia, and spent an interim period of exhausted timelessness in the stupefying heat and humidity of Port Moresby, where the corners of the terminal were splashed with what appeared to be gouts of blood. I was too wrung out to feel horror, but I was aware of a definite sinking sensation: I had read that the higher reaches of Papua New Guinea had been Stone Age and cannibalistic one generation before, but nobody said that public murder was commonplace in the capital city. Or maybe it was some kind of animal sacrifice, my muzzy mind suggested, citizens fearful of getting into a plane, ensuring their safe arrival. But in that case, shouldn't there be actual dead animals, or pens of live ones waiting . . . ?

My hallucinatory speculations were interrupted by a local, black of skin and short of stature, who strolled past one particularly gory corner and shot a precisely aimed red stream of spit on top of the stains.

Ah, yes: I'd heard of betel nut.

The plane out of Moresby was either Tuesday's very late or Wednesday's called early, I never learned which. In any case, it landed at a time no flight was scheduled to arrive, and apparently at an hour when any sensible human, expatriate or local, was sitting down to dinner. The airport was deserted. Dusk was settling in. It was raining and freezing cold.

The men from the plane hauled my bags out onto the ground, taxied around, and took off again, leaving tire tracks across one of the Samsonites.

I pulled my rain jacket around me, shivering and bewildered. This was an airport, and there were buildings all around; why, then, was there no sign of life?

I seemed to have two choices. I could sit down on my luggage and burst into tears, or I could go about finding humanity, and although the first option was hugely appealing, it was just too cold. And moving my belongings might warm me up.

I began to drag my luggage in the direction of what I supposed was the terminal. In no time at all, I was dripping and all the bags were splattered with mud; then one of the suitcases slipped from my frigid grip to the ground and vomited its contents onto the mud. After that, I admit, some of the wet running down my face was tears.

I managed to force most of the clothing back inside and was struggling with the clasp when a motion caught the corner of my eye, a scrap of yellow flitting rapidly behind the bushes and buildings. I slammed the lock shut, clawed my wet hair from my eyes, and waited for the vehicle to zoom on past. But in an instant it had careered around a metal shed and came roaring down the runway directly at me, as if intending to sprout wings and take off. Instead, it curved around and came to a halt next to my bedraggled self.

"You look rather stranded," the man behind the wheel said, understatement of the year.

He was a heavily tanned, clean-shaven, stoop-shouldered expatriate of about forty, high of forehead and bad of teeth; one glance and I was touched by a powerful aura of malaria-racked Victorian expeditions into West Africa, of the besieged administrators of troubled provinces, of wild-eyed Englishmen pressing into the desert on camels or the Antarctic on dog-sled—or into Highland New Guinea in an open-sided yellow Jeep. He set the hand brake and stepped jauntily from the open door, dressed in a button-down, short-sleeve shirt, flip-flop sandals, and the sort of shorts that everyone but that kind of man looks ridiculous in. He looked merely practical.

Later, making subtle inquiries that fooled no one, I would uncover few facts about him, and much rumor: He was Scots, or maybe a New Zealander; he was on the run from the law of Namibia, or was it Pakistan? He was the father of three, fleeing a dangerous marriage to a drug lord's daughter; or he was an aristocratic homosexual escaping repressive laws and social condemnation; or he was a mercenary wanted for war crimes in some dry African nation.

He was, of course, English, the sort of Englishman who could only have been formed on the playing fields of Eton, his spine stiffened by a regime of genial parental abandonment followed by institutionalized brutality: unsparing of himself, impervious to mere bodily discomfort, and always a step removed from intimacy with his peers. Later, I came to realize that both his bone-deep humanity and his utter disdain for authority had been driven into him by means of the same rods of discipline.

But I knew none of that then; I merely grasped that rescue was at hand. "Well, yes, it looks like I am kind of stranded. I thought I'd be met, but I don't know what day it is, and the plane seemed to just collect passengers and we stopped somewhere we weren't scheduled to—" I heard myself babbling, and shut my mouth.

"Well, we'll soon have you sorted," he said briskly,

and indeed, half my possessions were already inside his vehicle. I handed him the plastic bag with my hair rollers in it, which I hadn't been able to fit back into the suitcase, and walked around to get in the passenger side.

"Just got in from Moresby?" he asked, putting the vehicle into gear.

"Right."

"Which mission are you with?" It did not occur to me to ask how he knew I was with a mission.

"The Lutherans."

"Which ones?"

"Um, in Wape . . ." My brain wouldn't give me the rest of the name; it probably wouldn't have produced my own name at that point. But the Brit seemed to know what I was trying to say.

"Wapeladanga? Father Albion?"

"I think so. Yes, of course. I'm sorry, I'm not too on the ball."

"Understandable. But you won't get a lift up there for a day or two, I'm afraid. The S.I.L. lost a plane, and they're flying in another from Oz."

Oz: Australia. *Lost*, as in plane crash. As in, the plane they'd apparently intended me to get into. "There isn't a car?"

The brown skin creased all over as the man laughed at my fine joke. "The only way you'd get a car up there is if you lifted it in by helicopter or had it portaged one piece at a time. No roads," he explained. I must have looked confused, or near to breaking down, because he suddenly grew more somber and put out his hand slowly, as you would to an easily frightened child. "Terribly sorry. Don't know what's happened to my manners. Gordon Hugh-Kendrick.''

I shook his hand and answered automatically. "Linda McDonald. Are you with one of the missions, then?"

"Oh no, no. Just a civil servant. Government employee," he explained. "Glorified clerk." He pronounced the word "clark." He loosed my hand to steer around the abandoned-looking terminal buildings onto the road. "You'll need a place to stay. You can contact the mission on the radio tonight and ask what they want you to do."

"If you think that's best," I said uncertainly.

"Happens all the time," he assured me.

"It must, if the airport is always deserted."

"No no," he said, sounding surprised. "I've never seen it that way. Must be something going on in town."

And no sooner had he said this than we cleared a corner and had to brake hard to avoid plowing into a vast crowd of the most colorful people outside Mardi Gras. Not so much the first ranks, the naked children and the drably dressed women laden with heavily loaded lumpy string bags draped from their foreheads. But toward the center of the crowd we came to the men, and although many of them were dressed in grubbier versions of what Gordon Hugh-Kendrick had on—along with a dozen or so men wearing the uniform of the airline, which accounted for the deserted air terminal—others wore colorful leaf aprons, magnificent headdresses, and elaborate necklaces. Most of the colorfully dressed men had some object strung through their noses as well, bright feathers, long twigs, or curling pig tusks. I gaped at these figures passing by and wondered aloud if we had interrupted a parade.

"Why, the dress? Oh no, they're just in town for market, wearing their best. *Gudai, yupela,*" he said to an ornately bewigged man outside whose head barely cleared the bottom of the window. "*Watpo algeta dispela manmeri i stap hia?*"

The man turned to glare at us, all dark eyes, hooded brows and wide mustache behind a brilliant yellow feather. Then the fierce face was split by a huge grin. "*Eh, Gordon pren. Langtaim mipela no see yupela.*" He shifted the stone ax he was carrying to his left hand and thrust his right through the window; Gordon shook it vigorously, and the two exchanged greetings in a language that I did not think was Pidgin, although at that speed, I could not have been sure. Eventually they slowed, and Gordon turned to me.

"Do you speak Pidgin?"

"*Liklik tasol,*" I said. Only a little.

Introductions were made, and then to my surprise, Gordon waved the man around to the back. The feather man and half a dozen others clambered inside, squatting down on my suitcases, examining the bag of hair rollers with curiosity. They smelled powerfully of wood smoke and damp, and they all carried some deadly object: stone ax, spear, dagger, or bow and arrow. Half of them were dressed in shorts, the others nothing but leaves on a belt, and it was difficult to know how to greet them without confronting portions of their anatomy I was not accustomed to greeting. I was also distracted by their hair decorations, which ranged from one man's short Afro

threaded with feathers and bright flowers to a three-
foot-wide crescent-shaped hat made of matted hair,
shells, and black, glossy feathers. Gordon announced
my name to our passengers and put the Jeep back
into gear.

The ensuing discussion was far too rapid-fire for
my kindergarten-level Pidgin, but by the time we
had cleared the crowd Gordon had found out what
was going on in the town.

"It would appear that a white man was
murdered."

"Good heavens," I said. "What happened?"

"They found him up the road with his head
bashed in."

I gulped. "Is this . . . commonplace?"

That sparked another discussion, after which Gordon said, "It would appear not. None of these gentlemen can remember when the last *waitpela* was
killed."

"And you don't remember it happening?"

He looked at me, startled. Then his face cleared.
"The last murder, you mean? Oh, I've only been in
the Highlands for a year or so—there hasn't been one
in that time. But you can ask Mrs. Carver. She'd
know, if anyone does."

"Who is Mrs. Carver?" I asked.

He turned hard down a street and came to a halt
in front of a low, wide building with a flat tin roof.
The door opened and a six-foot-tall, rangy woman
with graying brown hair stepped out, hands on hips
and a scowl on her face.

"That's Mrs. Carver," he said. "This is her boarding house."

My heart sank at the unwelcoming face and posture. The woman looked as if she would bite. But to my surprise, Gordon trotted around, caught up her hand, and kissed it. She melted instantly into a near simper; clearly, he was no stranger here.

Our passengers tumbled out of the back, each of them holding his weapon in one hand and something of mine in the other. They meandered toward the house to set down the bags in a heap near the steps before clambering back inside. Gordon turned me over to the woman, refused a cup of tea, walked back to the car in a hail of Pidgin, and drove off in easy camaraderie, one hand emerging from the window to wave a farewell.

I stood on the graveled walk in front of this nondescript house, the air filled with the foreign odors of rain and smoke and jungle, and watched his spattered Jeep drive away.

My introduction to New Guinea.

Things were sorted out, as they usually are. Mrs. Carver had either been softened up by Gordon or else the intimidating face was an act, because she proved more maternal than my own mother. She had the hot-water tank stoked up so I could shower, fed me a meal of rice and some stewed meat, and then sent me to bed, assuring me she would make radio contact with the mission during their set time that night. Twelve hours later, I woke to a cool, misty morning, the smell of wood smoke and diesel fumes in the air, the singing of children outside my window, a mechanical thumping from somewhere in the building, and a green lizard clinging to the wall above the light fixture.

There were six other guests in the dining room

when I came in, dawdling over their toast and eggs, and one topic of conversation: the dead *waitpela*. Introductions were brisk: an American couple, missionaries on their way to a month in New Zealand, a trio of Catholic priests headed for a conference in Goroka, and a breezy Australian with grime in his nails too ingrained for soap, whose proprietary attitude made one wonder about his relationship to the owner of the guesthouse.

This gentleman held out his hand for me to shake, and said, "Name's Barry. I service the planes here."

It was on the tip of my tongue to ask, "Including the one that went down?" but I was saved from that faux pas by the American woman, whose name was Molly.

"Did you hear about our murder?"

"The man who was found yesterday? I'm so sorry. I didn't realize he was a friend of yours." Although truth to tell, she seemed more excited than bereaved.

"Oh, he wasn't. He was something to do with the mines."

"Do they know what happened?" I asked, and she proceeded to tell me in great detail what they knew, which boiled down to little more than Gordon had been told by the men in the street the previous evening. The man's body had been found by some locals on their way home from the day's market, lying alongside a trail a hundred yards off the road, his head bashed in. Barry intimated that he'd known the man well, although as it came out, the man, Dale Lawrence, had stayed in the guesthouse twice and flown in one of Barry's planes a few times. Lawrence had been in the Highlands about six months, had worked in the upper Sepik River area before that, and nobody much liked him.

Mrs. Carver came in with my breakfast at the tail end of this discussion, and I asked her if she knew anything about the man who had stayed under her roof. She set the plate down sharply and said, "The man was not welcome here."

When she had left the room, Barry leaned over and said in a low voice, "Mrs. Carver doesn't like it when *waitpelas* are rude to her staff. And after she asked him to leave—this was about six months ago—we heard that he'd been in trouble in the Sepik."

"What kind of trouble?"

Barry's eyes shifted to the kitchen door, and he looked uncomfortable. "There wasn't anything against him, far as I know. But they said a friend of his attacked a woman there, a local."

"Attacked?"

"Raped," he confirmed. "And killed her."

"*Killed* her?" I squeaked. "And he was still walking around free?"

"They work for the mines," Barry said, as if that explained everything. "But truth to tell, the police couldn't prove Lawrence had anything to do with it. And you can't lock a bloke up for being friends with the main suspect."

"Didn't that man, what's it called? Implicate him?"

"Bloke died before he could testify. His company lawyer bailed him out of the *kalabus*, and he was found with his head bashed in the next morning.

Probably by the girl's relatives. It was a big palaver for a while, all kinds of accusations flying, nothing much came of it. Girl's name was Jasmine. I remember that."

The killer's head bashed in, and a few months later, Dale Lawrence. I looked at my plate, and shuddered. What kind of place had I come to?

Fortunately, the following morning I was greeted by the news that the mission's replacement transport arrived from Australia and would leave at noon. I packed my bags, thanked Mrs. Carver for her hospitality, and was driven to the airstrip, where I climbed into a plane so tiny they had to put off a sack of potatoes to allow my weight.

What, I chanted the entire terrible, jolting, earsplitting way there, did I think I was doing? Quite literally, God only knew. If my introduction to the country had been somewhat too dramatic, my commute to work was just plain terrifying.

But to my great relief, that remote mission on the top of a mountain proved a place of great tranquillity, and I soon settled in to my new home. Within weeks, it was the letters from friends and family that began to seem remote and exotic. I worked hard, ate simply, learned more than I taught, and made friends, not only with my white countrymen, but with the local people. These hillmen lived a small step outside starvation, surviving on corn, plantains, and the sweet potato they called *kaukau*, calories supplemented by the occasional scrap of protein brought home by the hunters. I was there to teach English and basic medical realities to tiny aboriginal people one narrow step out of the Stone

Age, whose parents vividly recalled the first white face to appear in their mountain fastness. I discovered a people filled with simple joy and hard truths, more alive, more human, than most of the college students I knew.

We were, as Mr Hugh-Kendrick had told me, all but unreachable by land, our only contact with the outside world the toylike plane that dropped twice a week from the heavens onto a patch of cleared mountaintop over a river to bring us necessities (rice and tinned beef) and luxuries (soap, weeks-old newspapers, toilet paper). Four of us ran this station: Albert Haines, known throughout the Highlands by the deceptively Roman nickname of "Father Albion," which fit him better than the more accurate Reverend Haines. He was a lively Chicagoan who admitted to sixty-five but was probably much older, and he had been in the country since before I was born. With us were his devoted assistants Alice and Tom Overhampton, who had been there for three and a half years, and me. Within a couple of weeks, my life in Indiana began to seem like a dream. I had never been happier.

However, happy or not, a person could stay only so long in the bush before she began to feel the jungle closing in. Only Father Albion seemed impervious to the claustrophobia of having one's every move an endless source of scrutiny and amusement to the locals, of being followed to the outdoor privy and back, of having even private conversations—in English—punctuated by the giggles of children who had snuck under the thin floors of the native-style huts we lived in. Only saints of God can put up with that for long.

So every few weeks, one or another of us would find some excuse to hitch a ride on the supply plane back to civilization, to the town of a thousand souls that boasted such cultural riches as one-channel television sets, cold Cokes, and hot showers. The fleshpots were restorative, necessary even to those doing God's work.

I'd been in PNG for two months, and it was my turn to venture into the big city and luxuriate in being clean and eating meals I hadn't eaten a dozen times before. I had spent three of my seven allotted days in Mrs. Carver's boardinghouse, drinking two cold beers each evening and taking two hot showers a day, when one of the other girls came into the communal dining room with news of a sing-sing being held about twenty miles away.

Now, I'd yet to see a sing-sing, but I'd heard it was an event not to be missed. And this was not the flashy, shallow performance put on for the tourist cameras down in Lae and Moresby, but the real thing, a rural spectacle of celebration and male vanity. A sing-sing brought together families for a marriage, or the celebration of a son's return from the university at Moresby, or the unexpected (and hence sorcery-induced) recovery of a valued elder. The men painted themselves, primped like Miss America contestants, stripped the forests of bird-of-paradise plumage, and generally made any woman in sight seem a dull sparrow indeed.

However, the high point of this sing-sing was a pig kill. Pigs were the traditional measure of wealth here in the Highlands, nurtured and sheltered and made more of in the family than a child. Men might own them, but women raised them, sleeping with them, coddling them, even nursing piglets at their breasts. The boar's huge, curving tusks were prized as ornament as much as their meat was valued in a land where protein was rare, and pig kills were a time of great celebration. Not that the people whose pigs were the starring players actually ate much of the meat. Instead, at the end of the sing-sing, a day or three after it had begun, each celebrant would set off for home with his portion of pig riding in his string *bilum*, and often use the meat to pay off lesser debts of his own. As the next creditor would then use it similarly, and probably two or three after him, quite often the stuff was pretty ripe by the time it reached someone who was either in the enviable position of not needing porcine currency, or who was too hungry to pass it by.

So that was a sing-sing, and five of us decided to go and stay with the local missionary until it had finished. I, however, needed to get back to catch the Thursday plane, so I borrowed an ancient four-wheel-drive Subaru from the local school principal, and early the next morning set off with Beth Vreiland.

We got lost. Easy enough to do, when none of the roads had signposts and the other half had neither beginning nor end, but it did not much matter, since there was sure to be someone around to set us back on the right path, and between us we spoke enough Pidgin to get by.

But after getting lost, the car hit a rock, sputtered, and died. The starter whined without catching, the bit of track we occupied seemed less populous than any other patch of jungle we'd seen for the last couple of hours, and Beth was beginning to get on my nerves.

We sat, debating options, or rather, Beth debating options with herself while I kept my mouth firmly shut lest an unchristian sentiment escape it. I knew more or less where we were. We just had to finish sliding down the hillside into the river and grind our way up the other side, and I told my passenger this. She unhelpfully pointed out that, while sliding down to the river was certainly still open to us, that the only thing grinding up the other side would be our teeth.

"Help you, ladies?"

We both yelped at the plummy English voice at our backs, then whirled and craned into the gathering gloom, where I saw, with a sensation of inevitability, Gordon Hugh-Kendrick, dressed as before except for proper shoes on his feet.

I found my voice first. "We were headed for the sing-sing, but the car seems to have other ideas. I think something's broken."

"Pop the bonnet," he instructed. I figured he was asking to have the hood opened, so I found the latch and pulled. He disappeared into the engine, where we, naturally, joined him. I was not surprised when the car succumbed to his charm within a few minutes: I could not imagine a mere internal-combustion engine thwarting the man for long. What did take me aback was looking up to find that Beth had submitted as easily as the Subaru: When he let the hood drop on the sweetly humming engine, she all but batted her eyelashes at him.

He merely gave her a distracted smile and turned to me. "Do you know where you're going, then?"

"I thought we did, but the instructions for Holyoke must have been wrong."

"Oh, you're just one turn off the mark. Shall I show you?"

"Where were you heading?"

"That's as good as any. I'll catch a ride back to Hagen from there."

"But where's your car?"

"Oh, I'm on foot."

I glanced at his shoes, which were rimed with a grayish mud and spattered with betel, and wondered how long he'd been on *wokabaut*.

After asking permission with a gesture and a tip of the head, Gordon got in behind the wheel and turned us back the way we came in a space I'd have said was too small for the maneuver. Half a mile back up the track, he launched us at a sparsely grown patch between two enormous trees, which turned out to be the beginning of the track to Holyoke.

That was not the name of the town, of course, but it was what the mission was called, due to a superficial resemblance to the local name. Holyoke was a larger mission than that of Father Albion in the hills, so Beth and I knew they would be able to accommodate two strangers, if need be—or, as it was looking now, three.

The Subaru and darkness reached the mission more or less simultaneously, and I let out the breath I'd been holding for the last hour. A night curled up in the car, even with a resourceful Brit on hand to conjure up fire and food, was not my idea of ideal sleeping arrangements. I was grateful for the simple meal and for the unoccupied corner of a bedroom.

I don't know where Gordon intended to sleep—in the car, for all I know. He'd said hello to the missionaries, who greeted him as a long-lost rogue of a son, but when they asked if he wanted a bed for the night, he shook his head and said he had some friends to stay with, then slipped away before they could press him further.

Beth snored.

Life stirred outside the mission houses long before dawn, a constant ripple of excited voices and movement. When the sun rose, I joined it, and found my hosts in the kitchen with an enormous pot of tea on the table and Gordon Hugh-Kendrick exchanging local news. He was clean-shaven and his thin hair had been combed, but his eyes were slightly bloodshot and his clothing gave off the unmistakable strong aroma of hut smoke: The friends he'd spent the night with had been locals.

Breakfast was reconstituted eggs and some of the rocklike but highly nutritious biscuits that a number of the mission wives were experimenting with, an attempt to make edible one of the few sources of protein that would grow in that place, the peanut. These were no worse than some I had tasted, although fairly insipid.

"They need salt," Mrs. Craddock pronounced.

Gordon nodded, his mouth somewhat occupied with the ground peanut cake.

"The problem is," she continued, "we're trying to

come up with a recipe that calls only for things the people can find themselves. They can grind the grain and nuts in a mortar and pestle and cook it on a heated rock if they haven't a pan, but I can hardly ask them to use half a teaspoon of Morton's iodized.''

"What about salt from the ponds?''

"I keep asking our people about it, but no one has any.''

"Oh, I'm sure they have it. It's just so laborious to produce, they don't want to part with any if they don't have to. I'll bring you a sample, if you like.''

Mrs. Craddock went off on an exasperated speech about the shortsightedness of the New Guinean natives, but personally, I thought that even with salt, the biscuits would be better fed to the pigs and eaten indirectly.

The sing-sing would normally have begun with first light, as soon as the men had their elaborate costumes on and the paint perfected. But because this was a Christian people, they waited until Reverend Craddock had conducted his Sunday-morning service, most of his congregation spilling out from the tiny church onto the rough football field below the church and its school. The liturgy was Lutheran and conducted entirely in Pidgin; the good reverend's sermon on John 15, the pruning of the vines, was enthusiastically preached *(Em i katim long han na troimoim long paia)* and accompanied by hacking gestures and the tossing of imaginary branches into the fire. It was well received, considering the congregation's eagerness to be about their colorful business and the distraction of the squealing pigs from the stakes that

marched along the football field. But I thought my
host was as eager as the others, because the sermon
was admirably brief, and all inessential prayers
skipped. Forty minutes, start to finish: a record, in
my experience, from an evangelical.

The drums picked up the crowd as it turned from
the church, calling them in, the men donning their
feathered headdresses and checking their makeup in
the hand mirrors they all carried.

Down in Moresby, I understood, sing-sings were
put on for the tourists, with clans of men in more
or less the same costume and regional differences
obvious—Goroka mudmen in one place, others festooned with shells from near the sea, and the Highland clans sporting variations on the same brilliant
feathers and rich furs. Here, it was every man for
himself. Anyone who could get shells to supplement
the pig tusks, did so, and emu feathers from Australia were considered a good investment. I even saw
one man with a dozen tiny plastic baby dolls around
his neck, which made me think of my college religion
classes and the figure Kali—although this man's ami-
able and toothless smile gave lie to the bloodthirsty
reference.

Beth had brought her camera and enough film to
stock a convenience store. Gordon was there for a
while, standing among the missionaries and chatting
politely, or squatting on his heels with the locals and
carrying on with greater animation. I lost sight of
him during the middle of the day, but he was back
again in the evening, when the smoke of the cook
fires gave an air of the netherworld to the slaughter-
ing of pigs. The sounds were appalling, shrill

squeals followed by the meaty thuds of killing clubs and the rip of blades through the meat, but in the end the hunks and quarters were ceremonially distributed, clan by clan. Lengthy speeches were made, and the dancing picked up again. That night, the noise from the assembly never died down, and the whole thing was repeated the following day. By the second evening, I hadn't slept, my head ached from the smoke and the noise, the spectacle was beginning to blur in my mind, and I needed to get back if I was going to catch Thursday's supply plane to Father Albion's. Unfortunately, Beth was not interested in leaving.

"What do you mean, you're not going back?" I demanded. Make that drive through the bush, all alone? No thanks.

"Not for a day or two. I, er, I heard there's a new group coming in tomorrow. I thought I'd photograph them."

I narrowed my gritty eyes at her, remembering the good-looking young pastor I'd seen her with most of the previous day. "You mean you don't want to leave Father Harmon yet."

"Yeah, okay, I'm interested in seeing more of him. What of it?"

Only Beth, I thought, would come to Highland PNG to look for a mate. I shook my head. "Okay. I'll ask around and see if there's anyone interested in a ride to Hagen."

"Gordon's probably ready to leave," she said, a clear note of suggestion in her voice.

"I'll do that," I said coolly. I, for one, was not in the market for a husband.

But Gordon was indeed ready to leave, and I was so grateful that I would not have to face that so-called road on my own that I agreed to be ready at first light.

Having slept only fitfully for the past three nights, I took little notice of our route. Gordon coaxed the little car up and down some tracks, and although they didn't look familiar, nothing much did. It wasn't until we forded a stream that I woke up.

"This isn't the way I came," I noted.

"This way takes about as long, and there's a couple of things along the way you might like to see."

"Not another sing-sing, I hope," I joked feebly. It was dawning on me that I was in a place that was the very definition of "remote," riding with a strange man whom no one seemed to know much about; I began to wonder if I hadn't been extremely stupid. But surely, I told myself, if this Englishman intended to leave my ravaged body under a tree, he wouldn't have begun by driving off in full view of twenty missionaries and some four hundred locals.

"It's warfare," Gordon said, inexplicably a few minutes later. We had climbed sharply out of the streambed and emerged from the bush onto what looked like a mountain-goat track beaten into the side of a cliff.

"Sorry?" I got out, somewhat preoccupied with holding the car to the track by fervent prayer and willpower.

"The pig kills—they're sublimated warfare. War had been the basis of Highland society for centuries. When the paleface came in two generations ago, clans defined themselves by their conquests—long-planned-out raids, where one clan would forge alliances with another to attack a third, stealing the women, killing and eating the men, raising the children as their own. Then the Ozzies came and said, 'No, you can't do that any longer.' So now the locals jostle for position economically instead. It's similar to the potlatch of your Pacific Northwest. You put on a huge feast for your neighbors—your primary rivals—which not only puts you one up on them, but also means they will eventually have to reciprocate and stage an even greater feast, even if it utterly ruins them and forces them to borrow from other clans so that their children are in debt for the next twenty years. Fifty years ago, the big men might have had a collection of human skulls. Today they all wear the *omak*—you saw those? That bib of *pitpit* cane? Each length of *pitpit* represents participation in a pig kill. Ten pieces would be the sign of a wealthy man." I had noticed them, simply because they were such unadorned decoration to find on a man with a bird-of-paradise breast on his headdress and six inches of pig tusk through his nasal septum. The bib worn by the headman of the pig kill had stretched down below his navel.

I chuckled, then laughed aloud at the absurdity of it. He took his eyes off the goat track to glance at me.

"It's true!" he insisted.

"I'm sure it is. I was just thinking, What if the US and Russia adopted potlatch warfare?"

"Aerial bombardment of canned hams and television sets."

"And for a really big strike, they'd drop an entire school or hospital: Take that, Commie scum!"

"Might have made quite a difference in Vietnam," he agreed.

"Were you there?" I asked. I'm not sure why I caught on to the revelation so quickly, other than it being my first chance to learn something about him that was not rumor.

"I was, yes," he admitted. (Reluctantly? Or was I imaging that?) "Three years as a military—"

But I was not to hear what his role in that bloody conflict had been, because with the sort of curse I hadn't heard for months, Gordon slammed his foot onto the brake and fought the little car to a standstill between the Charybdis of the river below and Scylla in the form of a four-foot-tall, leaf-clad individual with a spear in his hand, who materialized on our left. We missed hitting him, missed becoming airborne; after a few moments, my heart settled back into place.

The man had not moved a hair; the front bumper was two inches from the *bilum* of *kaukau* riding on his hip.

With admirable English aplomb, Gordon cleared his throat and addressed the local. *"Gudai, yupela."*

The small black figure replied, not with the Pidgin version of Good day, but with a statement. *"Mipela painim onepela waitpela long raunwara bilong sol. Em i dai."*

"I dai?" Gordon repeated in disbelief.

My startled brain slowly seized and fitted together the Pidgin words. The man was informing us—

informing Gordon—that a dead white man was in a salt pond. *Dai* can simply mean that a person is ailing or injured. However, the local's response came closer to settling it.

"Em I dai pinis."

"Dying finish" meant at the very least that the white man was mightily ill.

Gordon turned to me. "You'll have to go on without me. You go straight for half a mile and then the track gets—"

"Oh, no. I'll go with you. I'm a trained nurse—I might be able to help."

He looked dubiously at my footwear, but I already had the car's first-aid kit in my hand and the door open. I inched around the car to solid ground; I had no intention of driving ten feet down that goat track, much less half a mile. Without a word, the local settled his stone ax more firmly into his leaf belt and set off up the hill, Gordon on his heels and me trying to keep them in sight as we slithered up a clay trail as slippery as greased glass, then pushed through impenetrable bush to the accompaniment of cries from unseen birds and the buzz of a thousand varieties of insect. After forty-five minutes, the bush opened up and we were looking at an expanse of swampy gray water with a whole lot of dead tree trunks in it, some lying flat in the water, others hammered upright to fence off squares of various sizes. Two fires smoldered sulkily on the opposite bank, the smoke drifting around Gordon and half a dozen locals who were looking down at something in the water. I joined them, and wished I hadn't.

Little need for my first-aid kit on this *waitpela*.

The man had been gutted, at least a couple of days before.

We soon had a crowd, as the bush telegraph gave news of this interesting event. Men with hastily arranged decoration, women with *bilums* that bulged with *kaukau* and *pikininis,* older naked children at their feet, and the two of us. Everyone including Gordon assumed that the dead man was our responsibility and ignored my protestations that the police should be called.

"There'll be nothing left of him by the time they get here," Gordon told me. "And he's already spoiling the salt." He began to undo the buttons on his shirt.

"But surely these people . . ."

"They've gone for something to wrap him in, and they'll carry him down to the main road, but I'll have to get him out for them."

He handed his shirt to the man with the spear, slipped out of his shoes, and waded into the murky water. I scarcely noticed his manipulations of the bloody object, however, because as soon as he turned away from me my eyes were riveted by the skin on his back. He had been scarred, deeply and thoroughly, in a pattern of great raised welts that ran from shoulder to waist. I had read about this, the crocodile marks of initiation found among the people of the country's Lowlands, in the Sepik area and near the sea. Where the hell had he submitted to those? And why?

Gordon wrestled the slab of pale skin and red

interior to the bank, where a threadbare blanket had appeared. He rolled the body onto it, and other hands quickly joined in to wrap the victim in wool and twine, then lay alongside a pair of long, sturdy branches and wrap those up as well. Soon the sprawling, bloody corpse had been transformed into a package with handles; the only indication of its nature were the two feet emerging from the end.

With great good cheer, now that the body had been made into a ceremonial object, four men seized the ends of the branches and heaved it up from the ground. They and a dozen other men made off with it, chattering and shouting, most of the audience trailing along in their wake.

Gordon sluiced himself off with water from the cleaner end of the pond, then resumed his shirt, sitting down on the grass-covered bank to dry his feet and talk to the spear carrier about the discovery of the body. I wandered up to look at the fires and realized this was what Gordon had been talking about with the mission wife back in Holyoke, salt from the ponds. Logs were corralled in the mineral-rich water, weighted down until they had absorbed as much as they could, then dried and burned to obtain the resultant salty ash. I couldn't imagine the tidy Mrs. Craddock spooning the gray ash into her recipe for peanut biscuits, no matter how true to life it was. I also wondered, somewhat queasily, how long it would be before traces of the *waitpela*'s blood were rendered down into someone's salt ash.

While I wandered up and down examining the enterprise, I heard a smothered burst of laughter and glanced over to see Gordon sitting on the close-cropped grass next to a boy of about fourteen, their heads together as they watched me, their eyes sparkling with humor, identical boyish grins on their faces. Gordon got to his feet, clapping the boy on the back, shaking hands with the menfolk, rubbing the heads of the small children and taking verbal leave of the women in the background. He tucked his shoes under his arm for the slippery journey back to the Subaru. Once there, I scraped the muck from my shoes while Gordon washed his muddy feet with water from the five-gallon can in the back, and we continued on our way.

This time, I hardly noticed the precipitous cliff. The scars on my companion's back took up my entire mind; they seemed to press through the fabric of his shirt at me, and finally I couldn't bear not knowing.

"That scarring on your back," I said, then couldn't think how to phrase the rest of the question.

He shot me a rueful grin. "You know how sailors get to port and wake up with a tattoo? Well, I didn't realize how strong the local hooch was."

You'd have to be drunk for a week or two for that kind of cutting, I thought. "So, you were initiated?"

"More or less. None of us took it very seriously—once it healed, that is." I thought he was lying, but to what extent, or why, I did not know. Before I could go any further, he asked, "So, why did you come to New Guinea? You don't seem much of an evangelical."

"To tell you the truth, I caught my fiancé in bed

with my best friend, and this just happened to be the first out that presented itself."

My answer startled him into laughter, but before he could continue his diversion, I got my own question in. "And what about you, Gordon? Are you married?" The unexpected turn of my question caught him unawares, and the animation faded from his face. He paid close attention to the roadway for a while before giving me an answer.

"I was. She died."

"Oh, Gordon. I'm so sorry. What was her name?"

Again a silence, even longer this time. "Mary," he said at last. "Her name was Mary."

I had been in New Guinea long enough to hear the name as *meri,* and had a brief flash of reflection—*How odd, to name a girl "Woman"*—before my own language reasserted itself and identified it as a proper name. "Was she English?" I asked.

"No." The finality of the word made it clear that the topic was at an end.

When we returned to town, Gordon insisted on dropping me at Mrs. Carver's before driving on to the police station to report the death. Mrs. Carver asked him in, but he refused, not telling her that he needed to inform them quickly so they could meet the body when it reached the main road. I shivered as I watched him drive away, and continued to feel so shivery that Mrs. Carver called the doctor, to check me for signs of malaria.

I was feeling a little better the next day, when a policeman came to take my statement. I had little to tell him apart from having been with Gordon Hugh-Kendrick when the body was taken from the pond, but he wrote it down and had me sign it and then told me that there was no reason I couldn't get on the plane the next day.

But after he left, I could not stop thinking about all I had seen and heard. Gordon Hugh-Kendrick's initiation scars and his marriage to a non-English woman. His wife's death, and his subsequent arrival in the Highlands. The gray mud and splash of betel on his shoes the afternoon he appeared out of the bush. His easy camaraderie with black men who came to his chest.

Late that night, I asked Mrs. Carver if she could get a message to Gordon for me. She said one of her employees would be able to find him, so I wrote a brief note and put it into one of the guesthouse envelopes. *I need to speak with you before the plane goes tomorrow,* it said. I thought it would bring him.

And sure enough, he was there at first light, leaning on the side of the yellow Jeep and chatting amiably with one of Mrs Carver's houseboys. When I came out onto the veranda, his eyes lit on me, and he managed to dismiss the young man without seeming to do so.

We met halfway down the white gravel walk, as public as could be, although he did not appear apprehensive, or even very curious about why I had asked him to come. He looked merely tired, as if he had not slept in some time. As if he had just finished a long and arduous task and wanted to rest.

"I just had one question," I told him.

"And what was that?"

"Your wife's name wasn't Mary," I said, but he

just waited patiently for the question itself. "It was Jasmine, wasn't it?"

"No," he said. He drew a breath, as if his last as a free man, and told me, "Her name was Yasmin." And then he added the truly terrible thing. "We were expecting our first child when those three men came through. They were scouting for labor. They found her."

One of the most difficult precepts of the Christian faith is that of forgiveness. Who holds the power to forgive? When is a refusal to punish forgiveness and when is it cowardice?

I did not know what God wanted me to do with Gordon's confession; I still don't know. But at the time, it seemed clear that the three men had been given their chance to repent when their mighty corporation's lawyer bought them away from the meager authority of the local police; I was merely buying Gordon Hugh-Kendrick the same opportunity for repentance.

I raised my eyes to his. They were brown, I noticed in surprise, as dark as those of the local people. "Is that the end of it, then?"

There had, after all, been some apprehension behind the calm, because a faint flare of hope now showed through. "I have done what I needed to."

I held out my hand to him. "If anyone figures it out, it won't be because of me."

He took my hand, then leaned forward and kissed my cheek before climbing into the yellow Jeep and driving away.

The next time I came down from my mountain

perch, I heard that he had left the Highlands and gone home: to New Zealand, or England, or was it Scotland?

But myself, I thought that the home Gordon had gone back to was not to be found on the other side of a sea.

Author's Note

Pidgin English is a language spoken across Melanesia, based originally on the simple conversational needs of traders. The majority of words are easily understood if said aloud, although the "p" is softened toward an "f"—hence *paia* is fire, *waitpela* is white fella.

THESE CROWDED WOODS

Skye K. Moody

Eight hermits lived in Forest Woods. Each dwelt in splendid solitude, rarely communing with the others, except for Regular Fred, who enjoyed a dinner partner on occasion. The hermits lived simply, as Nature had intended, although one or two of them held jobs that required complex backatcha skills.

Marco Prendergast, for example. Marco lived in a tree house and telecommuted to a software firm in Silicon Valley. Marco had a strict rule that no human besides himself would ever cross his lofty threshold. None did, until the day Marco was found brutally murdered on the path to Fender Falls, just a stone's throw from old Winter Beacon's meadow, where Rosie, Winter's ill-tempered black-haired goat, had grazed peacefully for years until the road to Fender Falls got clogged with the hermit influx. And then Rosie had stopped producing milk for Winter's breakfast gruel. But that's getting ahead of the tale.

The first to die was Wren, a frail girl with beady

gray eyes and a tiny beaklike mouth. Wren lived in a small cottage with a round door and a thatched roof, the same cottage she'd occupied when, according to Forest Woods gossip, her doting sugar daddy—some rich townie she'd sleazed into at Buck's Tavern—died suddenly of heart failure one stormy night in Wren's bed. As fortune so often favors sweet young things, Wren's sugar daddy left her a financial bonanza. But fortune wasn't enough for Wren. She craved fame, a condition that often eludes hermits. Unwilling to stride out into the world and forge the reputation she so desired, the clever Wren dipped into her inheritance, ordered up a sophisticated computer and digital camera system, finessed an online photography course, downloaded images of Forest Woods to a photo agency in New York, and in the wink of an eye mutated into a renowned nature photographer without ever once leaving the woods. With the remainder of her fortune, Wren planned to purchase every acre of these remote woods, evict all the other hermits, and make Forest Woods her private sanctuary. On the rare occasions when one hermit spoke to another, when Wren's name was uttered, the same remark was repeated like a litany: "Thinks she can own these woods, she does. Fortune 'n' fame turned her rotten. Somebody oughta do somethin' about that."

Somebody did. She lay, apparently bludgeoned, on the road to Fender Falls when Marco Prendergast came upon her stinking corpse. Marco must have intended to run back down the trail and report his gruesome discovery, because when his body was found just twenty yards from Wren's, his feet were pointed in a downhill direction. This, too, is getting ahead of the tale, for five hermits haven't even been introduced.

James Woolhouse was a latter-day enviro-hippie who, like Marco Prendergast, dwelt in arborea, only James lived in a canvas tent perched between the branches of a two-hundred-year-old cedar. James's needs were few, beyond basic necessities like toilet paper (any brand would do), Tom's spearmint toothpaste, and the occasional Atkins Advantage bar pulleyed up to him by his supporters. And bullets. James's raison d'etre was protecting the life of the ancient red cedar that he lived in, that same tree that forestry officers thought should be chopped down to make room for a hikers' way station, the same tree coveted by a certain Japanese billionaire who had offered the state two million dollars to evict James Woolhouse and turn over the beautiful wood for the construction of a Shinto shrine in Nogota. James guarded the old cedar with a nine-millimeter gun that he legally owned but had never yet fired. Other than infrequent trips to Fender Falls to bathe and shave (when Marco, before he was murdered, took James's place occupying the cedar, waving the nine-millimeter at anything that moved), James Woolhouse wasn't budging. Already, three times he had spied the same Japanese businessman lurking in the woods with a pistol aimed toward his treehouse. Even if it meant a shoot-out, James would die before anyone would chop down this old cedar.

Aggie Lund, the second eldest hermit in Forest Woods, collected mushrooms, illegally harvesting fungi off federal forest land. Aggie sold the mushrooms at market, which required a semimonthly trip to town in her ancient red pickup truck with rusted fenders. Few of the Forest Woods hermits owned vehicles, and Aggie often carried tagalongs on her trips. Aggie was old and crooked and the grumpiest of all the hermits. The others called her "old crank," but only behind her back because she was, after all, transportation.

Fred Morgan lived in a cave overlooking the forestry access road. Fred hadn't shaved or cut his hair or bathed in seventeen years. His fingernails and toenails resembled parrot claws. A convicted felon, Fred had served his sentence for breaking and entering and was thoroughly disgusted with human society, including himself. The story goes that back when Fred was a pristine young man of twenty-two, he had opened his apartment door one morning to find balloons festooning his porch, big bright things. From behind them a voice said, "Are you Fred Morgan?"

"Sure."

"Well, Fred, congratulations! We are the Prize Patrol and you have won ten million dollars."

At that very same moment, Fred had a sudden urge to go to the bathroom. When it hit, it hit, regular as clockwork, and Fred couldn't stop the action, so he slammed the door and ran to the toilet. Five minutes later Fred was back, but not a soul nor a balloon festooned his doorstep.

This was the moment of Fred's downturn, for he believed that the world owed him that ten million bucks, and he robbed and pillaged until finally he was caught and put away for enough hard time to totally pickle his world view. Now Fred kept a pistol underneath his pillow because he feared his dreams as much as he feared reality. The other hermits called him "Regular Fred," and clucked over his hygienic backsliding.

Rodney Herman was a young man of nineteen years with all the ambition of a tree sloth. Having fled the city at sixteen, Rodney recently had passed his third year as a hermit dwelling in a stone cottage in Forest Woods. Rodney's hand-carved driftwood panpipes sold well at the town market, providing him cash to buy the weed he needed to stay sane. Pot was Rodney's only vice, unless you counted his almost insatiable appetite for red meat. He ate nothing else. Often Rodney was seen combing the ocean beaches that bordered the woods, seeking driftwood for his panpipes and the occasional elk or bear to shoot and eat. Elk and bear were scarce now in Forest Woods.

Earl Monroe, pronounced MON-roe, was born and bred in Forest Woods, had never lived anywhere else and never intended to. Earl's parents had been tree farmers, and when they both died in a fiery crash—their pickup's brakes had mysteriously failed and they'd collided with a dairy truck on the access road—Earl inherited the small tree farm and the family's log cabin. Earl continued to live simply, except one day a year when he celebrated his parents' violent deaths. On that anniversary, Earl traveled into town and drank himself stupid.

The oldest hermit in these woods, Winter Beacon, was seventy-seven, and the largest man you could imagine, a giant whose footsteps terrified every living thing in his path, the single exception being his goat, Rosie, who feared no one and nothing. Winter's flannel shirts were the size of bedsheets and they billowed as he tramped through the forest on his daily rounds, which included a visit to Fender Falls, where he would bathe in the icy froth, then to the meadow glade where he would check the meadow pond's temperature, then to the crest of Hogback Hill, where he would check the position of the sun, when it was visible, then to the pasture where he'd check to see if Rosie's milk had come back, then to the ancient cedar, which lately harbored the tree sitter James Woolhouse, where Winter would knock on the cedar's trunk twelve times, then walk around it fourteen times, and then back home to his cottage deep in the woods, where Yaog, his Australian shepherd dog, awaited his return.

So these eight hermits lived in Forest Woods: Marco Prendergast, the telecommuting software programmer; the fragile, scheming Wren; the armed and vigilant enviro-hippie James Woolhouse; the mushroom thief, Aggie "Old Crank" Lund; Regular Fred Morgan, who hated himself and feared his dreams; youthful pothead Rodney Herman; Earl MON-roe, the tree farmer who celebrated his parents' violent deaths; and Winter Beacon, the oldest, grandest hermit of them all.

They knew little about one another until the day that Rodney Herman stumbled over Marco's and Wren's bodies in the woods.

That hot, dry summer morning, Rodney had set out along the path to Fender Falls, intending to have his annual shower. He'd spent the night quartering and field dressing an elk he had illegally killed the previous afternoon, and he had blood on his hands. Hiking along the path to Fender Falls, Rodney got about halfway there when he tripped over something solid that lay across the path. It turned out to be Marco Prendergast. Marco was as dead as a doornail and his bloated, blood-caked remains had already been visited by something with teeth. In fact, the only reason Rodney knew it was Marco was that he recognized the knapsack as the bag Marco always toted around with his software inventions stuffed inside.

Rodney got one look at where Marco's face used to be and lost his breakfast. Dazed, he wandered a few yards up the trail and came upon Wren's corpse. Even the buzzards had abandoned it, but it was Wren all right. Rodney recognized the signature Fluvog shoes that she liked to say were charmed.

Their magic hadn't worked this time. Rodney turned and ran downhill, passing Marco's corpse without stopping. In the dim morning light, he thrashed through the woods until he reached the cabin nearest to Fender Falls. Winter Beacon's cabin.

Winter heard Rodney's hollering and came out on his front stoop. Winter had long white hair that he wore in a flowing bob and white whiskers that reached down as far his chest, which often protruded between the unbuttoned sides of his flannel shirts. He had just finished a breakfast of boiled oats drizzled over with maple syrup, and his whiskers hung heavy with the remnants. Winter's dog, Yaog, scrambled up behind his master and growled at Rodney until Winter raised a gnarly hand as if to strike Yaog's muzzle. Yaog whimpered and slid his limp tail between his legs.

"Calm down, Rodney," said Winter Beacon. "Whatever it is can't be that bad."

Rodney gulped and finally managed a gargled, "They done it. They finally done it."

"Done what, Rodney? And who?"

"Wren. They killed her 'fore she could take over the woods. And Marco, too."

"What about the old bastard?" Winter called everyone an old bastard, except women. He called women bitches, slurring to make it sound like "britches," or "witches."

"Dead," Rodney said. "Wren and Marco. Both of 'em."

Winter studied the distant sky. A cloud bank was forming above his back meadow, dark buffalo-shaped billowing things that Winter knew carried rain. Drought had all but burned his upper meadow grass off and already Rosie had lost five kilos. Between drought and human encroachment, Rosie's territory had shrunk and shriveled, and Winter worried over her gauntness and the dark way she watched him from the barren slopes, her udders dry and shriveled as prunes.

"S'God's truth, I swear, Winter," Rodney said. "Both's dead. I saw their corpses. You gotta go for help."

Winter owned an aged Harley that he used on occasion to fetch supplies from town, but it had a flat tire.

"You got a telephone?" Rodney said.

Winter shook his head.

"We gotta report this, Winter," said Rodney. "Else someone might blame one of us."

Winter rubbed his sticky beard. Behind him, Yaog thrashed his tail and barked. Whenever Winter rubbed his beard it usually meant food was imminent. Yaog barked again and Winter kicked the dog. He yelped and slinked back inside the cabin. He cast a reproachful look at Winter, and for the first time, Rodney saw how the dog had one gentle brown eye and one icy blue.

Winter gazed out over Rodney's head and saw the dark clouds moving in faster now, with intent. "Who saw them last?" Winter said finally. "I mean, alive."

Rodney scratched his smooth cheek. "Dunno about Wren, but last time I saw Marco, he was with Aggie Lund. Saw the old crank's pickup on the highway heading toward town. Marco was hitchhiking. It was yesterday morning. Aggie stopped, picked up Marco, and they drove off into town. I saw that. Then, later on last evening, I was waitin' for Marco to meet me. We had an elk to kill. But when he never showed up, I went down to Regular Fred's in case Marco might've gone to Fred's for supper like he does some of the time. But he wasn't there. Fred told me that Marco's electric generator had broke down and he'd gone into town for parts. And Fred told me he saw Aggie on the road coming back again, heading back into the woods. She was alone, Fred told me. No Marco. But Fred'd been drinking mojitos with Wren, 'cause I saw her in his cabin hiding in the shadows, just lurking back in there, like with a guilty conscience, like she'd got somethin' on her mind, and then she called out from the shadows, claimed that Marco was with Aggie when she come back. But, you know, Wren was as drunk as Fred, so how would I know who to believe?"

Winter said, "Maybe they made it all up. Just to cast suspicion."

Now Rodney pleaded with Winter. "We got to do something, else we'll get blamed."

Winter grunted and said, "Where'd you get that blood on your hands?"

Rodney looked down at his hands as if seeing them for the first time, as if they had just now grown there. "What?" he said, surprised. "This blood? Hell, Winter, this here's elk's blood. I killed me one yesterday, butchered and dressed it over the night. See, I was headed up to the falls to wash off."

Winter chortled behind his beard. Like he didn't buy Rodney's story, like he had found it humorous.

Rodney shivered. "Winter," he said in a high, tight voice, "you don't think I killed Wren and Marco, do you? Just 'cause I got elk's blood on my hands? Just 'cause I come across Wren's and Marco's corpses don't mean I killed them. Why would I come for help, then? Hell, anybody coulda' come upon that on the path to Fender Falls. You don't think I killed them, do you, Winter?"

Winter tugged at his whiskers. Like he had to think it over. He had a habit of sucking air through the spaces between his teeth, and now he sucked air so loud that Rodney thought at first he heard the waterfall. Finally, Winter turned slowly around and headed back inside his cabin. Over his shoulder he said to Rodney, "You go on, now, Rodney. Play your little games on someone stupider than me."

"No game, honest to God . . ."

"Go on now, Rodney. I've seen enough of you for one day. Hurry now. It's gonna pour buckets."

Winter closed the cabin door firmly, and Rodney heard the wood bolt slip into place. A gust of wind came up and danced across Rodney's back. He could smell the rain coming, and he could smell danger.

Half an hour later, when Rodney arrived at Aggie Lund's cabin, the air had grown cold, the sky had turned black, and rain was falling in sheets. The forest floor had turned to thick mud, and all Rodney could think about was the two corpses up there on the path to Fender Falls and how they lay there on the sodden ground that surely by now had turned to muck. Rodney should have moved Marco's body, or covered him up, or, hell, done something. He didn't care about Wren. She could rot where she lay. The hell with land-grabbers. But he cared about Marco. At the very least, he should've covered him up. Instead, he had just let the body lie and had run to Winter Beacon for help. Big damn help.

Aggie came to the door. "Hell and tarnation, Rodney Herman, are you out of your skull? Get in here out of the rain. It's about to drown you like the rat you are."

Rodney shook off before entering Aggie's cabin. It was warm inside, a big fire blazing in the stone fireplace, the soft glow of oil lamps flushing the room crimson and gold. Rodney felt like he'd gone from hell to heaven. He dropped down before the blazing fire and held his hands to the flames.

Aggie brought him a towel. "Now, go on into the pantry and put these things on." She tossed a dry flannel shirt and a pair of trousers at him.

Rodney stood up and carried the clothing into the pantry. When he returned to the main room, dressed in Aggie's pants and shirt, the old crank was seated in a wing chair by the fireplace, her apron lap filled with mushrooms, a basket at her feet. She sorted the good from the rotten, tossing the rejects directly into the fire where they sizzled and shriveled to nothing. Once again, Rodney dropped down onto the hearth, his teeth chattering, despite the dry clothing.

"What's got into you, young man?" Aggie asked him.

Rodney wept and told Aggie about finding Wren's and Marco's corpses.

Aggie listened intently, and when he had finished his tale, she said, "Smoking too much weed's your problem. Marco can't be dead. I rode him into town yesterday morning and I rode him back to the woods yesterday evening. And when I left him off on the road, I saw Wren standing on Regular Fred's front stoop, and Fred was there, too. I didn't bother to wave, but I saw them. You're hallucinating, you ask me."

Rodney begged and pleaded with Aggie to believe him, but the old woman insisted that he had concocted the terrible tale in a marijuana stupor. When the rain let up, Rodney thanked Aggie for the loan of dry clothing and left her sitting by her warm hearth sorting mushrooms and clucking about juvenile delinquency.

Rodney loped down the path, wearing Aggie's shirt and pants, his own drenched clothing tucked into a canvas Doubleday Book Club bag that Aggie had provided. Soon as he rounded the bend out of sight, Aggie put down her mushrooms and prepared to go out. She donned her light summer cape, the one with all the secret pockets where she hid mushrooms from the forestry officials who lurked in these woods. Lacing up her Doc Martens, she locked her cottage door, stepped onto the rain-muddied forest path, and hiked three miles uphill, grumbling all the way about how osteoarthritis was eldercide perpetrated by Gen Xers in a race with crows to dominate the world. Aggie huffed and puffed and cursed her aching kneecaps.

At a fork in the road, Aggie turned left and followed the narrower path toward Fender Falls, a steep, rocky path, slick now from rainfall. Climbing cautiously, her mud-caked boots seeking purchase on slippery stone outcroppings, Aggie suddenly had the sense that someone or some thing stalked the woods nearby. She looked straight ahead, pretending not to notice the flickers of shadowy movement between the trees to the right of the path. She hiked until she heard the waterfall; then she turned suddenly and faced the shadow in the woods.

"Come on out now, MON-roe," she hollered.

Silence. Just the soft swoosh of the waterfall.

Once again, Aggie yelled, "You come on out, MON-roe. I know you're back in there. I can smell ya."

Earl Monroe poked his head sheepishly around a broad fir trunk. He grinned, showing all his empty gums, and raising one gnarly brown hand, he wiggled his fingers at Aggie. "Hey, Aggie," he said. "Wasn't spyin', swear to God."

"Well then, what'd you mean creepin' and crawlin'

in there like a snivelin' snake, you sonofabitch? Now, come out and face me like a man."

Earl Monroe skulked out from behind the fir and loped down onto the footpath. His waterlogged clothing clung to him like a wrinkled skin and his red hair hung wet and stringy over his forehead. He pushed it back and tilted his head, unable to form the words he wanted to say.

"Speak up, you nincompoop." Aggie folded her broad arms across her chest.

In that summer cape, Monroe thought, Aggie resembled a pup tent. How do you talk to a pup tent? Finally, the words came and Monroe said, "He's bad. Real bad."

"Who, damn it?"

"M-M-M-Marco. Real bad."

"You saw him?"

Monroe nodded and rotated his head some more. Aggie grabbed him by the wet arm. "You take me there, MON-roe. Hurry now."

Monroe shrugged. He didn't want to go back there. Too ugly. "Can't," he said. "Made me puke."

Aggie grasped him harder. "Where's yer gumption, MON-roe? Now, march."

Monroe paid attention to Aggie's steel grip as she pushed him ahead of her up the path. When they finally reached Fender Falls, Monroe jerked his head sideways and said, "Over yonder."

Aggie tightened her grip on Monroe's arm. "You take me there."

Monroe shook his head from side to side. "No way, Aggie. I ain't seein' that corpse again. I ain't pukin' again. You go on over there by yerself. I be right here waiting for you."

Aggie snorted. What in the world was wrong with chicken-hearted young folk? MON-roe had the nerve of a slug. She let go of his arm and went off by herself in the direction MON-roe's head had jerked.

Monroe watched the old crank disappear around a bend. As soon as she was out of sight, he drew a pistol from his trouser pocket and set off on a trail parallel to the one Aggie traveled.

The woods were silent except for the whooshing of Fender Falls. Aggie plodded toward what looked like a log fallen across the path. Then, from the near distance came the cracking sound of gunfire. Aggie paused, listened. Silence again. The gunshot had come from somewhere to her left, not far from the path to Winter Beacon's cabin. Could be the old man finally got sense and shot that beastly hound Yaog. Could be.

Though she hadn't heard a death yelp. Aggie turned her attention back to the thing lying across the road, approaching it with caution. Bending over the thing, she immediately smelled death, and when she looked at the corpse's face she let out a tiny cry. Who in hell would want to murder Rodney Herman? He lay across the footpath, deader than stone, an expression of astonishment frozen on his face and the imprint of a cloven hoof on his forehead.

Aggie reached down and closed the boy's paralyzed eyelids. Other than the mark on his forehead, she couldn't find any injury on his body, no blood except for some dribbling from his mouth and ears. No bullet holes, nothing cut and dried that said how Rodney Herman had met his fate. She drew his splayed arms up across his chest, and that's when she saw one hand had been chewed off. Removing her cape, she spread it over Rodney's corpse, and as she did so, tiny teardrops slid down her cheek. She grieved for young Rodney Herman less than for the ruin of her favorite cape.

Aggie continued on because she had to see for herself if it was true about Marco Prendergast, if he really lay dead near Fender Falls, his face torn off. And if it was true about Wren, that someone had finally done what Aggie had dreamed of doing.

Sure enough, when Aggie reached the spot Rodney had described, she found the corpse of Marco Prendergast, its face missing and the most godawful smell emanating from it. Aggie reeled backward. Moving up the trail, she spied Wren's body, got close enough to ascertain that the girl was indeed dead. She waited half an hour but MON-roe never showed up, so she hiked back down the trail, pausing to whisper over Rodney Herman's corpse. "Stupid pothead," she said. "Serves ya right fer killin' poor Marco."

Of course, she didn't know for certain that Rodney had killed Marco, but with both of them dead, and with Rodney's checkered lifestyle, it only made sense that one had killed the other and then Satan had come and taken the killer's body to hell. Even left his mark. Maybe Rodney had killed Wren, too. "It's what you get for selling yer soul to the devil," she grumbled over Rodney, and then she followed the path back home, where on her porch, rocking in the slider sat Regular Fred, the ex-con who had snubbed the Prize Patrol. Fred pointed his gun at Aggie.

"Don't shoot me, ya goddamn criminal," growled Aggie. "And what d'you mean sittin' up there on my porch without my permission?"

Fred stilled the slider and put the gun away. Standing to his full height, about five-foot-four, Fred said, "Thought you was dead, Aggie. Thought I just now saw your ghost."

"What the hell are you talking about, Fred? I'm as real as you are."

"But I saw you up there on the path, dead. A big mark on your forehead. Like Satan's mark."

Aggie said, "You idiot. That was Rodney Herman wearin' my clothes."

Fred followed Aggie inside, "So, then, who killed MON-roe?"

Aggie squinted. "What the hell are you sayin', Fred? That MON-roe's dead, too?"

Fred sucked in air, pissed it out slow as a leaky tire, and said, "That's why I come over here, Aggie. About Earl MON-roe. He's dead up near Fender Falls. Over on the back side, y'know? I found him on Hogback, way up above Winter Beacon's land. Dead as they come. Had a gun in his hand, too, like suicide, but I didn't see bullet holes, just that mark on his forehead, like he'd been kicked silly. And both ears chewed off. So then I'm comin' back down toward your place, 'cause Winter wasn't home when I stopped, and I like to tripped over what looked like you lyin' in the path. But now you tell me that was Rod Herman wearin' your clothes."

"You sure it was Earl MON-roe?" Aggie pawed in her closet for her other cape, the winter cape, made of yellow canvas, waxed.

"Totally. Can't mistake that red hair. And he had on that old flannel shirt he always wears, you know the plaid one, always smells like cow puck?"

Aggie knew the shirt. "Now, listen here," she said

as she tied the winter cape around her shoulders, "we're going for help."

Fred shook his head. "Don't know, Aggie. I'm nervous. Real nervous. You know how the law treats an ex-felon. I don't want nothin' to do with cops."

Aggie grasped Fred by the arm. "C'mon, chicken-shit," she said and pulled him out the door and onto the path, Fred whimpering like a scared puppy. They hadn't walked a mile when they came to the old cedar occupied by James Woolhouse. They stopped and Aggie yelled up to James, but he didn't answer. She yelled and yelled, but James didn't once show his face or in any way indicate his presence. Aggie turned to Fred. "You go on up there," she told him. "See what you can find."

Fred reeled backward. "Hell, Aggie, I can't climb up there. What if James is the killer? What if he's layin' a trap? He's got a gun, you know."

"So do you, you sniveling wimp," snapped Aggie. "All right, then I'll climb up there. You stay down here and keep watch. Satan's in these woods. I can smell it." Under her breath she mumbled an apology to the late Rodney.

James Woolhouse had made a little rope ladder that hung halfway down the cedar's trunk. Grasping on to the rope, she found purchase with her foot and climbed up into James Woolhouse's tent. What she saw made her gasp.

"You come up here right now, Regular Fred Morgan," she yelled down. "There's badness up here, and I need a witness."

Fred balked until Aggie emerged from the tent carrying James Woolhouse's shotgun. Aiming it down at Fred was enough to convince him to climb. No telling what the old crank might do with a loaded gun. Fred climbed up and peered into the tent.

What Fred saw was two bodies slumped over James Woolhouse's little table. One was James. The other was a Japanese man dressed in a dark business suit, starched white shirt, and a black tie. His shoes were polished to a high gloss like the hair on his head. From the positions of their corpses, it appeared the two men had struggled with each other. James had two black eyes. The Japanese businessman had a broken arm and from his hand dangled a small pistol.

"Look at their faces," said Aggie grimly. Fred looked at the men, hard as it was, and saw they both had the same cloven hoof marks impressed on their foreheads. He looked up at Aggie. The old crank nodded.

"Satan's mark," she said confidently. "Someone in these woods has made a pact with Satan and's killin' us off one by one."

Fred said, "But these two, they musta' been fightin' the way they look."

"Sure they were. But then the killer got 'em both." Aggie gestured with the shotgun toward the tent door. "Let's get on down and go for help."

The two hermits scrambled down the cedar trunk and continued along the road. Aggie always kept her pickup truck at the head of the access road, where, when it snowed, she didn't get stuck.

Aggie turned out her palm. "Think about it, Fred. There's you and me. We've been together this past hour. Who's dead? Marco and Wren, Rodney, MON-roe. And now James and that Japanese feller. Who's left?"

Fred thought it over. "Naw," he said. "Couldn't be. He wouldn't do this, not Winter Beacon."

Aggie grimaced. Fred was so stupid. "Well, then, who else?" she asked him irritably.

Fred shrugged. "A stranger. Some serial killer's got loose in these woods. Plenty of them in that place I was locked up in. Some of 'em bound to be out by now. Ask me, this has serial killer written all over it."

Aggie gripped Fred's arm tighter than ever. "We're going for help. You get in the pickup now, Fred."

Aggie and Fred drove along the access road a half a mile to the highway entrance. Traffic was light, but Aggie couldn't turn off right away because the setting sun glared straight into her windshield, blinding her. She squinted until she could see, and when the traffic cleared, Aggie put her foot on the gas pedal. At the same instant, Aggie and Fred saw the thing come crashing through the windshield, Fred thinking at first that it was a huge meteorite.

"Good hell," cried Aggie, and that was the last thing she ever said. The thing struck Fred's forehead first and Fred died instantly. It took three strikes of the cloven hoof to finish Aggie off.

At sunset, Winter Beacon came around a bend in the Forest Woods access road and saw Rosie nibbling at a dry bush.

"So there you are, Rosie," said Winter, patting the goat's shiny black coat. "Always scroungin' for food, ain't ya?" Winter took a good look at Rosie. "Why, girl, you've gained some girth since yesterday.

Musta' found you a fine grassy meadow somewhere."

Rosie tilted her head up to Winter. The old hermit stroked her pointy beard and doing so, noted red stains on its hairs. Looking down, he saw that Rosie's front hooves also bore red stains.

Winter grinned. "Found you some red clover, did you, Rosie?"

Rosie snorted and pawed the earth, and then Winter led Rosie up home. He couldn't help but notice Rosie's udders, full and soft and round, and Winter thought how delicious fresh goat's milk would taste on his breakfast gruel.

BAD-HEARTED
Brad Reynolds

Old Stories of Isidore Pete
Translated by Lizzie Karl and Alice Pitka
Mrs. Baird, 8th Grade

A.P.

Me and Lizzie interviewed Isidore Pete for our Eskimo Elders project in Mrs. Baird's class. We were going to do my app'a, but Mrs. Baird said no relatives. Then we thought Anna Felix. But Ralph and Sonny had her already, so we said ok to having Isidore Pete. But I still don't know why we couldn't do my app'a, because he has good stories and, besides, is nicer.

L.K.

Isidore Pete was born in Eqtarmiut in 1921, but he doesn't know the month. Maybe October, because he told us it was Cauyarvik, which means "the month

of drumming in Eskimo dances." It was a lot different back then, and he told us some of those things
he remembered. He lives with only himself in the
old house that is away from the others, down by the
slough, past those willows on the other side of Mar-
tina Lincoln's house. His place never got water like
the new housing, so his honey bucket smells really
bad, but after a while we were used to it, and besides, his house was dirty already. There is only
some chairs and a table and his bed. But no mattress,
just blankets and a bearskin on top that is dirty and
has holes. But he has electricity and can watch television when he wants to.

Besides being very old, Isidore could tell us about
his past-life experiences and how they lived in the
old days. He knew lots of stories. I think he was
trying hard to scare us and sometimes I was scared.
Even if he said they were only stories, I wondered if
sometimes they were true. This is because of how his
eyes looked when he said those stories. Sometimes
you can see the truth in grown-up eyes when they
tell you things and sometimes you can see when they
are just lying. I thought maybe he was saying more
truth than lies. But Isidore told us we had to give
him money first. Mrs. Baird said no money for stories
so we told him that, and then he changed and said
just *agutuq*. So my mom made Eskimo ice cream and
then he ate it and he told us some stories.

I.P.

My Yup'ik name is Paluqtaarlek, but just my family
called me that and they are all dead, so now I am

only Isidore Pete. So old I was born in 1921, maybe while it was Cauyarvik, but I don't remember for sure. Our village was called Eqtarmiut, but there is nothing left there. I got only five white hairs on top of my head that you can see. There's more, but they're somewhere down below and you kids can't see those. Otherwise maybe they would lock me up.

I can remember lots of the old stuff to tell you about.

A.P.

And you know stories?

I.P.

Yes. But in the old times those kids never would interrupt their elders. They only sat quiet and listened to what they had to tell them and did not butt in with other words. Only the elders said words and the kids just listened. It was really different back then.

OK then. So when I just started noticing things I was still with my mama and not living in the *qasegiq* with the other mens. We didn't know about snow machines, and whenever we had to go anywhere we either walked or sometimes had sleds with lots of dogs. When I first became aware of myself I remember my mama putting me in our sled and tying a big bearskin around me. The black hairs were tickling my face, but it was snowing hard, and my father was holding on to the barking dogs, tying them to the sled. My sister wasn't born yet, so it was only me and my mama who got in the sled that time, and my father ran behind and sometimes he rode. I don't remember where we went that time. I can remember smelling my mama there on the sled and hearing the dogs when they were barking. My father would shout whenever they slowed down.

Now, I should tell you about some of the winter rules that I remember. These are rules about when you travel outside the village.

The old times had a rule about when you get lost in the tundra and there's too much snow. If you will die by yourself you make a hole in the snow and try to put in some grass or maybe small bushes to cover the bottom. And get a pole or stick. Then close the opening over your head so you are inside the snow and it is warmer down in there than up above in the wind. You won't freeze right away. But keep checking with the stick to make sure there is a hole so you can breathe. And on top of the stick you should tie something you are wearing. So if someone is going past you or even looking for you, they will see the clothes and know you are inside the hole. Then they dig you out and even if you aren't awake they can take you back to the village and make you warm and you will live. That is one rule.

Another rule is for when you fall through the ice. When you are stuck and can't climb out, take off your pants or your shirt. They are wet already so it don't matter. Hold on to it tight and slap it hard on the ice in front of you. It will freeze on there in a minute, and then you can use your clothes to pull yourself out of the hole. That is a really good rule, and I know it works because once I had to do that.

So when you are wet and out of the hole, get grasses or willows. Take off all your clothes and wring out the water. Then put them back on but with the grasses or willows between your skin and the clothes. They will be puffing out and not touching you so even if they are really wet those clothes won't touch. And if they freeze and turn hard, no wind can get inside and make you freeze worse. But you need to hurry home then and not keep hunting. These are old-time rules and good ones to know about, even today. Or else you might die someday.

OK. That's enough for rules. *Tuaii.* Now I'll tell you a story you asked for, even though you gave me no moneys.

A.P.

We gave you *agutuq* from Lizzie's mom.

I.P.

OK then. But you don't remember what I told about not interrupting, do you, little thing? Maybe I should tell you about the baby that had the biggest mouth and what happened. Would you like to be scared? No? OK then. When I was first in school I had an Eskimo man who taught us with a stick. If we cried or misbehaved, he hit us on the head really hard. Even if I was only beginning I never forgot what he taught. We had only flat rocks and we wrote our alphabets and numbers on those. We didn't do school until Vivik, the beginning of circling the year.

And we were finished in Tengmiarvik, when ducks fly back.

L.K.

Vivik is what we call December now, and Tengmiarvik might be in April. I did not say this on the tape recorder when he was talking so Isidore couldn't scold me. I only wrote it later on.

I.P.

We learned to write *qaneq* for eyes. *Nuyat* was hairs and *qengaq* was nose. These were words I wrote down when I was a beginner. I remember older boys wrote *qurrsuti*. You girls know that word, I bet you do. Even if it's a bad word about boys, I bet you sure know it. And they wrote *ningi*. That means horny. That Eskimo teacher broke his stick when he saw what that rock was saying. He was really pissed off at those boys.

When we got a *gussuk* teacher the first time, he told me my name was Isidore and I was ten. Even if I was older than that, he still said I was ten. This was not at Eqtarmiut but somewhere else. By then I had dogs for my own sled, which is how I know I was more than ten. Even if I was young I had seven or nine good dogs. They ate mostly fish, but by Tengmiarvik that was gone and I hunted for other foods to give them, rabbits with mush and flour or heads off ptarmigan. Anything you could get and didn't eat, you fed to the dogs. If not, then you had to get rid of some and even feed the rest with the ones you got rid of. That's just the way it was.

It was harder then and not as easy as things are now. We had no electricity, so in the night it was dark outside. My mama never let me go outside at night because peoples or monsters could kill me. Even in the *qasegiq* the monsters could try and come in from the floor. If the shaman didn't try to stop them, they could tie a rope around a man's neck and then kill him at night. And at night I was not supposed to go in other houses. Because if you find something that is not yours and you take that, people will think bad about you. Even if your hand reaches out for money that is not yours, you should not take it. My mama said teeth would catch my hands. But they never did. And at night we were not to touch other people or kids or be too friendly. Again our hands would get bitten by the teeth and the people would get mad. Those were the rules at night when it was dark.

This story is not about me but about another. When this boy's father ran away, maybe to another village to have a new wife, he felt lonely even if he still had his mama. But there was no man to hunt them food to eat and the boy's mama went back to her own parents so that his grandfather, his *app'a*, started to be his father. And the mother was pregnant, too, so that later she had a baby girl and the grandparents started to bring that girl up like it belonged to them. And then the mama died. Maybe it was alcohol. All that booze was killing her after her husband ran off to that other woman.

The boy's *app'a* used to take the boy to the *qasegiq*,

the men's house, and they started to sleep there with the other men. The boy was missing his mama, but if he cried his *app'a* would shout and maybe even hit him sometimes. If he tried to sleep when it wasn't night, he would poke the boy with a sharp stick, making him cry more. If there was snow, the boy was sent outside to push it away from the doors so the men could get out and so women could bring in the food to feed their husbands. Although there was lots of food then, the *app'a* hardly gave the boy any. He started to get really skinny then. One time he caught a crane with a bow and arrow and took it to his grandmother so he could eat. She skinned it and cut off its throat and put it on the boy's throat. Then she said, "Boy, may your voice be strong like this crane's, and even if nobody can see you, they will hear your voice from a long distance." When she cooked the crane, her husband would not let her give the boy even a taste. That *app'a* was very mean to that boy.

One time the boy went to the *qasegiq* and was going to try and sleep there. Only when he got in the door he saw his *app'a* sitting in the corner. That old man was the only one in there. The boy started to go to him to ask him if he could sleep even in the day, but when he got close he saw the man's eyes were closed. He was sleeping. He was carving something and got tired and put down his knife next to him. The boy saw that and picked up the knife to look at it. If it was good and sharp, he was thinking he might take it for a while. But then his *app'a* woke up and saw the boy holding his knife. He shouted out and tried to grab the boy, but the boy was too quick for the old man and jumped back. The grandfather stood up and ran to the boy, but then he tripped on something lying on the floor, maybe the thing he was carving and the knife went into the old man and he fell down on the floor. There was blood coming out from him, where the knife went into him, and then his mouth. Then he died.

The boy got scared and ran out of the *qasegiq* and back to his grandmother, but he didn't say nothing about what happened. Then later some other men came and told his grandmother that her husband was dead. They said he fell on his knife because they saw how he tripped on that thing. The boy said nothing, even though his voice was now as strong as the crane's. That is the story. *Tuaii.*

If you want another one, it will be about a little girl this time.

A.P.

Yes, we want one.

I.P.

OK then. A young girl was walking in wintertime and she only had a grass basket. There was nothing like backpacks or purses back then. And she had a woman's knife, an *ulaq*, in the basket. When she starts going between the two mountains, she trips and falls into the snow. She gets up and finds what made her trip. It is a thick string. One side is from the muscle of reindeer and it goes all the way to the mountain. The other side is made from fish skin and it goes to that other mountain. So she opens her basket and uses the *ulaq* to cut the string. Then she keeps walking past those mountains. Only she hears a voice behind her. "Hey! Hey, girlie, you should come back here." She starts to turn around, and another voice says, "Don't listen to her. You should come to me." The first voice says, "He's lying. He'll piss on you when you're sleeping." And the second voice says, "She is a liar. She'll kill you and eat you if you go to her."

The girl turns around and sees the boy on one mountain and the girl on the other one and both of them are chewing something in their mouths. The young girl tells them to show her what they are chewing. Remember, this is before gum, so it wasn't that. The boy was chewing walrus skin for gum, and the girl had a human person's ear for chewing gum.

The young girl thought about both those kids and then went over to the boy chewing walrus skin. He got very happy and took the young girl over the mountain to his house on the other side. They run down to the house and go inside, and the boy's grandmother is very, very happy. She gives them good food to eat and tells the young girl she can have a bed to sleep in. Only she says never to go outside at night. "If you need to go to the bathroom, you should use the honey bucket and not go outside," she says.

So the young girl starts to live with the grandmother and the boy.

One night when the girl wakes up she has to go to the bathroom. But the honey bucket is very full so she has no place to go. Even though the grandmother warned her, she went outside. The moon is bright and she can look around and see things. When she is finished, she looks around and sees something shining. It is that other girl with the human ear from the mountain. The ear girl puts two of her little fingers in her mouth and sucks and when they get real wet she wiggles them at that young girl. And even though she doesn't want to, her legs start running right toward that ear girl. When she gets there, she is carried over the mountain to the ear girl's house and they go inside.

Her grandmother is lying on the bed inside, and she is happy to have another little girl. She says she can stay and have a bed to sleep in. So the girl lies down and though she can't fall sleep for a long time, eventually she does. When she wakes up it is still dark, but she can hear someone doing something with metal. With moonlight coming in the window she can see the old woman is holding the *ulaq* she took from the young girl's grass basket. Quickly, the young girl changes places with the ear girl and she puts on the other one's clothes. Then she pretends to be asleep.

The grandmother whispers, "Granddaughter, are you awake yet?"

The young girl says quietly, "Now I am."

"Is that other girl sleeping?"

"*Iiii*," the young girl answers, "I guess she is."

"Good," the grandmother says. "Now, put some of those cardboards underneath her bed."

A.P.

Cardboard? How can there be cardboard if this is an old story?

I.P.

Damn it! When you keep talking you make me forget part of the story. It was a dry sealskin, not a cardboard. OK then. She put down that sealskin under the bed, beneath the ear girl's head. Then the old woman came over and looked down. "She looks like my granddaughter," she said.

"Even if she does," answered the young girl, "she isn't. You should do it quickly before she wakes up."

So the old woman used the girl's *ulaq* and cut off her granddaughter's own head.

"*Aren!*" she cried. "There is too much blood! Run outside and fetch me that bucket."

So the young girl jumped up and ran outside. She got the bucket and threw it into the house beside the old woman. "Here," she said, "put it under your granddaughter's head to catch her blood." Then she started running away, and behind her the old woman was screaming about what she had done. The young girl ran all the way to the other mountain and down the other side and into the house. The grandmother and the boy were sitting in their beds, crying. But as as soon as they saw that young girl they both jumped up with joy and were happy. "We thought you would be dead," said the grandmother. "Now you are back and can stay with us. But never go out again at night, even if you want to go to the bathroom.

Always stay inside.'' So the young girl was happy for a long while and stayed with that grandmother and the boy after that. *Tuaii iqukllituq.*

L.K.

Quyana cakneq.

I.P.

You're welcome, little thing. That's a good story I can remember.

A.P.

Why did that one girl chew the human ear? Was her grandmother making her do that?

I.P.

No, not at all. That one girl was bad-hearted. And the boy knew it, and that's why he wanted the young girl to stay with him and not go to her. He always knew when someone was bad-hearted.

A.P.

How? How did he know?

I.P.

Aren! You ask me so many questions. He knew, OK? He always knew when people were bad-hearted. Even when he was a little boy, he could tell that. His whole life he had to live around bad-hearted people.

That's why his life was so sad to him. Only his mama and his grandmother were not bad-hearted. But everyone else was. He felt that very, very much. They made him mad and then maybe even he got bad-hearted.

Tuaii! Enough questions now. I will tell you how that boy finally turned into a bear.

L.K.

We had to stop that day because A.P. forgot to bring more cassettes for our tape recorder and Mrs. Baird was already gone from the school. So we had to wait until the next day to get cassettes and go back to Isidore's house. He got mad when we had to leave him and told us we couldn't come back. But we took more *agutuq* and some moose meat so he let us come into his house the next day.

A.P.

L.K. is always a blamer. I wouldn't have forgot the cassette if she didn't make me hurry up. And the moose was from one my brother shot.

I.P.

OK, this is my last time for telling you stories. I don't care if you got cassettes or not, so maybe you should just listen with your ears instead of that damn machine. You little things might learn some lessons then.

I was going to tell you about that boy becoming a

bear, but first maybe you should know about the girl
and how she started to live.

One time there was a young girl without no family
and she got adopted by an old woman and her
grandson. They lived way out by themselves somewhere. Maybe folks did not live by them because the
grandson was so strong and becoming a giant. I don't
know about that. But when they got older the boy
decided to marry the girl. But she refused him. All
the time he would try to marry her, but she kept on
refusing. She liked her dog better than she liked him.
Finally the boy got pissed and said, "Maybe you will
marry your dog someday!" That dog got up and
shook himself all over. He understood what the boy
was saying.

When it was night and they were about to sleep,
that dog would go over to the girl's bed and crawl
right into it and sleep with her. So the boy decided
they were already married and the girl's husband
was that dog.

When that girl got pregnant, the grandmother was
pissed off because she said the babies would be like
dogs and not human people.

One day the boy went to the river with the dog
husband and told him his wife was waiting for him
on the other side. He had the girl's baby and he put
it in a basket he tied on the dog's back. "You should
take your baby and go see your wife," he told the dog.
"Maybe it's time for her to nurse it." Then he put rocks
in the basket, too, and sent the dog across the river.
He watched him swim and how much that dog kept
swimming. Finally the dog got tired. The boy thought
the dog drowned, so he went home and the dog never

came back. That girl cried for her husband a long, long time. Then the grandmother made her some *agutuq* and she ate it and was happy again. *Tuaii iqukllituq.*

A.P.

Wait a minute. That boy killed that girl's dog?

I.P.

Because it was trying to be her husband, that's why.

A.P.

And the baby?

I.P.

It weren't no human. It was just an animal. That's the story.

A.P.

I don't like that story. It's not a nice one.

I.P.

I don't care if it's nice, that's the story I'm gonna tell about. You asked me for stories, right? OK, then, I'm telling you. If you don't want them then go away and don't come here no more. I never invited you.

L.K.

No, no, it's OK if you tell that story. Alice didn't mean to say that. You tell good stories. *Quyana.*

I.P.

OK then. I'm only saying how life was in those times. Peoples lived like family and they had to respect one another. Children grew up and they were supposed to marry and love one another and stay together and not do anything to hurt or disappoint one another. Even when they are separate they stay kind and don't talk about one another to other people. The woman is supposed to have great respect for her husband and not criticize or rumor him. Even if he shouted she never should talk back. A woman never did that to her husband. You young things need to listen to how wonderful it could have been in those old days. Maybe then you will understand. OK?

A.P.

Even when Lizzie pinched me I didn't say anything back to him. Isidore was scaring me. But I never liked that story and I still don't.

L.K.

Mrs. Baird, I never pinched A.P.

I.P.

This last story is called Bear Man. Now listen close so you things can learn something.

A long time ago a man and a woman were living across this river in a pretty nice place beside two mountains. And they had a couple of kids that were good. Both of them were boys, and they never did

anything to make their dad too upset with them.
They were pretty good kids and not bad-hearted, you
know. Anyway, their father would go away to hunt
for them. Sometimes he used a dog team and sometimes he just went by himself. He used a boat in that
river sometimes. After one or two nights he always
came back home and gave his wife what he brought.
They always had food.

One time that man got finished hunting in the afternoon and he came home and looked in his house.
His kids were in there, but the woman wasn't. He
looked all around but never saw her. Finally she
came home at night.

"Where were you, wife?"

"Oh, I was walking by myself and got lost," she
told him. "I looked around and found my way back
here." Then she cooked the ducks he brought and
they ate some dinner.

The man went hunting again. This time he caught
muskrats really soon that were down by the river
and when he brought them home that wife of his
was gone again. Those two boys were still in the
house. They had bowls that were empty, and the
younger one was crying because he sure missed his
mama. The father told him to stop and so he did.
Finally she came back and cooked the muskrats.

"Where were you, wife?"

"This time I went on the other side of the river
and couldn't find a way to get back across," she said.
He knew she was excusing herself, and it pissed him
off but he didn't say anything. He only went to bed
and acted like he was asleep.

The next morning the man said, "OK then, it is

time for me to go hunting again." He put his stuff in the sled and hooked up all his dogs. "Maybe I will come back in two days," he told his wife. "But maybe more." Then he left.

Only he didn't go hunt but went around one mountain. Then he got down by that river and hid where he could watch his house. Sure enough, his wife came out and she went up the other mountain and he started following. After she climbed over and went down the other side the man followed and looked down and there was another house. He looked at it for a while and then went home. His two kids had bowls of food in front of them, but they weren't crying yet. When it got night they went to sleep, but the man never did. And in the morning when it was real early, he got up and went back over the mountain to that other house. He watched for a little while and then the door opened and another man came outside. He pissed in the snow and then went back inside. Later the door opened and his own wife came out and she did some things and then went back in the house.

He went back behind the mountain then, to where he lived with his wife and two boys. He looked inside the cache he put up on poles and found a black bearskin he hunted. He carried it in the house and gave those boys some bowls of food and then got that bearskin soft. Then he climbed into that bearskin. He got two sticks and pounded nails in them for claws and broke his wife's knife for teeth. Then he went straight back over that mountain.

The man waited until the door opened and that other man came out. He followed him into the trees and then let that bear attack him. It pounded his body with the sharp claws until the snow was red with blood. Then it chewed the man's neck clean through. After that the bear went back to the house and pushed in the door. The man's wife was still in the bed and she didn't have no clothes on. The bear jumped on that bed and started clawing off her skin and biting her. She died right on that bed. Then the bear went crazy and ripped up that house. It was still plenty mad, so it came out and went back over the mountain to that other house. When it was there, it pushed in the door and found that woman's two boys still sitting there in front of their bowls of food. That bear was so angry it pounded those two little boys and spilled their food and then tore up that whole cabin. When it was done, it made a fire and burned everything.

From then on he never went back there. That man was not human after that, but was always a bear. Other hunters looked for him, but he was too smart because he used to be a man and he knew what to do. You know what? He disguised himself to look like a man again. Then he went to another village and started staying there and acting like a human again. Only he was still a bear, but no one knew. They never caught that bear, even until today. But he was not always happy thinking about what happened and about those two boys in front of their bowls of food. *Tuaii.*

That was a hard story to tell because the ending isn't so happy. I think stories should end good so people feel happy from them. But sometimes they don't. Like in that one, right? But that's just the way it is. OK then, I'm tired and I got no more stories now. You two little things should turn that off and go home. Tell your mamas *quyana* for the *agutuq* and the moose.

A.P.

What are you going to do?

I.P.

None of your business, nosy little thing. Go on out. Your visit is over.

L.K.

Quyana for the stories.

I.P.

Iiii. Tell your teacher these stories I said were only made up ones. Remind her they are the old stories of Isidore Pete. But even if they are made up ones, you little things should remember this lesson I'm telling to you. Try to stay away from bears. And from bad-hearted men who might become one.

Tuaii. You go home now.

BIRDS OF PARADISE
S. J. Rozan

The sky was dazzlingly blue, the air was shirt-sleeve warm for the first time this season, and as I drove up the highway beside the Hudson I could see two hawks circling a distant hill. In the expansive early-Sunday, early-spring silence, with the hillsides yellow-green and the streams rushing with melt-water, it was easy to believe that at least some problems, like the one I'd been called upstate to help out with, could be solved.

I turned off the highway onto the county route that would take me to Hanover, to the cheerful neighborhood of wood-frame houses where Pearl and Harry lived. I didn't go through town; we'd go into town later, when Harry was ready to open the store to show me the phenomenon he'd brought me up here to see.

Harry Hershkowitz sold hardware in Hanover, which he'd always said qualified him to join the 4H Club. Not that he ever had: "From the end of the horse that eats the oats, I wouldn't know." Hanover, a big town for this part of the state—it supports an elementary school, a synagogue, and eight churches—is a forty-minute drive from the cabin I have two counties over. It was a drive I'd learned to make after the locals had let me in on the secret: For three-penny nails or hacksaw blades, the Agway was fine, but when you needed just the right bracket or reverse-threaded screw, you needed Hershkowitz's.

And now, according to Harry, Hershkowitz's needed me.

The door to the small, neat house opened as I pulled up the driveway. Harry, bent, bald, spry, and smiling, trotted down to the car, shook my hand, tugged me through the door and directly back into the sun-filled kitchen. Pearl, also wrinkled, also smiling, kissed my cheek, poured me coffee, and ordered Harry to leave me alone until I'd eaten. I surveyed the kitchen table: platters of smoked fish, tubs of cream cheese, a mound of sliced tomatoes, and a basket of seeded rye and bagels crowded together as though they had stopped jostling each other for position just before I walked in.

I turned to Pearl, feeling a little helpless. "I ate," I said. "Before I left."

"So?" Harry pulled out a chair. "This means you can never eat again?"

"Sit." Pearl smiled. "Drink your coffee. Nibble. Harry doesn't open the store until noon on Sundays, and the preachers don't come until eleven thirty, the earliest, so what would be the point in rushing?"

So I sat, sipped Pearl's strong coffee, and arranged tomato and smoked trout on a slice of bagel. "Tell me about the preachers," I said.

Pearl made a disgusted, dismissive sound. She poured Harry coffee; he wagged his finger at me. "I'm telling you, it's people like this who give men of the cloth a bad name."

"I didn't know men of the cloth had a bad name," I said. "I think they're generally pretty well-respected."

"Of course they are," Pearl said. "The way they should be. We've always gotten along so well with our neighbors, such nice people in this town. Our children went to day camp at the Y. This is why Harry doesn't open the store until noon on Sunday, from respect for their church services. And all the customers understand we don't open on Saturday. Never a problem, always everybody with their differences living side by side."

Harry picked up the story. "For thirty-five years. Until suddenly comes this ganef, he—"

" 'Ganef'?"

"This thief, this fast-talking con man, Gull. The Reverend Lester Gull, you should excuse me. He could steal the words right out of your mouth, the Reverend Lester Gull. Do you know the Aerie Motel?"

"Up on Route Six? Restaurant and a dozen little cabins? Abandoned?"

"Not abandoned anymore. The Reverend Lester Gull bought the whole place last spring. Did a little bit of fix up, reopened as the Heaven's Messenger Bible School. Bible school! The man wouldn't know from a Bible if one fell out of Heaven and hit him on the head."

"This, of course, is not true," Pearl interrupted. "The Reverend Gull is a very learned man. He quotes his Bible all over the place, from memory. Which only proves that learning and wisdom are not the same thing."

"All right," I said to Harry. "So we have the Reverend Lester teaching the word of the Lord up in the old hotel. What's the problem?"

"Up in the old hotel, there wouldn't be a problem. In front of my store, there's a problem."

"Which is?"

Harry sighed. "Hershkowitz's sits, which of course you know, in the best spot on Main Street. Right on the corner. Nobody has to walk too far—you could get there from anywhere. A store so perfect it's historic, on the National Register if you please. Also on the National Register should be the oak tree that grows on the sidewalk in front of the store. Two hundred years old. It was growing in that spot when the British were here. Which I don't, by the way, remember, no matter what Pearl tells you."

Pearl patted Harry's cheek.

"I know the tree," I said. "The sidewalk widens there to let you walk around it."

"Right!" said Harry. "Which is what people do, now that the Reverend Lester Gull has come to town."

"He tells them it's the will of God that they should walk around the tree?"

"Don't joke. This is not a funny situation."

"I apologize." I grinned. "Please continue."

"Lester Gull," Harry said with great dignity, "doesn't even come down to the tree himself. Except to stand in the crowd. It's his students who make my customers walk around the tree."

"Harry—"

"Harry, please, you're giving the man heartburn. You eat, I'll finish the story." Pearl turned to face me. "Reverend Gull is training—what do you call them? They preach on TV."

"Televangelists."

"That's right. Such a silly word. Maybe they believe what they say themselves, maybe they don't. But the religion part, that's not what they learn from Reverend Gull, anyway. From him they learn how to ask for money."

"Specifically?"

"You bet specifically," Harry broke in. "How to stand under my oak tree on Sunday afternoon and harangue my customers. They preach and they preach and they ask and they ask, and the customers get so upset they don't come on Sundays anymore, which of course is my biggest day because all the weekend people, like you, when else are they going to come? But now they don't come. They shouldn't have to know from the Reverend Lester Gull's students doing their homework."

"That's what it is, their homework?"

"Homework," Harry asserted. "Their assignment, should they choose to accept it, is to make people feel bad until they give money. Last summer they started this, this practice for picking your pocket. Over the winter they don't come, but last month they were back like the birds flying north. My customers are too smart to give money to a fake"—he said this proudly—"but they're too good not to feel bad when someone says they're no good unless they give money. So what happens? My customers, they need a left-handed wall stretcher, they come to Hershkowitz's. While they're there, it shouldn't be a total loss, they buy paint, they buy brushes, they buy hammers, they buy nails. But now, the preachers yell at them, Fire and brimstone and give us money. The customers say to each other, 'Paint and brushes and hammers and nails we can get at the Agway. Those guys won't bother us.' So to Hershkowitz's they don't come anymore, unless for a left-handed wall stretcher. And you can't make a living, my friend, selling those."

Harry finished his tale, looked at me mournfully.

"You've talked to the sheriff?" I asked.

"Don Brown. I voted for him four times already. 'Harry,' he tells me, 'I'm sorry, but they got a right. The old oak's in front of your store, but it's public property. People got a right to give any kind of speech they want there. Nothing I can do.' "

"And you talked to the Reverend Gull?"

"The Reverend Gull"—Harry was affronted—"suggested I consider joining his flock. He said I had the makings of a first-class TV preacher. Can you believe this? I told him—"

"What you told him," said Pearl, "you will not repeat in this house, in front of our friend. It was not nice," she added to me.

"I'll bet," I said. "So. What do you want me to do?"

"Something smart," Harry said. "You're a big-city private eye, a very smart man. I want you to think of something very smart to make the Reverend Lester Gull and his phony preachers go away."

Harry and I walked through Hanover to the center of town. Kids rode bikes and dogs chased after them through the bright sun and sharp shadows. Tulips and daffodils glowed in front gardens and curtains billowed out from open windows.

As we turned onto Main Street a block from Hershkowitz's, I saw the oak tree and the crowd. The tree was huge, the crowd was small, but the preacher on his box under a drooping branch was giving them his all: the arm waving, the shouts that dropped suddenly to whispers, the finger pointing and the burning eyes.

Harry scowled, looked meaningfully at me; then he turned the lock on Hershkowitz's door and disappeared inside.

I listened for a while and watched the crowd. The text was from Matthew, the preacher reassuring the onlookers that they were of more value than many sparrows. From that came the pitch: As you have value to the Lord, you must demonstrate the value of the word of the Lord to you; as the Lord sees each sparrow fall, He will see the strength of your faith in the size of your offering. It was a good tie-in, though I didn't see many takers. What I did see was what Harry was complaining about: people crossing the street, or cutting behind the back of the tree, to avoid the preacher altogether.

I followed Harry inside the store, between shelves jammed with hinges and hacksaw blades, knobs and chains and gardening gloves. Harry was leaning on

the counter in front of a wall of tiny drawers that
held bolts and nuts and washers of every imagin-
able variety.

"So?" he said as I reached him. "Did you save
your soul?"

"I haven't even seen my soul in years," I said.
"Are all the preachers that good?"

"That's good?"

"Terrific," I told him. "Is Lester Gull out there?"

Harry craned his neck to peer through the window. "No. The chicken. He probably knows you're
in town."

I cocked an eyebrow. "Did you tell him about me?"

"I told him I was going to get someone to fix his
wagon. How, I didn't tell him."

"Good, because right now I don't have a clue how.
Is it okay if I use your phone for a while?"

"Please, be my guest. You thought of a clue?"

"I'm going to look for one."

I called some people I knew in New York and in
Albany. Because it was Sunday, everything took
longer than it might have, but in the end, because
computers never sleep, I got what I'd asked for.

"Doesn't do us much good, though," I had to
admit to Harry, toward the end of the afternoon.

"What good were you looking for it to do us?"

"I don't know. An outstanding bunco warrant on
the Reverend Gull would have been nice."

"But no?"

"But no. The school is a legal setup, a tax-exempt
nonprofit religious institution."

"But religion he doesn't teach! He teaches how to
make a profit. This makes him a nonprofit?"

"Well, maybe there's something you could do with that, but it would take time to dig around and then go through channels. You'd have to complain to the attorney general, things like that."

"Time, my friend, I don't think I have. A whole season like this, I'm out of business. Where are you going?"

"To the lion's den," I said. "The belly of the beast. To the cedars of Lebanon, where the birds make their nests. I'm going to see the Reverend Gull."

The golden sun was getting ready to sink comfortably behind the hazy hills when I reached Heaven's Messenger. On a new painted sign by the side of the road a dove flew out of an open Bible. The old restaurant building and the cabins wore fresh coats of green-trimmed white paint and the front door had a shiny brass doorknob. I wondered, admiring its glow in the low sun, if it had come from Hershkowitz's.

My ring was answered by a thin, beak-nosed man whose smile sprang to life half a second late, as though he hadn't decided whether to activate it until he saw who I was. "Welcome, my friend. Welcome!" His bony hands grabbed mine, pressed and pumped. "Heaven's Messenger welcomes you. You've come for the month's session? Or perhaps the two-week intensive study course? Please come in. You're the first of your class to arrive. I'm Lester. Reverend Lester Gull. You're . . . ?"

"Not here to study with you, Reverend Gull. Bill Smith. I'm a friend of Harry Hershkowitz's. Is there somewhere we can talk?"

"Oh." Gull's eyes filled with sympathy. He

stepped out onto the porch, shut the door behind him. "Mr. Hershkowitz. I did suggest gently to Mr. Hershkowitz that if he were to come to the Lord—"

"Harry has a Lord he's fond of, Reverend. He also has a business he's been running in Hanover since before the flood. He'd like to keep it going."

Gull shook his head sadly. "The concerns of man are so temporal, aren't they?"

"And your concerns?"

He smiled, his lips curving up under the sharp point of his nose. "At Heaven's Messenger, we are concerned with souls. With preaching the word of the Lord throughout the land. Isaiah 61:1, 'The spirit of the Lord is upon me; because the Lord hath anointed me to preach good tidings to the meek.' "

"Uh-huh," I said. "Well, some of the meek aren't getting it. I've spent the day tracing a random sample of your graduates. Four have phone-solicitation businesses—one also runs a phone-sex line, by the way—two have pulpits in churches with shaky charters, and one is wanted by the Feds, something to do with mail fraud. And those are just the ones easy to trace on a lazy Sunday afternoon. Not a very holy bunch, Reverend."

Gull's eyes grew gently sad again. "It's tragic but true. Some of my flock have strayed. It's always the way, and it causes me great pain, but I can hardly be held accountable. Genesis 4:9, 'Am I my brother's keeper?' "

"Well, I wouldn't know, but I do know you're getting rich off your brother. I checked you out, too, Reverend. You're worth quite a bundle."

"Ecclesiastes 5:19. 'Every man to whom God hath

given riches and wealth, and hath given him the power to eat thereof, and to take his portion, and to rejoice in his labor; this is the gift of God.'" He smiled benignly. I felt my blood begin to boil. I lit a cigarette to give myself time to cool off.

"Mr. Gull, sir," I said, "I was baptized Catholic and raised Baptist. I can tell a can rattler from a man of God; you don't even make it hard."

His face saddened. "Your lack of faith is distressing, Mr. Smith. I do think a course of Bible study here at Heaven's Messenger would do you a world of good."

"I doubt it, but I won't argue. Right now I'm just here to ask you to move your final exams to a different place and time. Harry needs his Sunday business and you're ruining it."

"Alas, the Bible says nothing about preaching the word at a time and place convenient for the heathen. Quite the opposite—Romans 1:15, 'So, as much as is in me, I am ready to preach the gospel to you that are at Rome also.'"

"A block up from Harry's store is still Rome."

"Ah, yes. But that magnificent old oak is at the center of Main Street. That's the perfect spot. The Sabbath is the perfect time. A hostile shopkeeper and an indifferent crowd are excellent practice for my students. That's why they come to me; my training methods ensure their success. No, I'm sorry. I've found what I need." He gazed out over the darkening hills, watched the red-streaked sky with a satisfied, proprietary air.

"If I have to," I said, "I'll keep digging. I'll turn up something on you that will wipe you out."

Gull smiled again. "I think not. I'm a careful man. I'm well-established here, and prospering. All my sessions are full; Heaven's Messenger is doing quite well. No, Mr. Smith, I believe I'm here to stay."

Gull's sharp, smug face was too much of a temptation. I had to leave or take a swing at it. Halfway down the front path, I turned.

"Jeremiah 5:27." I said. Gull's eyebrows lifted. "'As a cage is full of birds, so are their houses full of deceit: therefore they are become great, and waxen rich.' And check Matthew. Something about camels, needles, and rich men going to Heaven."

Gull seemed disconcerted. As I drove off, leaving him staring after me, I hoped that was true and not just a trick of the fading light.

I went back to Pearl and Harry's, reported the results of my meeting with Gull—"He won't quit and he won't move"—begged off dinner, and drove over to my cabin with Harry's worried look and Pearl's confident smile lingering in my mind. "Leave the man alone," Pearl had commanded Harry. "He can't think with you hovering like a vulture." To me she'd said reassuringly, "Go home. Sleep on it—tomorrow you'll have an idea."

I wasn't so sure, but I didn't have any other idea where to get an idea. At the cabin, I settled myself on the porch with a bourbon, watched the fresh spring evening. Then I went in and tried the piano. I played for a while, Schumann and then Liszt. I played well and felt good about it, but it didn't give me any ideas. Finally I gave up, folded myself under the quilt, and went to sleep.

In the morning I didn't have any ideas either. I took my coffee out onto the porch, watched the pale sun burn off the mist, listened to the chatter of the birds. It was a busy time, an early-spring morning, birds in pairs and flocks staking out territory, grabbing up the best places to nest and feed. They hopped on branches, dove through the air, flicked to the ground. I sipped my coffee, tried to think.

A sudden screeching made me look up. Two birds, small and large, soared, swooped, hurtled through the blue of the sky. The large one, a hawk, circled, faked, and cut back, aiming for the branches of a great ash tree. The small one, screaming and flapping, wouldn't let him near it. The battle was ballet-like in elegance and dead serious in content: a mother bird protecting her young from a predator. It was over fast, and the smaller bird won. The whole thing became too much trouble for the hawk; he circled, lifted onto an air current that took him over the trees and across the valley. The mother bird disappeared into the branches of the ash.

I stared after her for a moment, then laughed. I was still laughing as I pulled the car out of the driveway, heading for Hershkowitz's.

All over the world, hardware stores open early. Even upstate, even in Hanover. It was eight thirty by the time I got there, and Harry's day was already well begun.

"Okay," I said. "Time to get to work."

"One of us is already working," Harry pointed out. "Where's your nearest lumberyard?"

"Sheppard's, off the highway. You had an idea?"

I was moving through Harry's shelves, grabbing what I'd need. "No," I said. "Divine inspiration."

I spent the rest of the morning hammering, sawing, gluing. Out on the porch of my cabin I had quite a little assembly line going. It occurred to me halfway through that I probably could have just gone to the Agway and bought these things, but I decided I liked the personal touch better anyway. Just after three I pulled up to Hershkowitz's again, trunk and backseat crowded with the work of my hands.

I stuck my head in the hardware store door. "You have a ladder?" I called to Harry.

"This is a hardware store. I better have a ladder. How long?"

"Long."

"What are you going to do?"

"Climb the tree."

I climbed the ladder and climbed the tree, twelve times altogether because I couldn't carry much each time. Luckily I only needed to work in the lower branches; ten to twenty feet above the ground, I reasoned, was just about what this plan needed. When I was done, Harry and I stood back and admired my craftsmanship.

"This will work?" Harry asked.

"Harry," I said, "this will work. Isaiah, 31:5."

Harry gave me a sideways, appraising look. "I didn't know this about you, that you know so well the Bible."

"I looked it up."

I had dinner with Harry and Pearl, warned them it might be a week before they saw any results from my installation, maybe longer before it had the desired effect on the Reverend Gull's students.

"It will take work," I warned Harry.

"I am prepared," he replied solemnly.

Two Sundays later I went back up to Hanover, to see how things were going.

I left midmorning, had a leisurely drive. The Hudson flowed high in its banks and the yellow-green of the hills had deepened to a glowing emerald. The air smelled sweet, early flowers and damp earth. By the time I got into town it was after twelve. I parked up from Hershkowitz's, sauntered down the block, checked out the tree. Everything looked good to me. In the store I found Harry behind his crowded counter.

"Hey, look who's here!" he greeted me. "Mr. Smart Person! Why didn't you tell us you were coming? Pearl would have made breakfast."

"I'm still full from last time. How's business?"

"Like the garbage man, my business is picking up. Which, by the way, is not so funny. This plan of yours makes a mess."

"You can't make an omelet without breaking eggs."

"Don't talk about breaking eggs! I—oh, oh, look at this," he interrupted himself.

I turned around to face the window, saw what he was seeing: Across the street, two shiny, late-model cars had pulled up. From them, dressed in their dapper Sunday best, emerged the Reverend Lester Gull and six other men.

"Harry," I said, "I think I feel the need to hear the word."

"Definitely," said Harry. "Me, too."

We left the store, stood waiting as Gull and his

entourage strode toward us. I lit a cigarette and smiled at Gull. He smiled back.

"Mr. Smith, isn't it? What brings you back to Hanover? Good day, Mr. Hershkowitz." He turned his smile to Harry.

"I'm like a homing pigeon, Reverend," I said. "You preaching today?"

"No, no. Mr. Vogel is going to share some thoughts with us this beautiful afternoon." He turned to one of the men beside him, a short sour-faced man in a pale gray suit. "What's your text today, Al?"

"The Book of Job," the man replied, squaring his shoulders in a self-important way.

"Job," I said. "I like that. Some of my favorite verses are from Job."

"Oh? Which might those be?" Gull asked pleasantly.

"There's 12:7," I said. "And 20:5 and 7. Those, Reverend, particularly make me think of you."

Gull's face clouded. He fixed me with angry eyes; then he nodded curtly and turned his back. With a smoothly reassuring smile he said to the little man, "Whenever you're ready, Al. I know it's your first time; don't be nervous. Just preach as the spirit moves you."

Gull and his friends, Harry and I, and a few stray shoppers stood in a semicircle around the tree as the little man began his sermon.

"Must be a beginner," I whispered to Harry, watching Vogel shift uncomfortably, start in a voice too soft, lose his thread. He glanced at Gull, who smiled. That seemed to give him courage. He set his shoulders again and warmed to the full force of his argument, which was that although the purposes of the Almighty are not always apparent, nevertheless faith is required of the faithful—Harry lifted his eyebrows at that—and that support of a preacher like himself is a tangible sign of that faith.

As a pitch, I'd heard better, but anyway that wasn't why I was here. I was waiting for my reward from heaven, or at least from the sky.

And it came. A few minutes into his talk, Vogel, without missing a beat, brushed something from his hair. A minute later, something else. Then he waved his arm to make a point, stopped horrified as a wet white lump landed on his sleeve. He twisted his head to look up into the tree just in time to catch a sunflower seed in the eye, but that was good, because it made him jump back fast enough to avoid the next big white splotch headed his way.

Someone in the crowd stifled a laugh. Everyone looked up into the tree. And the tree was full of action.

All the feeders I'd built were full, overflowing with nuts, seeds, crumbled bread. Harry had been assiduous. I'd built the feeders flat, to make it easier for the birds to toss what they didn't want over the side. They were busy tossing, eating, digesting. In the next higher set of limbs they were living: wrens, robins, sparrows, crows, and finches flitted around, hopped in and out of birdhouses, landed on nesting platforms. Five pigeons sat cooing on a branch.

"I didn't know you had pigeons up here," I said to Harry, as Vogel, out of the line of fire, frantically scraped at his sleeve with a handkerchief.

"I got everything," Harry said proudly. "But I'm

telling you, cleaning up under that tree every day is a pain in the neck. Seeds and crumbs and what do you call that stuff, guano?"

"In the Bible," I said, in a voice meant to carry to where Gull and the others huddled in hasty conference, "they call it dung."

Gull spun and glared at me. "You did this!" he accused. "You did this to keep us from spreading the word of the Lord!"

"No," I said, "I did it to keep my friend Harry from going out of business. You said this was the perfect spot. I disagree. I think this spot is for the birds."

Gull paled with anger. He turned on his heel, stomped off to his car. His flock followed. They all slammed their doors as they screeched away.

"That man is not happy," Harry said.

"No."

"What if he comes back in the middle of night and poisons all my birds?"

"Harry, as long as you keep those feeders full, you'll have a waiting list. If Gull poisoned all these guys at midnight, you'd have new tenants by dawn. He knows that. He won't be back."

The crowd that had gathered was dispersing, smiling and glancing into the tree. One man asked Harry if he was open. "I just need some wing nuts," he said with a grin. "It's no big deal, but as long as I'm here."

"I'd better go back inside," Harry said to me. "The customers might come back, now that there's nobody yelling at them. But you better come for dinner, or I'm in big trouble with Pearl."

"Sure. Thanks."

"Wait," Harry said. "Those verses from Job that you told him you like. What do they say?"

"One was for me. 'But ask now the beasts, and they shall teach thee; and the birds of the air, and they shall tell thee.' "

"And the ones you said made you think of him?"

" 'The triumphing of the wicked is short,' " I quoted to Harry, " 'and the joy of the hypocrite but for a moment. He shall perish forever like his own dung; they which have seen him shall say, Where is he?' "

Harry grinned, and I grinned. With a wave he turned back and disappeared into Hershkowitz's.

I stuck my hands in my pockets, ambled down the block, enjoying the sun and the breeze and the songs of the birds in the small-town morning.

THE QUIET COLD
James Sarafin

The plane came in first, well after midnight, landing without lights and in silence except for the crunch and schuss of the skis over the wind-hardened snow on the river. Karuk waited in the moon shadows along the bank while the Cessna 206 turned and taxied back toward his position. Over its stuttering engine, he could hear the higher-revving sound of snow-gos coming up the river. Five of them arrived, and the riders got off and exchanged a few words with the pilot. And Karuk waited. Waited until they had transferred all of the cardboard cases from the plane to the sleds hauled by three of their snow-gos.

He could stop the plane from taking off by pulling his own snow-go in front of it. But he really needed to bust the local ring, and the pilot might not know very much. So he announced his presence by starting up and driving toward the dark figures standing on the ice.

One of their flashlights illuminated the City of

Nuyaqpalik Police Department logo on the front of his snow-go. They scattered for their machines, but he thought he could cut them off. Then one of them started shooting; a bullet struck the fiberglass cowling in front of Karuk with a loud crack.

His hand released the throttle lever and dove into the parka pocket where he carried the Glock .40. His hand stopped there.

Was this really worth shooting someone over?

Karuk had never killed a man. His machine slid to a stop, and he watched the five bootleggers go skimming across the snow, engines roaring, their snow-gos jumping and long shadows leaping and skittering in their headlights. A breaking laugh, high, almost falsetto, sounded across the expanse of snow. Then they were gone around a bend in the river. Behind him he heard the roar of the plane taking off.

Steam poured from under the cowling, seeped through the cracks in his helmet and mask, brushing warm and wet against his face and carrying the smell of antifreeze. The bullet had punctured the radiator or a water line. In the motionless air near the riverbank, the steam hung in a little cloud about head high; as he watched, the cloud froze into tiny ice crystals that settled sparkling in his headlight beam. He shook his head, turned the key to shut down the engine, and climbed off the disabled machine. It had taken a lot of work in his off time, tracking in his headlight beam through the almost unbroken night of Arctic December, to find the bootleggers' probable rendezvous. And half a dozen long stakeouts in the cold, getting up to dance and fling his arms around whenever he grew sleepy.

From his parka zipper hung a plastic thermometer given to him by his nephew; it was bottomed out at twenty-five below, the limit of its gauge. Even in this temperature, he probably could not make it back to Nuyaqpalik without the engine seizing up. The town's budget had been gutted by loss of state grants, due to declining oil revenues, and the police department could ill afford costly repairs or an engine replacement. His handheld marine VHP radio was line of sight, out of range of town.

Working quickly, doing one thing at a time and warming his hands in his pockets between doing them, he set his helmet and mask on the seat, put on his headlamp, and tied down the hood of his wolverine-ruffed parka. Then he took a small pack holding survival gear and a thermos from the underseat compartment and put it on.

A three-quarter moon was high over the bluff to the south as he started downriver. His breath smoked blue in the moonlight. The wind had not left any depth of snow on the river, and traffic had made firm footing on the trail. Each footfall sounded with that squeaky crunch only expressed by hard-packed subzero snow. The stars overhead rippled through the dense, cold atmosphere, and he saw the faint point of a satellite tracking to the northwest. Once he caught a whiff of distant wood smoke from some homesteader's or trapper's cabin. But the exercise kept him warm, and he didn't bother looking for it.

Hours later he had left the bluff behind him, and the country leveled and flattened all around. The riverbanks rose no more than waist high, and nothing protruded from the dim whiteness of the snow except for the occasional tuft of tundra vegetation. The moon had set, and he moved under starlight.

He came to where the river made a long loop to the west and went on in that direction for several miles before it turned back to the south. The trail left the river here, headed due south. He knew the bootleggers had come this way; he and they were going to the same place. Town. The only place for them to dispose of their cargo.

They always brought in the same kind of booze: cheap vodka, gin, and whiskey, packed in cases of twelve and bottled in shelf-brand "traveler's" plastic, to cut down on weight. Probably bought retail in a warehouse store in Anchorage or Fairbanks; all the taxes paid, so no reason to interest the Feds. The kind of liquor that might be of concern only to local police—if it was being sold for two hundred dollars a bottle in an Eskimo community that had voted itself dry under Alaska's local option law. As Nuyaqpalik had done, following the murder of Karuk's predecessor, the town's last chief of police, in a bar two years ago.

Karuk knew just how the *taannaq* would smell. How it would taste, on the first drink, how it would taste on the ones after, then how cool and slick it would feel in the throat when you couldn't taste it anymore.

He had to toil harder in the deeper snow, his boots sometimes breaking through the packed crust on the trail and sinking thigh deep. His legs moved ceaselessly, and in the faint starlight he saw his breath appear and vanish and appear and vanish over and over. The vapor of his breath coated his lower face with ice and froze the ruff of his parka hood to both sides of his jaw. Still, he wasn't cold as long as he kept walking, except for his feet. When he topped a rise in the tundra plain he could see the morning lights of town, far across the dim expanse of the Sound, shimmering like the stars in the cold thick air.

The tundra plateau sloping below him showed the dark lines of many snow-machine tracks converging toward the crossing to town. The tracks of the bootleggers mingled there with those of hunters, trappers, travelers, and sport riders. Just about everybody in town had a snow-go. He tried the radio, but picked up only static; he must have neglected to recharge the battery, or else it had been weakened by the cold.

Beside a tussock that showed its head of dried, brown grass above the white surface, one of the bootleggers' machines seemed to have left the trail and bogged down in the deeper, unpacked snow. He twisted on his headlamp and stopped to study the signs. It looked like the others had circled around so they could help push and dig the stuck machine out. Most of the tracks were unreadable in the deep, light snow; but he found a single clear footprint where one of them had stepped on the trail to mount his machine. It looked like the bootlegger was wearing sneakers.

Sneakers? In this weather? Some of the newer machines came equipped with hand and foot warmers—so you could ride in sneakers without losing toes to frostbite. Still, the risk of a breakdown made it foolhardy to go so far out of town without a pair of insulated boots. Maybe the bootlegger was too drunk himself to know better.

He went on, and the sky grew brighter, with the blush of false dawn on the horizon ahead, to the south. The wind picked up as he approached shore, gusting, throwing up dervishes of dry powder that marched across the pack ice and up the beach, where they died against the heavier snow on the tundra. His breath plumed pinkly in the dawn light, and he stopped to break the ice away from his face and take a long drink of tepid cocoa from the thermos. His slight hope of finding someone to give him a ride the last five miles to town faded; there was no one else or sign of movement or other living thing anywhere in sight. The roseate glimmer of dawn had moved slightly west along the horizon, turning into the magenta of dusk, as the sun sank away from the world again. The stars reappeared, twinkling thickly; and it was night again.

The snow creaked faintly under his boots as he hit the trail across the sea ice. The trail curved back and forth to skirt the leads and jams caused by the tides, which broke and shifted sections of the pack ice around as if in reduced representation of the tectonic plates of the earth. After a time he heard the faint crackling of the aurora, and when he paused to look up, the stars directly overhead had vanished behind a wide shimmering band the color of jade that streamed like some enchanted river in the sky.

His feet were slowing, beginning to stumble, when he came into the north end of town under the big floodlights of the dock. Some of the houses along the shore had strung up Christmas lights, but the barge office was undecorated and showed only a dim glow from inside. He climbed up the short, steep beach and noticed someone standing in the shadows by the door, as if waiting for him.

"Charlie?" the man called to him, in a familiar voice. "I wondered who was walking out there." Rich Stahl, the barge company's watchman, stayed on the payroll year-round, even after the ice shut down the sea lanes.

To Karuk's birth certificate, his driver's license, credit cards, mortgage on his house, and magazine descriptions and junk mail, and every other thing brought by the European Americans, he was Charles W. Henderson. The only other living person who used his Eskimo name was his mother.

Of course, there were still the dead to answer to. Even if they never spoke. The whites did not believe, but the Inupiat could sometimes see ghosts. Charlie knew a man's friends and relatives—and perhaps his enemies—could come back from the other side.

"Do you know what time it is?" he asked.

"Almost six p.m.," Rich said. "Where have you been? Nick and Carl must have asked everyone in town, looking for you since this morning."

Charlie told him, and Stahl shook his head. "Jesus, you mean you just came more than twenty miles on foot? It's thirty-eight below."

Charlie went into the barge office to use the phone. The heat burned on his face, and he had to open his parka immediately. He accepted a cup of old, burnt-smelling coffee and passed it gingerly from hand to hand. The air seemed far too warm in the office, and while he was waiting for Nick he went outside, the coffee steaming madly in the mug, to watch the aurora. It looked pale and washed out now, beyond the lights of the town.

Even at full blast, the defroster in the police Blazer was losing its war against the cold; only the center of the windshield remained clear of frost, through which Charlie peered as if out of a tunnel. Officer Nick Totemoff, an Aleut from St. George Island, drove the creaking vehicle delicately on the gravelly ice that constituted the normal winter surface of the town's streets, as if he were afraid it might come apart on one of the deeper ruts. Which it well might.

They pulled into the police station and picked their way across the parking lot to the front entrance. Cold weather had come right on the heels of a heavy fall rain, leaving the parking lot covered with a sheet of ice that hadn't yet lost its slick surface to winter wear. Nick opened the door, said, "Oh, I forgot to tell you—your nephew's been by to see you three or four times since school let out."

Charlie went into his office. He looked at the log, shook his head. Two domestic-violence calls, a drunk-driving arrest, two young men picked up for a drunken fight at the bingo hall—all in the last twenty-four hours. For a year or so after the vote to go dry, things had been quiet, people had treated each other decently, the community hardly seemed to need a police force anymore. Now it was almost as bad as in the old days, when they had been running three or four drunk and disorderlies a day, a murder or suicide every month. If he could stop this new bootleg enterprise, the town might make it through winter without any more deaths.

He was about to leave when he glanced at his calendar. Damn. It was Friday, and that council meeting was tonight at seven; the mayor had made a point of asking him to be there. Now he didn't even have time for a shower, just maybe a bite of food if he hurried.

In the lobby entry his nephew was stamping snow off his boots.

"Johnnie, I've got to run to a meeting," Charlie said. "I'll catch up with you later, okay?"

"But it's important, Uncle Charlie!"

Charlie put his hands on the boy's shoulders, trying not to sag. Johnnie's father had left years ago, and his mother, Charlie's older sister, had taken to drinking and snorting cocaine, not staying in town for more than two weeks at a stretch. Four years ago they'd found her strangled in a Fairbanks park, her skirt pulled up to her chest and panties twisted around one ankle. Johnnie, now thirteen, was living at Charlie's mother's. He said he wanted to be a cop. If he kept getting the good grades, Charlie knew he could do better.

Charlie could feel the warmth of the room bringing the weariness out of the depths of his bones and into the surface of his face. He had been walking for sixteen hours, without sleep for thirty-five. He had to stay alert for the meeting, but all he wanted was a quick meal and the moment of collapsing into bed.

"John-guy, let's talk tomorrow, okay? I'll come to dinner at Grandma's and we can talk then."

The boy started to object again, but then nodded. He stood outside to watch Charlie leave in the Blazer. The lights were on in the second-floor council room when Charlie reached the City Offices building. Clouds had moved in overhead, the temperature seemed to be rising slightly, and the wind had started blowing out of the Sound. Looked like more snow on its way.

Charlie was a few minutes late, but he had arrived before three of the council members. He found a seat among the audience chairs. The minority group of whites on the council always thought it important to start on time; they fidgeted, sighed, glared at the clock.

Charlie's eyes would not stay open, and he tried to keep awake by concentrating on the sounds in the room. The rising wind rattled the panes of the front windows. Two steps on the upper part of the stairs squeaked every time someone came up. The old-style radiator heaters creaked and groaned constantly as they shed heat into the drafty room. Like most of the town's structures, the City Offices building was poorly constructed, thrown together in haste by an outside contractor who hadn't lingered one minute after his final payment.

The last member arrived, and the council moved through the agenda. Finally, the mayor called to Charlie.

"Chief, what's going on with these bootleggers? I heard there's a lot of new liquor coming into town for the holiday parties."

Charlie told them about the preceding night's events.

"You shouldn't have gone out there by yourself, with them carrying guns," one of the Eskimo women said.

"Two of our officers are out with the flu," Charlie said. "Which leaves us shorthanded, even with Nick pulling overtime. I couldn't go out there without leaving someone behind for the town." ·

"I've said this before, but the police have better things to do," said Will Davis, one of several council members who had formerly owned interests in liquor establishments. "Al and I bowed to the will of the majority and shut down the Seal and Harpoon when the vote came in, but the city won't never stop people who want to drink. Prohibition just don't work."

Al Briggs, one of the white members, who still owned the town's general store, leaned forward, rested his elbows on the table, and put his chin in his hands. "Well, I agree people ought to have a constitutional right to drink in the privacy of their homes. But we've got to try to stop the bootlegging, so long as it's against the law. Though I am skeptical we'll succeed."

"At least you found where they're landing, how they're bringing it in," the mayor said. He had been a strong supporter ever since Charlie had tracked down and brought in the boy who murdered Chief Tigges.

"Yeah, but it doesn't mean much," Charlie said. "They'll just find another place to land the plane now."

"No offense, Charlie," Briggs said, "but these bootleggers always seem to be one step ahead of you. I think once the holidays have passed, maybe we should ask the State Troopers to come in on this investigation."

"Why wait until after the holidays?" asked the white woman who was married to the local Presbyterian minister; the couple had been leaders of the prohibition lobby. "I should think we'd want to stop this *before* all the holiday celebrations."

"Because the troopers will probably be too busy dealing with things in Anchorage and Fairbanks until then," Briggs replied. "But after the holidays, we might have a chance to get a couple of them up here."

"They was here two months ago and didn't find nothing," the mayor said.

Charlie shrugged; he was so tired he could hardly make out their words. "The bootleggers just hole up, stop bringing in the booze and selling it while the troopers are here."

"Well," Briggs continued, "again, meaning no offense, but maybe you're just a little too close to this problem."

Everyone was silent. They all knew Briggs was referring to the time when Charlie drank, even as an officer on the force. When they were likely to find him, had anyone bothered to look, drunk in the office or in his truck or in a bar. Back in the days when he'd begged drinks or dollars, at various times, from most of the people in the room.

"That's not fair," the mayor said. "You always liked the bottle pretty good yourself, Al."

"I said I didn't mean any offense."

The rest of them waited, apparently for Charlie to make some response, to defend himself or deny or explain or even, in the way of the reformed alcoholic, acknowledge Briggs's statement; but he had nothing to say. The council moved on to other matters, tabled all outstanding issues until the January meeting, and adjourned promptly at eleven o'clock. Later, Charlie couldn't even remember going home, undressing, and dropping into bed.

He woke at five thirty a.m., wondering if his body had forgotten how to sleep, and was in the office by seven. Charlie and Nick left town across a new layer of snow to retrieve the broken-down snow-go. They rode double on Nick's machine to reach the site, and had the damaged machine towed back to town before the twilight of dusk had faded.

They drove to the big four-bay garage shared by the police and fire departments, and Charlie went in through the side to open the overhead door on one of the vacant bays. Three firemen were playing cards at a table in the rear with Carl Baldwin, the day-shift police officer. The four men stopped in midbet as Charlie came in and hit the door switch. After Nick pulled the two machines in, Charlie hit the switch again to close the door and turned around. The four were still looking at him.

"What's up?"

The firemen looked down and Carl cleared his throat.

"Uh . . . Charlie, I tried to reach you on the radio. Your nephew, Johnnie—we found him this morning, on the shore under the dock. He's . . . dead."

In the cavernous garage Charlie heard the groaning of the water pipes that ran along the inside wall and the slow ticking of Nick's snow machine engine as it cooled. The telephone jangled eight or nine times over the intercom speakers; no one moved to pick it up.

"Oh, shit," Charlie finally said.

"He didn't come home last night—your mother said he was supposed to be staying overnight at a friend's. Apparently, he never made it there. It looked like he froze to death, but . . . no results from the medical examination yet."

The phone started ringing again.

"Mink, will you get that?" Charlie said; then, to Carl: "What else were you going to say?"

"Well, uh . . . it sort of smelled like the kid was drinking." Carl paused, then went on. "The mayor said to call the troopers, so I did. Two of them are coming up tomorrow from Anchorage, if they can get here."

"You sure it was him?"

Carl nodded. "Your mother confirmed the ID. I, uh . . . took her statement. Hope you don't mind me doing it."

"No." They both knew it was better if a relative didn't do it.

Charlie went through the door that connected the garage to the police station. Drinking? Johnnie? He had always been a good boy, never in too much trouble, never doing anything real bad, past the point of normal boy mischief. Where would he have gotten anything to drink? It didn't make any sense.

He caught himself; he sounded like all the other

parents and relatives, whenever one of their kids got into trouble.

He checked the messages left on his desk. Two, no, three calls from the mayor. One from the troopers. Another from . . .

His mother.

He turned and found Carl standing in the doorway, watching him.

"Charlie . . . your mother said he was excited about something yesterday. She didn't know what, but it was something he saw on the way to school— something to do with the bootleggers."

"Great. And he did try to tell me." Charlie rezipped his parka and headed out into the cold. He did not bother with the Blazer; he had less than half a mile to go. The hardened snow on the street squeaked under his boots. An intersection streetlight glowed out of a broad halo of ice fog settling downwind from the station's boiler emissions, the fine crystals chillingly brushing his face as he passed.

All Charlie would have had to do was listen to Johnnie—and the boy might still be alive. What if his death had been no accident?

He went by several small businesses: a welding shop, a florist, a septic service for homes not connected to the city sewer system. At the third intersection he went left, toward shore. Just ahead was the general store, its parking lot well illuminated by the overhead and storefront lights. The boarded-up bar across the street lay in darkness.

As he passed the store, a group of teenage boys came gunning out of the lot on four snow-gos, nearly running him over. They took a long look at Charlie and throttled back.

"Oh, sorry, man," one said.

"Joey, you boys better take it easy," Charlie said, glad for the distraction. "Hey, that's a brand-new 'Cat, ain't it?"

The boy nodded, his face invisible behind the tinted helmet screen. "Nice. Your dad's?"

"Mine." Joey paused. "Got it with my NANA dividend." The Native regional corporation recently had made good money on sale of oil exploration rights and royalties from the zinc mine; annual shareholder dividends had been the largest in years. Charlie had not yet decided how he would spend his own, but had been thinking of a vacation to someplace warm and exotic. Costa Rica, maybe. Anywhere to get away from Nuyaqpalik for a while.

The four boys pulled slowly into the street, came to a full stop at the intersection, and signaled a left turn. They were half a mile down the road before he heard their engines rev up to a full-throated roar. Charlie walked on, passing some of the town's older homes, the low-lying wood shanties that were barely removed from the sod dwellings their ancestors had sunk into the tundra only a few generations before. A block from shore he turned right down a narrow street, toward the house at the end of a cul-de-sac. The house looked dark, uninhabited; no lights shone from inside. He knocked lightly on the front door, then opened it and went in. The floor at the entry sagged under his weight. He had been meaning to replace the joists that were rotting there.

She was sitting in the kitchen beside an old Franklin stove, looking out the window through which could be seen, between two other houses, the lighted surface of Shore Avenue and nothing but the darkness of the ice beyond.

"Mother," he said in Inupiaq, "I say you should lock your door. These aren't the old days anymore."

The light of the fire flickered faintly out of the stove's air vents. Her face looked cracked and yellowed in that light. He would have thought that she had expended all her tears long ago, for his father, his brother, and his sister; but the tracks glistening down her face said otherwise.

"It's so quiet here again, Karuk. I don't think I can stand the quiet anymore."

He wanted to ask her questions—when had she last seen him, where was he supposed to have been, when was he expected home? But Carl had already asked the questions and the troopers would come tomorrow or the next day and ask them all again. If he asked, she might think he was blaming her—when really only one person might be at fault for Johnnie's death: he, Karuk, Charlie Henderson.

"If only he'd worn his parka," she was saying. "He went out with just his jacket. How can he do that? I always tell him, 'Wear your parka.' But these boys, they don't listen to an old woman."

He pulled a chair from under the table and sat with her. After a time she rose to offer him tea, and then food. Later, when she asked if she should make up his old bed, he did not refuse.

The chief of police couldn't get a drink even if he needed one badly. Most of the people in town, including some who had helped vote it dry, probably had a bottle or two, smuggled in past the airport search or mailed by friends in other places. Even those who didn't keep their own bottle, including the other police officers, would know someone who did. But not Charlie; he had deliberately avoided such knowledge, and others had wordlessly joined in that objective.

That lack of knowledge might have been the only thing that kept him from going on a binge the next day. Usually, when the thirst hit, he would force himself to wait until it went away. But drinking this time would have been too easy—compared to driving to the morgue.

"His blood alcohol was .531," said the doctor who served as the local state medical examiner. "More than five times the limit for drunk driving. The kid must have drunk a whole bottle by himself—or more. I still haven't decided whether to list this as death by hypothermia or acute alcohol poisoning. That much alcohol would have killed him at any temperature, probably."

Johnnie's body looked as pale as any white boy's under the bright fluorescent lights. His clothing had been removed and placed in labeled bags. *This is not him*, Charlie told himself. *Johnnie has gone someplace else.*

"Looks like he got in a fight earlier," the doctor added, looking up from the chart in his hand. "See the bruises on his face? And there's a patch of hair ripped out of the back of his head."

Charlie moved slowly to the head of the table and forced himself to look closely. *It's not really him. . . .*

"He didn't die from any fight injuries, though," the doctor continued. "The bruises had time to form, so they had to have been made several hours before death. There's no sign of concussion or skull frac—"

"What caused this?" Charlie pointed to thin bruised cuts, curved and less than an inch long, running along the center of the boy's upper and lower lips.

The doctor shrugged; he wasn't long out of a California medical school and had already seen more than a few Eskimo boys laid out on his table like this. "I assume that maybe he was punched by someone who was wearing a ring."

Maybe. A memory suddenly flashed out of the days that were mostly lost to the alcoholic haze: walking in the dark somewhere, the bottle tilted up— and running into the side of someone's truck. Leaving a cut like that on Charlie's own lip; he saw an image of himself inspecting it in the mirror of a gas station restroom.

"Could a bottle do that? If it was forced into his mouth?"

The doctor shrugged again. "Maybe. What kind of bottle?"

"How about one of those hard plastic traveler's bottles the bootleggers sell? I can probably turn up an evidence sample if you need one."

"Uh, I can probably find one around." The doctor's face reddened slightly. "Your theory is he was forced to drink it? Look, Chief Henderson, I know he was your nephew . . . but that would be hard for someone to do."

Charlie was looking at the boy's arms. "What could make those round bruises on the insides of his wrists?"

The doctor looked. Then he straightened and swallowed. "A knee. Knees, I mean."

"Like maybe two guys were kneeling on his wrists, while someone else poured?"

"The officer who brought him in didn't say anything about treating this as a possible homicide. I thought this was just another . . ."

"Dead drunk?" Charlie finished.

The doctor pulled off each latex glove with a snap and flung them in the trash can, shaking his head in disgust. "I'm sorry—at least I don't usually ever make the same mistake twice. There's some dried blood under his fingernail—I did at least collect a sample, and I'll get it rushed to the lab. Any idea how soon you might need the results?"

Charlie turned to take his parka off a hook. "I'd appreciate knowing as soon as possible."

He went out and sat without starting the Blazer. So many of his family and friends were gone, and several of them his fault. His younger brother, lost overboard when they'd both been drinking and Charlie's boat hit a snag in the river. His sister, whom he might have saved if he'd tried harder to keep her in that rehab program. Tigges, the last chief of police, killed by a knife that Charlie could have taken from the killer. He had seen some of their ghosts. None of them had ever come back to blame him—Tigges had actually returned to say that it wasn't Charlie's fault. But the weight of all those dead . . .

And now Johnnie—dead because Charlie hadn't bothered to listen to him for five minutes.

Carl or Nick would know where he could get a drink.

In the spring when he was twelve, Karuk and another boy lay on the offshore ice beside a seal hole, holding an old pump .22 rimfire. They could not shoot the seal as soon as it came up for air, or it would sink; they had to wait for it to come out all the way to lie in the sun. Then Karuk would try to shoot it in the brain. They had waited a long time when they saw the white bear coming across the ice. The other boy urged Karuk to leave and walked away in a direct line from the bear, in the way they had been taught, to minimize the sense of movement. For some reason he could never explain, even to himself, Karuk stayed. He watched the bear grow larger, quickening its pace, breaking into a charge at a hundred yards. Karuk saw the bear's breath steaming, gobs of saliva dropping from its gums. A bright metallic taste filled his mouth, as if he held the rifle there instead of in his hands.

Later, the men could only look from the great dead bear to the toy rifle and shake their heads. It was then that Karuk started getting the reputation as a wild, wild boy. And only much later, when he remembered how he had waited for the bear, that he discovered how to wait before taking a drink. If you could wait a moment, you could wait another. You could wait for an hour. And then another hour after that. Just keep waiting.

He wanted to drive on, and on—but the roads all deadended within a few miles of town. There was nowhere to go. When he found himself at the north end of town, by the dock, he parked and knocked on the office.

"Hi, Charlie," Rich Stahl said through a crack in the door. "What's up?"

It didn't look like he was going to be invited in. Charlie asked if he could see where the body had been found.

"I already showed Carl. And answered all the questions."

Charlie said he'd like to see the place for himself anyway. Stahl went to get his coat, then led the way down the steep narrow beach and under the dock and pointed his flashlight to rest on a point between two pilings. The snow had been depressed there, but no clear markings had survived the new and drifting snow. The wind whipped along the shore, funneled by the dock. Hard, crystalline flakes stung Charlie's face; he turned to put his back to the wind and face Stahl.

"When did you find him?"

"Like I told Carl, I got up yesterday morning, went out to make my rounds, and just saw him lying there."

"Huh." Charlie tried to look thoughtful.

"Something the matter with that?"

"I was just wondering why you'd go look under the dock."

"Sometimes I do. Just to check things out. That's my job."

"Uh-huh. Find any tracks?"

"No." Stahl shrugged. "Nothing that looked fresh. It was blowing, drifting almost as bad as right now." The snow on the beach was cratered with numerous old footprints; several sets of snow-go tracks had been drifted over and filled in. No way to be sure if they had been made the day before or weeks earlier.

"You didn't see or hear anything at all that night?"

"No. Well, not really. I forgot to mention to Carl that I did hear some kids fooling around on their snow machines on the beach."

"Why do you think they were kids?"

"I don't know." He was shivering. "I didn't get a look at them or anything."

"Did you hear them say anything?"

"Uh . . ." Stahl closed his eyes and his face cinched up. "I guess I heard a couple of them yell at each other. Just sounded like kids, teenagers, you know?"

Stahl shrugged deeper into his coat; he kept looking away, maybe trying to keep his face out of the wind, too.

"You got something else to add, Rich?"

Stahl tried to smile. "Yeah, well . . . if your family sues over this, it could mean my job."

"Any reason for someone to sue the barge company?"

"No. Oh, hell, Charlie—you know everybody sues over everything these days."

No use in hanging around here longer. Carl would have taken a look when he recovered Johnnie's body; there was nothing about this place that told Charlie anything now. And he had heard the plane from Anchorage come in and land, which meant the troopers would be waiting for him.

Charlie recognized them in the airport lobby, the

same ones who had come before, now wearing two of the heaviest parkas he had ever seen. They had just picked up their bags. The two white men each stood well over six feet tall and almost a foot above Charlie's own head. Outside they grunted at the cold, threw their bags in the backseat, and both squeezed shivering into the front of Charlie's Blazer. One of them asked if Charlie had learned who the dead boy had been with last, and Charlie shook his head.

"No. But I think he was murdered."

The troopers looked at each other, and the one in the middle of the seat said, "Why do you say that, Chief?"

"I saw the body this morning." He told them about the bruised wrists and lips. "I think they held him down and made him drink it."

"He was your nephew, wasn't he? Lived with your mother?"

"Yeah." Charlie pulled into the office lot and shifted into Park. "Did you read the witness reports we faxed?"

The officer next to the passenger door, the quiet one, hesitated before getting out. His hand had cracked the door open, then just held the handle. "He told your mother he'd seen something about the bootleggers. You could be right. I can't imagine how a kid wouldn't pass out before he could drink that much on his own. Even if he was a hard drinker with a lot of tolerance for the stuff."

"He didn't drink at all."

In the morning when he went out on the porch of his mother's home the temperature had dropped again, though the air was still. Ever since awakening, Charlie had been nagged by the feeling that he was missing something important. He paused to zip the parka before going toward the main street. When he looked up he saw someone walking ahead of him, passing into the range of the streetlight at the intersection. Someone familiar.

It was Johnnie.

Charlie paused only a moment. When he had seen the ghosts of his brother and friend Tigges, they had simply come to stand in front of him. Johnnie's was walking away.

"Hey," Charlie called, "where are you going?"

Johnnie stopped to look at him. There was no sign of the boy's breath condensing under the streetlight. The air was still, yet Johnnie's light jacket flapped and ruffled as if a strong wind were coming up the street from shore.

Charlie waited; the dead, he believed, always had a reason to come to you. But Johnnie wouldn't say it, for the dead do not speak.

Johnnie turned and went down the street, hunching his shoulders away from the wind that touched only him. Following silently behind, Charlie noticed that Johnnie carried his school pack on his back. They went a few blocks; then Johnnie turned right down an alley that ran beside the general store and passed out of view behind another building. Charlie hurried to catch up. He looked down the alley, but couldn't see Johnnie anymore.

Charlie ran forward, his boots slipping on the icy patches of street as he tried to keep up. He paused only briefly to check the intersection with another alley that ran behind the store—empty—and ran on. He went all the way to the next street, then came back to the intersection and checked again. Johnnie was gone. All he saw was the Dumpster and the double doors at the rear of the general store.

It was not enough for a cop to know. What Charlie knew would do no good without admissible evidence to prove it in court. A few confessions would work fine; but suspects didn't usually confess just because they were arrested. Most would only protest their innocence, would even continue protesting throughout their prison terms, as if by the sheer persistence of the denial they could rewrite their own history. Unless—sometimes—they knew you could tie them to the physical evidence.

Charlie drove his repaired snow-go to the north end of town around eight o'clock that evening. The light glowed dimly through the curtained window of the barge office. He knocked, waited, saw the curtains move, knocked louder.

"I'd like to talk to you some more, Rich," he said through the crack of the door. Stahl let him in and immediately took a seat at the little kitchen table with his back to the wall. He waved for Charlie to take the other chair. A pot of coffee was cooking on the burner and a half-full cup was in Stahl's hand. Charlie couldn't smell a trace of booze in the room.

"You look tired, like you're not getting near enough sleep," Charlie said. "Maybe you need to tell me what really happened that night?"

"I don't know what you're talking about."

"The cold really bothers you, doesn't it, Rich?"

"Maybe more than some people, yeah. So what are you getting at?"

"Well, it's just sort of funny. Cold and blowing like it was that morning, I can't see you going down to the beach to take a look under the dock."

Stahl's poker face collapsed. He put his elbows on the table and dropped his face into his hands. "This is really eating at me. I told you and Carl I really didn't see or hear anything. . . . I'm sorry, Charlie. This'll cost me my job . . . but it's my fault Johnnie Lee's dead."

"Maybe, maybe not. But tell me what happened."

"That night . . . it was late, around midnight. I heard snow machines come down the beach and . . . when I heard those kids arguing, it sounded like they were under the dock. Then another machine came up the street and went down there, and I heard his voice—*that* was an adult man, though I didn't recognize it. I got bundled up and went out with the flashlight, and then they took off. It was blowing snow and real cold, like you said, and I . . . just went back inside." He lifted his head and struggled to look directly at Charlie. "So it's my fault he's dead."

"What do you mean?"

"If I'd just gone down there, shined the flashlight under the dock . . . They must have left him behind. Johnnie froze to death . . . because I didn't even check."

After a few minutes of both men looking at the floor, Charlie finally said, "I think he was probably dead already then, and they would have hid him in some better place, if you hadn't shown up. But do you know what time this happened?"

"Well, it must have been a bit after eleven, because I always go to bed then, but I hadn't fallen asleep yet."

"Did you hear what the man, the one on the fifth machine, was saying?"

"A little bit. You know how the wind can snatch up a conversation and carry it? When I opened the door I heard him shout, 'You used it all? My last bottle?' Or something like that. He was definitely mad."

"This is real important. When they took off, which way did they go?"

"To the south, back into town."

"You didn't hear any of them go north, across the Sound?"

"Don't think so. No, they all went south."

Charlie had to get up, move his feet, toward the sink. He dug out a cup that wasn't too dirty, then looked back at Stahl. "Now, this is important, too. Last night or the night before, did you hear anyone come by, heading north?"

Stahl shook his head firmly. "And I'd know, 'cause I haven't been sleeping very well—like you said, Charlie."

Charlie poured himself some coffee, then retook his seat. "Could be a long night, Rich."

"What do you mean?"

"We'll just wait here and listen."

"For what? They won't come back here, will they?"

Charlie couldn't tell Stahl that they were listening for a snow-go heading north, that the snow-go would come, he was sure, sometime—if not tonight, then within the next few days. Charlie would wait here every night for a month if he had to. But he could not explain this to Stahl, because Nuyaqpalik was a small town, and if it didn't happen tonight, he wanted to make sure it had the chance to happen tomorrow night or the night after.

"Actually, I should make a call first," he said. "You got a phone back in the bedroom?"

Stahl nodded, and Charlie shut the bedroom door, then called Nick at the station.

"You know Joey Hensen and the boys he hangs around with, playing video games over at the store?"

"Sure. You mean those cousins of his?"

"That's them. I'm down here on stakeout at the barge office. If you get a call from Rich later tonight, you and the troopers should go round up Joey and the others. One or more of them should have fresh scratches, and ought to match the blood samples the medical examiner has."

Charlie went outside, lifted the cowling of his snow-go, and yanked out the headlight wires so it wouldn't go on when he started up. He and Rich went through most of a fresh pot of coffee, and it was almost midnight when he heard a single machine come down the shore below the dock and head off across the ice.

"Well, thanks, Rich," Charlie said. "I'm in a hurry, so will you give Nick a call?"

"What should I say?"

"Just that I told you to call. He'll know what to do." Charlie shrugged quickly into his parka. "Oh— and you can tell him I'm going to pick up the son of a bitch that killed Johnnie."

He started his own machine down the shore and onto the ice, cautiously at first as his eyes adjusted. But a nearly full moon hung to the south, and the light was good enough to follow the trail easily.

Half a mile ahead, Karuk could see the other machine's light moving across the ice, then up the far shore, the light bobbing over the rolling tundra, darkened plumes spraying to both sides of the track. He closed in and by the time the other machine was slowing he was only a hundred yards behind. He hit the kill switch as soon as he saw the other one come to a stop on the trail. The man removed his helmet and stepped to the back, then took something out from under the seat. He turned and dug in the snow behind the machine, knelt, and reached into the hole. He got up and put something in his left pocket, then something else in the underseat compartment. His feet kicked snow back into the hole. Then he stopped, apparently seeing the dark form of Karuk's machine on the trail. Karuk started the engine and closed the distance, stopping about ten feet from the other man.

Karuk took off his own helmet. "I figured you'd be getting thirsty pretty soon. . . ."

"I'm stuck," a familiar voice replied. "I'm trying to dig out."

". . . but I was afraid you might wait until the troopers had gone."

" 'Fraid I don't know what you mean, Charlie. Last time I checked, in this country a man's still free to go for a ride when he wants to."

Karuk let go of the handlebars, flexing his fingers. "Nick and the troopers should be picking up those boys of yours right about now. I expect they'll be saying plenty by morning."

"What boys?"

"I should have figured out that much when I found that sneaker print out here. Even if you've got foot warmers on your machine, only a teenage boy would be careless enough to go riding like that. I knew you liked to drink, but I didn't think you were the kind who'd get kids mixed up in bootlegging."

The man froze; the moon shone on his face, but only his head and upper body were outlined above the dark form of his machine. "Look, I don't know what you're accusing me of, and I'm not admitting anything here. I'm just stating an opinion. Most of these local kids are going to leave town someday. Maybe for good, maybe just to go to school, but they're going to leave. Then they'll have to cope with the real world—and liquor is part of that world, and if they haven't learned to handle it they'll be in big trouble. Look at you, Charlie. No offense, but if you'd learned when you were younger how to handle it, you'd have been fine."

"Yeah. Johnnie Lee learned, didn't he, Al?"

"Goddamn it!" Briggs said. "I'm sure tired of hearing how down-trodden you people are, every time some Eskimo drinks himself to death. This country is founded on individual rights, and the last time I looked at the map, Nuyaqpalik was still part of the U.S. of A. If a few kids got to celebrating and one of them drank too much, don't go blaming somebody else."

"That's not the way I heard it." Karuk still made no move to get off the snow machine.

"No, no, sorry, Charlie. These boys you've mentioned, who've supposedly been helping the bootleggers—I'd think if that was true, they'd be prepared for getting picked up and questioned. They would have been told to just demand a lawyer. These hypothetical boys wouldn't say anything."

"I didn't hear it from them." Karuk waited. The white man shifted on his feet. He didn't want to say anything more now, but Karuk thought he would. Finally, he did.

"All right, we don't need to play games. So who said different?"

"Johnnie Lee."

Briggs's shock was visible in the moonlight. It must have been the one thing he couldn't have been sure of—whether Johnnie had talked to anyone before he died.

"When you and those boys were coming back from your pickup the other night," Karuk continued, "you probably weren't sure how far behind I'd be. You knew I might be able to radio ahead to have someone watch for you coming into town. So you had to hide the booze before you got there."

"You've got some imagination."

"By the time you finished and made it to the rear of your store, it must have been around seven or seven thirty in the morning. Some of the boys must have been excited at almost getting caught, and you were probably yelling, too. And then another boy happened to walk by, cutting through the alley on his way to school. A boy who never did a damn thing wrong in his life, but just happened to be in the wrong place.

"There's just one thing I'm not sure of, and I really want to know, Al. Did you just tell them to go get him drunk and find out how much he heard—and they got carried away pouring that vodka down his throat? Or did you mean to kill him that way, so he couldn't talk? Would you really take a life, just to get away with your bootlegging?"

Briggs laughed up at the smeared and shimmering stars. His left hand steadied itself on the shovel handle; his right was in his pocket. Karuk could hear a rushing in the distance like the wind, though the air remained still. He took off his right outer mitt and the inner glove and laid them across the handlebars. Then he put his own hand in his parka pocket.

"Okay, Charlie, let's stop the fantasy bullshit. We both know I'm no bootlegger, and I'd never have a kid killed. But let's say you were to search me and you found a bottle or two. All right. I'm not the only one in town. So I'd turn it over and pay my fine and promise not to do it anymore."

"I'm not talking misdemeanor possession, Al. Either way, it's likely to work out to some degree of murder. Or felony murder."

"All you've got on me is two bottles, Charlie."

He could feel it gathering now, rushing from out of the low tundra hills all around, from out of the depths of the pack ice behind.

"And a bunch of cases right under your feet. You couldn't leave the trail to hide it because I'd have seen the tracks. So you buried it *under* the trail, next to this tussock, then rode over it with your machines so it just looked like someone had gotten stuck here. Once you dig it all up, Joey and the other boys will

talk all night. If they don't, their lawyers will tell
them to do it tomorrow."

Briggs shifted again, turned slightly. "You know,
if those troopers can't find the booze, they'll have to
let the boys go."

When he was twelve and the bear had come at
him, Karuk had felt no urge to run, no fear, only the
sense of an inevitability so vast it reduced all human
will to nothing. A seal broke surface and blew when
the bear was fifteen feet away. The bear skidded to
a stop, claws digging at the ice, swung its head to
look at the seal. Karuk slid a little forty-grain bullet
in through its right ear, and the bear collapsed without a sound.

"Get your hand out of your pocket, Al."

It was rushing in from all sides. Karuk could taste
that old .22 in his mouth, and he waited. For Briggs
to take his hand out of his pocket.

Flame spouted from Briggs's extended arm, and
Karuk was standing astraddle the snow-go, Glock in
his hand, and the roaring filled his ears.

He guided the three machines in with his headlamp, then waited, watching one of the troopers get
off on the wrong side and flounder into the waist-
deep snow. Standing up on their machines, the other
and Nick both shone their flashlights around on the
snow.

"So where's the booze?" the trooper asked.

"I figure we dig just about where he's lying,"
Charlie said.

The other trooper had climbed back over and gotten off on the firmer snow on the trail. Through the

spider-webbed windshield, Charlie saw him walk up to Briggs.

"Looks like you drilled him right in the forehead."

"What was he packing?" the trooper on the machine asked.

The one in the trail knelt and unclenched Briggs's right hand. "Walther PPK. Pipsqueak James Bond gun."

"Wouldn't carry one myself." The trooper still on his machine lit a cigarette and nodded at Charlie's windshield. "No penetration. Looks like his bullet just deflected off the Plexiglas."

The one in the trail was checking the angle. "What happened, Chief? You must have stood up and shot over the windshield, huh?"

"I . . . guess so. I'm not sure I can remember."

The trooper nodded. "I've heard it can be like that. Well, there will have to be an inquiry, but it sure looks like a justifiable shoot to me. One thing they might ask about—if you don't mind my saying so, it doesn't look real smart—is your coming after him all by yourself like this. He might have killed you and stuffed you in a snowbank out here."

"I didn't know for sure he'd be coming out tonight. Besides, there was something I needed to know."

"Yeah, and how would *we* have ever known what happened if he'd killed you?"

"Oh," Charlie said, "my ghost would have showed you."

The troopers looked at him, then smiled. Nick knew better.

WRECK RIGHTS
Dana Stabenow

A twenty-four-year-old woman in a 1991 Ford super-cab pickup had been driving back from the liquor store that pretty much justified the existence of Crosswind Creek. She was there because she'd run out of whiskey, and not because she'd been serving it to guests.

Her drinking was no longer a problem. Sergeant Jim Chopin of the Alaska State Troopers wouldn't have minded so much except that on her way out of the liquor store's parking lot she'd T-boned a 1994 Dodge Stratus four-door sedan with a mother, two children, and a set of grandparents inside. The grandfather was DOA. The thirteen-year-old had a chance if the medevac chopper made it to the hospital in Ahtna in time.

The rest of the living were on their way to the hospital via ground transportation and the dead were in body bags when the second call came in. Another accident, this one about halfway between

Tok and the Ahtna turnoff to the Park. A forty-three-year-old man driving a 1995 Toyota 4Runner had collided with a nineteen-year-old man driving a 2001 Ski-Doo snow machine. The snow machine driver had been on his way to visit his girlfriend in Glenallen, and from the tracks at the scene, had been operating his vehicle along the side of the road as he was supposed to until he came to the Eagle Creek Bridge. Eagle Creek was narrow and deep and fast and never froze up enough in winter to take the weight of a snow machine, so the driver had come up off the trail next to the road to use the bridge. Demonstrating a totally ungenerational care for his hearing, he'd been wearing earplugs, which was probably why he'd missed the sound of the oncoming pickup, which, again according to the tracks, had seen the snow machine only at the last minute, when it had been too late to swerve and there wasn't any room to swerve anyway. The weather hadn't helped, a day of wet snow followed by a night of freezing rain, resulting in a road surface suitable only for hockey pucks.

The 4Runner driver was dead drunk, with three prior DWIs to his credit, not to mention a suspended license. The snow machiner was just dead.

Jim had barely contained that scene when a third call came in, this one from just south of the Park turnoff. Kenny Hazen, Ahtna's police chief, was already there when Jim's Blazer slipped and slid to a stop. Hazen, a big, square man, hard of eye and deliberate of speech, met Jim halfway, ice crunching beneath the grippers pulled over his boots. "The Ford Escort was making a left on the Glenn when the asshole in the Chevy pickup T-boned her. Near as I can figure, he was doing about ninety-five. And you know that curve. There's that hill, and you can't see a damn thing around it, especially on a winter night."

Jim knew the curve. "Alcohol involved?"

"Smells like it."

Jim sighed. "My night for drunks in pickups."

"Every night's a night for drunks in pickups," Hazen said. "The woman driving the Ford Escort is dead. So's the eleven-year-old riding behind her. The teenager riding next to her has at least a broken arm. The baby was in a car seat in the back, for a miracle buckled in correctly; it seems okay. The pickup driver's stuck, can't get either door open. The fire truck and the ambulance are coming from Ahtna, I—"

The rest of what he had been about to say was drowned out by the sound of shrieking brakes and skidding chains coming at them fast from up the hill and around the curve. Jim didn't wait, he dove for the ditch, and he'd barely hit snow when Hazen's massive figure hurtled over him and landed two feet west with a solid thud and a grunt. Jim had maybe a second to admire Hazen's 10.0 form before the semi currently screeching sideways down the hill slammed into the snow berm above their heads. For another very long second it seemed as if the berm would hold, but no. The double trailer, already jack-knifing, broke apart. The rear trailer rolled right over the berm and the tops of their heads, the ditch providing the minimum amount of required shelter. It rolled downhill twice more until a grove of pines slammed it to a halt. Its sides tore like paper, and pallets broke open, cases of canned goods going everywhere, a box of mandarin oranges nearly braining Jim when he stuck his head up to take a look.

The front trailer teetered on the edge of the road about fifty feet down the hill from where the rear one went over. Jim thought it might have had a chance if the snow berm had been higher. As it was, inertia and momentum took charge, and over it went, rolling at least half a dozen times, the doors bursting open and more pallets breaking apart and more boxes flying everywhere to explode upon impact. Cans of soup and green beans and tomato paste, bags of pasta and popcorn and potato chips, sacks of rice and sugar and flour, six-packs of juice and pop, bottles of vanilla and soy sauce and red-wine vinegar, boxes of Ziploc bags and Equal, packages of toilet paper and paper towels, it all tumbled down in a runaway landslide of commercial goods.

Jim, watching from the safety of the ditch, said in an awed voice, "I've never really appreciated the phrase 'bombs bursting in air' before."

"It does kinda look like Da Nang," Hazen agreed.

When it appeared certain that the semi tractor was going to stay on the road, Jim and Hazen climbed out of the ditch and over the berm. The tractor was jammed against the side of the hill out of which the road had been cut. The motor was still running, the headlights still on. Hazen climbed up and opened the passenger-side door. "Hey, you all right in there?"

A low moan was his reply. Hazen climbed inside the cab. "She smacked her head pretty good," he said, "but I think the rest of her's okay. Get on the horn, why don't you?"

On suddenly shaking legs Jim walked to his vehicle and raised the Ahtna emergency response team, who didn't sound thrilled about a fourth call out in as many hours, especially one in which no bodies were involved.

At dawn, Jim was even less happy to be able to supply them with one.

As usual the news hadn't taken long to get around, and by the time the sky lightened to a pale gray the hillside was swarming with Park rats picking over the detritus.

"They're like seagulls," Jim said.

"Except they don't shit all over everything." Hazen yawned, resettling his cap against the steady drizzle. Traffic swished by on the damp pavement behind them, vehicles slowing down when they saw the police cars pulled to the side of the road. The semi was long gone, towed to Ahtna. Hazen had taken the driver to the hospital there, along with the victims of the previous accident, and returned to the scene before daylight. "You talked to the shipper?"

Jim nodded. "Yeah, I called Anchorage. They called the store in Tok. I think they're trying to decide whose insurance company is liable for damages."

Hazen jerked his chin at the swarm on the hillside. "Think we should stop them?"

"Think we could?" Jim said.

"Probably not."

"Not wading around in hip-deep snow that's

mostly ice by now anyway," Jim said. "They'd be gone before we got down there. Besides, the shipping guy said not to bother."

"Not like it hasn't happened before," Hazen said, nodding. "They're performing a public service. Cleaning up the mess so the shipper or the state don't have to."

"What about the trailers?"

Hazen snorted. "What about them? Couple of Budds, straight haul, look about thirty years old. You could pick up a couple more just like 'em off the Internet for seventeen, eighteen hundred dollars." He saw Jim's look. "I did some driving, back when. Anyway, the tires might be worth something, but like you were saying, you'd have to be willing to climb down and wade around to get them. Not to mention haul them back up. Easier just to buy 'em new and already on the trailer. Hitch up and go. No missed deadlines that way, and believe you me, truckers are all about deadlines."

"Yeah." Jim frowned. "Did you hear that?"

Hazen's brows drew together. "Yeah, sounded like a scream. Look." He pointed. "Somebody's waving at you. I think they want you down there."

Jim regarded the waving and screaming at the bottom of the hill with distinct disfavor. "Why me and not you?"

"This is a state highway," Hazen said virtuously, and grinned when he saw Jim's expression. "I wouldn't dream of overstepping my authority, which after all, stops at the Ahtna city limits."

"My ass," Jim said.

He heard Hazen chuckle when he began the slippery descent of the hillside below the highway. It was one long wet slide punctuated by tree trunks that had an uncanny habit of leaping out in front of him just when he'd achieved too much momentum to stop. It didn't help that the spruces among them were beginning to ooze sap. He was covered with it by the time he reached the small knot of people clustered around a tiny hollow, all staring down at something, which accounted for the ill humor in his voice when he said, "All right, what's the problem?"

They turned as one and stared at him out of wide eyes. Some he knew; a few were unfamiliar. Marty and Dickie Grayling were regulars at the Roadhouse. A girl had her face tucked into Marty's armpit; all Jim could see of her was a lot of black hair. Her shoulders were shaking. A heavyset man with a permanent scowl turned that scowl on Jim, like the girl crying was Jim's fault.

Jim didn't take it personally, having a lot of experience with shock in all its various forms. More gently this time he said, "What's the problem?"

Another woman, this one older and thicker through the middle, her ruddy cheeks leeched of color, motioned with her hands. The circle parted, to reveal the body of a man, mostly white, maybe some Native if the straight black hair was an indication, the fleshy nose of the drinker beneath eyebrows so stingy they looked moth-eaten. A slack mouth sat over a receding chin with a faint down of ragged beard that looked more like neglect than fashion. He was probably in his late thirties, wearing jeans, blue plaid flannel shirt, thin nylon Windbreaker and high-top tennis shoes over thick socks.

No hat, and no gloves, either, although Jim had to turn him over to tell because his hands had been tied behind his back with the same kind of rope that bound his ankles.

"So whaddya think, suicide?" Hazen said, after they'd put the victim in a body bag, tied it off to a length of polypro, and hauled it to the road.

"What was your first clue," Jim said, "the bullet hole in the back of his head?"

They stooped to examine the entry wound. "Twenty-two?" Jim said.

"Handgun," Hazen said, nodding. He turned the body face up. "And no exit wound. We got mob in Alaska?"

"Not so's you'd notice," Jim said. He looked back at the body. "Up till now."

Hazen jerked his head. "Took a look at the skid marks."

"Oh yeah? Anything left?"

"Enough. There was no reason for her to slam on the brakes the way she did. Some black ice, sure, here and there, but she had her chains on, moderate rate of speed, fair visibility. I checked her driving record. She's clean. Got a good rep with her outfit. I talked to her boss, and he's ready to take her back on as soon as she gets out of the hospital."

"Let's go talk to her," Jim said.

The semi driver was lying in a bed in the Ahtna hospital, brow bandaged, both eyes black and swollen. "When the fuck do I get outta this place?" she said when Jim entered the room.

"Beats me," he said, removing his cap. "I'm Sergeant Jim Chopin, with the Alaska State Troopers."

"I know who you are," she said malevolently. "The so-called Father of the goddamn Park. I want my goddamn pants."

Hazen nudged him in the back and said in a stage whisper, "That's got to be the first time you've heard a woman say that."

Jim moved into the room. "If I find you your pants, will you answer some questions?"

She glowered at him. She was short-limbed and thickset with pale, freckled skin and fine orange hair cut like a marine's. "Find me the pants first."

There were the usual objections from the hospital staff, but in the end the nurse wilted beneath one of Jim's lethal smiles and produced the clothes: black jeans and a navy blue sweatshirt advertising Hulk Hogan and the WWF. Nobody had washed them, and the dried blood did not add to the semi driver's manifest charms. They turned their backs without being asked as she dressed. When they turned back, she said, "Got a smoke?" Hazen produced a pack of unfiltered Camels and she lit one and expelled smoke with a voluptuous sigh.

Her name was Bertha, Bertha O'Shaugnnessy. "Call me Bert," she said, the flame eating halfway down the cigarette on the next inhale.

"Okay, Bert," Jim said. "Why'd you hit the brakes?"

She narrowed her eyes against the smoke. "So I wouldn't hit her."

"Hit who?"

"Whaddya mean, who? A woman ran out in front of the tractor. I hit the brakes so I wouldn't hit her." She looked from Jim to Hazen. "What, you haven't talked to her?"

"This is the first we've heard of her, Bert," Jim said.

Bert stiffened. "She was like inches off the goddam front bumper. I hit the brakes and jacked the wheel around. There's no shoulder on that sonofabitchin' hill or I might have saved the cargo." She saw their expressions and her voice rose. "There fucking was a fucking woman, goddamn it!"

"What did she look like?" Jim said.

Bert shrugged. "Shit, who could tell at that speed?" She sucked in smoke. "Skinny, dark clothes—why I didn't see her until the last minute."

"You sure it was a woman?"

"Long hair flying out behind her like a goddamn kite. Don't know many men with hair that long." Bert shook her head. "She was a woman. She moved like one."

"Did you hit her?"

"No, goddamn it, I didn't hit her, I put the cargo over the side of that fucking hill so I wouldn't hit her."

"Would you recognize her if you saw her again?"

She shook her head. "It was too dark and everything happened too fast." The cigarette burned down to the end. Bert tossed the butt on the floor and ground it out beneath her heel. She looked at Hazen and tapped two fingers against her mouth. Hazen tossed her the pack and the matches. "Keep them," he said.

"Thanks." Bert lit up again. The fingernails of her stubby hands were stained yellow. She walked to the door and they parted so she could get to it. Halfway through, she paused. "Funny thing."

"What?"

"She didn't look scared."

"You didn't see her long enough to recognize her again," Hazen said, "but you saw her long enough to see she didn't look scared?"

Bert frowned, not rising to the bait. "She didn't *move* scared, I guess is what I mean. Something sort of, I don't know. Deliberate? When she showed up in the headlights." She stuck the cigarette in her mouth and dropped her arms to her sides, bending her elbows into right angles and clenching her hands into fists. "Like she was in a goddamn race instead of getting the hell out of my way." She shook her head, ash dropping off the end of the cigarette clamped in a corner of her mouth. "Crazy fucking story. I don't believe it myself. Probably losing it. Thanks for the smokes."

He heard her footsteps long before she appeared. His mouth went dry, his breath shortened, and his heart might even have skipped a beat. Was that any way for a grown trooper to behave? Thank God Hazen was back in his office making some calls. It certainly wasn't any way for a grown trooper to be observed to be behaving by a fellow law enforcement professional.

The door swung inward and there she was, all five feet nothing of her. A short, sleek cap of hair as black as night framed a face with tilted hazel eyes, high, flat cheekbones, and a full, firm mouth. She wore a dark green parka with a wolf ruff around the hood open over a white T-shirt, a navy blue fleece vest, and faded blue jeans tucked into Sorels.

She had to be the only woman alive capable of looking sexy in a morgue. Somehow the scar that bisected the otherwise smooth, golden skin of her throat literally from ear to ear, faded from its original ugly red gash to today's thin white rope of skin, only added to the effect.

There was a scrabble of toenails on linoleum and a gray furry torpedo launched itself at him. "Okay, Mutt," he said, fending off the attentions of the 140-pound half husky half wolf. A long pink tongue got in several swipes before she was satisfied and dropped back down to all fours. Her big yellow eyes were filled with love and her tail was wagging hard.

He looked up and swallowed, trying to work up some saliva. "Kate," he said, and hoped it didn't sound like the croak he was sure it did.

She gave a short nod. "Jim." Her voice was a low husk of sound, the effect of the scar. She nodded at the body beneath the sheet. "That him?"

He took a deep and he hoped unobtrusive breath. "That's him."

She walked to the table. He followed, coming to stand opposite to her. He raised his hand to lift the sheet, and paused. She met his eyes. "It's all right," she said. "Go ahead."

He raised the sheet. She didn't flinch. She did sigh and shake her head. Mutt curled her lip and went to sit down next to the door, her back pointedly to them. "Put it back."

He did. "You know him?"

She nodded. "It's Paul Kameroff. Some kind of third cousin's son to Auntie Vi." She sounded tired. "How did he die?"

"A bullet to the back of the head. No exit wound."

Her gaze sharpened. "Small-caliber weapon?"

"A twenty-two, we think. Haven't recovered the bullet as yet."

She was silent for a moment. "Where'd you find him?"

"At the bottom of Hell Hill."

She frowned. "Someone shot him and then tossed him out of a car window?"

"Looks like. We'd never have found the body if it weren't for a semi jackknifing over the side on top of him."

"Another one? That's the fourth this winter."

"And the state says there's nothing wrong with the grade of that curve," he said. "So anyway, the seagulls were out, scavanging like mad, and some of them stumbled over Paul here. His hands and feet were tied, by the way."

"Tied, and then shot, and then tossed," she said.

"Yeah. What was he into?"

"Nothing." She saw his expression. "I mean it, Jim. Nothing. Paul was, well, to tell the truth, he wasn't too bright. He was a couple of years behind me in school, and he never would have made it through if his sister hadn't carried him. Sonia," she added. "They were a year apart, I think."

"He live in the Park?"

"She stayed, he left when someone—probably Emaa or Auntie Vi—finagled him a Teamster's card. Last I heard, he was working roustabout for RPetCo up in Prudhoe Bay. Week on, week off, free food and board while he was working, good salary, pretty cushy deal all around. Paul might not have been very bright, but he was smart enough not to screw that up." She looked down at the body. "Or so I would have thought."

"What does a roustabout do?"

She shrugged. "Whatever they ask him to. Oil field cleanup, moving flow pipe around the Stores yard, on the emergency-response team for fires, loading and unloading luggage for the charter, driving crew-change buses, supervising the stick pickers."

"What kind of trouble could he get into on that job?"

"I told you—"

"Yeah, you told me." He jerked his chin at the body. "And yet here he lies with a bullet in his brain." He let the silence lie there like a wet, heavy blanket, and knew a fleeting gratitude that at least she didn't turn his knees to water when he was on the job.

"Let's go out there," she said.

"Out where? You mean where we found the body?"

"Yeah."

It was as gray and drizzly at the scene as when he and Hazen had left it. You wouldn't have known that a ragged ridge of tall mountains was holding up the edge of the eastern sky if you hadn't seen them on a clear day, or that a river draining twenty million acres of national park was winding its serpentine way through the valley below. No, this was just a barely two-lane road hacked out of the side of a steep hill, with one too many switchbacks in it for safety.

As witness the wrecks of the two trailers below. "You're not going to make me climb down there again, are you?" he said dismally, but she was already over the snow berm and scaling the snow-covered hillside. Mutt gave a short, joyous bark and leaped the berm in a single bound, vanishing into the underbrush in search of the elusive arctic hare. Sighing heavily, Jim followed less gracefully, grabbing for bushes and tree limbs to slow his descent. He reached the bottom of the ravine just as she was climbing inside the remains of one of the trailers. "Kate," he said sharply. "Wait. Don't go in there. The whole damn thing's probably ready to collapse."

She went in anyway and cursing, he followed. "For crissake," he said, picking a gingerly path through twisted boards and splintered pallets, "what's left to look at? Everything got tossed outside when the trailers went over."

She'd brought the flashlight he carried with him in the Blazer, and she was quartering what was left of the floor of the trailer, not an easy task because the trailer had come to rest upside down. He crunched through a pile of chocolate chips, fuming. "What are you looking for?" he said. "What the hell's the wreck got to do with Paul Kameroff?"

She clicked off the flashlight and clambered back outside. He gritted his teeth and followed her through the trees still standing to the second trailer. This one was resting on its side, or what was left of it. Jim noticed that, like the other trailer, all the tires were missing. The Park rats hadn't wasted any time, but he did wonder what they thought they were going to use them on. It wasn't like you could mount the tire of an eighteen-wheeler on a Ford F150 pickup truck. Not and go unnoticed, at any rate.

He had time to think all this as he slogged through the knee-deep snow, and time to wish he'd never called Kate in, or better yet, never met her in the first place ever in his whole life. Trouble, that's what she was, nothing but trouble. And the proximate cause of his boots being wet through to his socks. He swore.

"Give me your hand."

He looked up, and she was standing in the hole of the trailer, looking perfectly natural surrounded by twisted metal and torn wood. "Why?" he said. "Wasn't anything in the other one. Everything this trailer was hauling is now piled up in some Park rat's cache. What the hell is there to see?"

"Come up and find out," she said.

It was a challenge, and he took her up on it, using her hand and the rickety side of the trailer to pull himself up. A can of cream of mushroom soup came rolling out from a dark corner, and he stumbled over it to bump into Kate.

He froze.

She smiled up at him, not moving. "Gosh," she said, "you've picked up some snow, Jim." She leaned over to brush a clump that clung to his pants leg, and she took her time standing up again. There was the inevitable reaction, fight it though he would. He stood very still, his jaw working. She smiled again, and the pitiful thing was she wasn't even working him at full power.

"What," he said through his teeth, "was so all-fired important in here that you just had to see?"

"Over here," she said, leading the way.

The surface beneath his feet shuddered and shook. He wasn't sure if it was the wreck or him. *What's the difference?* he thought, and almost laughed.

She played the flashlight over an intact corner of the trailer. "Look. You see it?"

Jim tried to focus. "What? Wait." His voice sharpened. "What's that?"

"Blood, I think. On what used to be the floor."

Jim had a lowering feeling that he knew what she was getting at, but he said stubbornly, "So what? Maybe there was a side of beef strung up in that corner. Maybe it dripped a little."

"This isn't a reefer, Jim. It's straight storage. Nothing but dry and canned goods. I think you should take a sample and get the lab to run it through their magic machines."

"You're a witch, aren't you?" he said two days later. "Go ahead; you can say it. I won't tell. I may personally burn you at the stake, but I won't tell."

They were sitting at the River Street Café in Niniltna, where Laurel Meganack presided over grill and table and dispensed not awful coffee out of a large stainless steel urn. The village of Niniltna (year-round population, 403) wasn't large enough for a street sign, but the Niniltna Native Association board of directors, which had been persuaded to front the money for the café against their better judgment, didn't want to be publicly coupled to the business. The Kanuyaq River was about twenty feet from the front door, and there was a game trail that ran between the two, and that was enough for Laurel.

"Whose blood was it?" Kate said.

Mutt sat between them, pressed up against Jim's leg, looking back and forth between her two beloveds. Jim gave her ears an absentminded scratch. "It was Paul's," Jim replied. "But then, you knew that."

"I thought maybe," she said.

"Yeah. So his body wasn't on the ground when the trailer went over, it was in the trailer and got thrown out when the trailer hit bottom and broke open."

"Yeah."

"So Paul Kameroff wasn't killed in the Park. He was probably killed in Anchorage and loaded into the trailer there." Jim brooded over his coffee. "To what purpose?" he said. "To be unloaded with the rest of the groceries in Tok?"

"It doesn't seem likely."

"No." Jim sat back and looked at her, and there was no trace either of seduction or of a susceptibility to seduction in his steady gaze. "You want to tell me what the hell is going on?"

Laurel Meganack swished by with the coffeepot and a bright smile. "You sure you folks don't want something to eat? I make a mean asparagus omelet."

Jim had a hard time controlling his expression. "Thank you, no."

Kate didn't bother hiding her grin.

"What?" Laurel said.

"He hates asparagus," Kate said.

"Hmmm." Laurel topped off their mugs and said to Kate with a grin of her own, "And you would know this how?"

Jim noted with interest the faint color in Kate's cheeks, and kept watch as she became involved in doctoring her coffee with evaporated milk until the coffee was a nice tan in color. After that came the sugar, a lot of it. Jim averted his eyes and tried not to shudder. "Ballistics took a look at the bullet."

"And?"

"They ran it through every possible database going back to the Civil War. No matches."

"There wouldn't be," she said. "This was a hit, Jim. Whoever did this was a pro."

He thought of the neat knots on Kameroff's wrists and ankles, the equally neat placement of the bullet in the back of the head. It was all very, well, neat. "Yeah," he said. "That's pretty obvious. Tell me something."

"What?"

"We got mob in Alaska?"

She considered. "We got the Aleut mob," she offered. "You don't want to cross them. They'll sic Senator Stevens on you."

When he stopped laughing, she said, "I been asking around since I saw you last."

"Asking who? And asking what?"

"Paul's family. Sonia, mostly, although she's not saying much."

"Sonia's the sister."

"Yes."

Her expression was unreadable. He waited. When nothing else came, he said, "And you found out what from all this asking around? Anything that will help us find out who tied up Paul Kameroff and put a bullet in his brain?"

She glared at him. "I don't need to be reminded of the object of the exercise."

"Funny, I thought you did. I won't let the Park's tribal loyalty screw up my investigation, Kate."

"Neither will I."

"Good to know."

She drank coffee, a delaying tactic to regain control over her temper. "For one thing, I found out that my information on Paul was out of date. He wasn't working for RPetCo on the Slope anymore. He'd moved to town."

"Who was he working for?"

"Masterson Hauling and Storage."

He paused in the act of raising his mug. "Really?"

"Really."

"That would be the same outfit that owns the two trailers that went over the side of Hell Hill a couple nights ago."

"It would."

"Well," Jim said, putting down his mug. "Isn't that interesting."

"You might even call it a clue," she said. "When do you leave?"

"Immediately." He reached for the cap with the trooper seal on the crown.

Mutt got to her feet, tail wagging. She was always ready for action. "Got room for two more?" Kate said.

He paused. "I meant what I said, Kate."

She replied without heat. "I did, too."

"I won't hide what I find, no matter who it involves."

"I know."

He put his cap on and tugged it down. "All right, then. Let's move like we got a purpose."

The Cessna was fueled and ready at Niniltna's forty-eight-hundred-foot dirt airstrip. Kate untied the mooring lines while Jim did the preflight, and they were in the air fifteen minutes later. He leveled them out at five thousand feet and set the GPS. It was only then that he realized he'd be spending an hour plus touching shoulders with the one woman in all the gin joints in all the world who was like to drive him right out of his mind. He could hear her inhaling over the headphones and clicked off the channel, but that didn't help because he could still see the rise and fall of her breast out of the corner of his eye. He knew she didn't wear perfume, but he could smell her anyway, an alluring mixture of Ivory soap and wood smoke that his renegade pheromones translated as all heat.

A cold nose against the back of his neck made him jump, and Kate laughed. It was a very seductive laugh, or so it seemed to him, and he found himself leaning forward into the seat belt as if he could push the plane along faster by doing so.

He was never so grateful in his life to hear Anchorage ATC come on the headset, and he burned up the Old Seward Highway like he was driving for NASCAR, only at five hundred feet. The landing at Merrill Field was a runway paint job and he was out of the plane the instant it rolled to a stop.

It didn't make him feel any better to see the tiny smile tugging at the corner of her lips.

*   *   *

Masterson Hauling and Storage was headquartered in a massive warehouse in midtown, off Old Seward near International. It was surrounded by a lot of other warehouses, car dealerships, a candy factory, a strip club, and the Arctic Roadrunner, home of the best cheeseburger in the state. "What time is it?" Kate said.

"Not lunchtime."

She gave him an exaggeratedly hopeful look. "After?"

Jim was partial to a good cheeseburger himself. "Works for me."

The reception area of Masterson Hauling and Storage was a small room behind a door with a window in it. There was a yellow-and-green striped love seat much the worse for wear next to a pressed board telephone stand laden with a phone and a phone book and a stack of *American Trucker* magazines. At a desk a young woman with bleached blond hair spiked into a Dali sculpture was applying more liner to brown eyes that already looked strongly racoonish. "May I help you all?" she said. She saw Mutt and the burgeoning smile went away. "I'm so sorry. We can't have animals in here."

Jim smiled down at her. "Sure you can," he said in a suddenly slow and very deep drawl. He let an admiring gaze drift down to the tight white man's shirt that was straining at its buttons, and from there to the nameplate on the front of the desk. "Candi."

Candi forgot all about Mutt, and when she spoke again her voice was a little breathless. Candi was not long out of the very deep American South and her R's had a tendency to defer to her H's. "You all are a trooper?"

"I am that." Jim didn't bother to introduce Kate, which was okay because Kate wasn't registering even on Candi's extreme peripheral vision. "Who's your boss, Candi?"

Her hands and eyelashes fluttered uncontrollably. "Why, that would be Mr. Masterson. Mr. Conway Masterson."

He let his smile widen. "I like the way you say his name, Candi."

More fluttering. "Why, I, why, thank you kindly, mister, officer—"

"It's Jim Chopin, Candi. Sergeant Chopin of the Alaska State Troopers. I'd like to speak to your boss for a few minutes, if it's convenient for him."

"Why certainly, Sergeant," Candi said, and reached for the phone. She missed it on the first try and blushing again, had to disconnect from Jim's eyes.

Jim looked at Kate. To his surprise, she was grinning and not bothering to hide it. "The Father of the Park has his uses," she said.

"I told you I never did deserve that title," he said.

She fluttered her eyelashes. "Ah, but did you earn it, Sergeant Chopin, sir?"

He thought longingly, not for the first time, just how much he'd like to wring her neck. Well. After.

Candi hung up and twinkled up at Jim. "Mr. Masterson can see you now, Sergeant Chopin."

"Thank you, Candi."

"Just on up the stairs now, first door at the top. And don't forget to stop off to say bye."

"I don't think any man worthy of the name could forget to do that," Jim said gallantly. Mutt was waiting for him around the corner. "What are you grinning at?'' he said to her, and escaped up the stairs behind a Kate whose shoulders were shaking slightly.

Conway Masterson's office was large and utilitarian, the desk piled with bills of lading and maintenance schedules and correspondence, more of the same stacked on top of a wall of filing cabinets. There was one window overlooking the interior of the warehouse, and one of the flourescent lights was flickering overhead. One wall was given over to a large dry board divided into grids indicating trucks out on runs to Homer, Seward, Valdez, Tok, Fairbanks, Coldfoot, and Deadhorse, including departure time, estimated arrival, and cargo. A radio was playing country-western music, which didn't add to the ambience, and Masterson himself was talking on the phone as they stood in the doorway. He waved them inside and kept talking. "Well, get to it. I've got four loads scheduled for the Fairbanks warehouse already this week, and I'm down two trailers." He hung up. "You're the trooper," he said to Jim. To Kate, he said, "Who're you? And who the fuck said you could bring a dog up here?''

Mutt's ears went back, and a low growl rumbled up out of her throat.

Masterson bared his teeth and growled back.

Kate put a hand on Mutt's shoulder before things got out of hand. Mutt stopped growling, but she didn't sit down and she didn't take her narrowed yellow gaze off Masterson.

"Kate Shugak," Jim said. "She's working the case with me."

"What case?"

"The murder of one of your employees," Jim said bluntly. "Paul Kameroff."

Conway Masterson was about fifty, with a W. C. Fields' nose barely separating small dark eyes, red fleshy lips, and a stubborn chin that looked days past its last shave. His comb-over extended from just above his left ear to being tucked behind his right ear. He wore a rumpled navy blue suit off the rack from JCPenney, an unknotted red tie featuring a Vargas girl, and a white shirt with the third button down sewn on with brown thread. His eyes met Jim's without a trace of awareness, but he took a little too long to answer for Jim's taste. "Paul Kameroff? Who the hell's he?"

"He used to drive for you," Jim said. "His body was found in the wreckage of that semi your driver put over the side of the Glen Highway three, four days back."

Masterson's eyes narrowed. "Bert's rig?"

"Bertha O'Shaugnnessy, yes."

"It's that fucking hill. What do my guys call it? Hell Hill, that's it. It's the worst stretch of that fucking road. We've put, I don't know how many goddamn rigs over the side there. It's so fucking steep we can't recover any of our cargo, and half the time the tractors go over the side with the goddamn trailers. Bert was fucking lucky. It's getting so I can't afford insurance on that fucking run. What the hell am I suppose to do, run everything going to Ahtna up the goddamn Parks through fucking Fairbanks?"

"What can you tell me about Paul Kameroff?" Jim said.

Again a slight hesitation, barely noticeable. "I run

a lot of trucks and a lot of cargo out of this warehouse. I don't know the name of every last fucking employee." He reached for the phone. "Candi? We got an employee named Paul Kaminski?"

"Kameroff," Jim said.

"Whatever," Masterson said. "If he's got an employee file, make 'em a copy." He hung up. "That all?"

"No," Jim said. "I'll need to talk to anyone who worked with Kameroff."

"What the fuck for? My delivery schedule's already down the shitter this month. I don't need you fucking around in the warehouse slowing things down even more."

"Nevertheless," Jim said, imperturbable.

"That didn't take long," Kate said as they sat down with loaded trays.

"No, it didn't, did it?" Jim said, reaching for the mustard. "Amazing how in a crew of only twenty, Masterson couldn't remember Paul Kameroff."

"Amazing how hardly any of that crew of twenty remembered that Paul existed," Kate said, and dug in. There was silence for a few bliss-filled minutes. Murder was a serious subject, but a good cheeseburger deserved attention and respect.

Jim grabbed a handful of napkins to clean the juice that had run down his hands. "Going to be hard to prove that anyone in that warehouse had anything to do with Kameroff's death."

"Next to impossible, I'd say," Kate said. She licked her fingers, one by one.

He managed to resist the urge to offer to do it for her. "There used to be rumors about the truckers in Alaska."

"There used to be fact about the truckers in Alaska," Kate said, sitting back in the booth. "They were a pretty rough crowd during the pipeline days. was just a kid when they first had oil in the line, back in, oh, June, July of 1977, I guess, but I remember hearing about how they expected a body to come out the other end with the first of the oil."

"Did it?"

"No. If there were any bodies, there's almost six hundred thousand mostly uninhabited square miles out there to have dumped them in."

"Which naturally begs the question, why was Paul Kameroff's body dumped in the back of a trailer that was going to be unloaded in Tok the next day?"

Kate met his eyes. "Whoever killed him wanted his body to be found," they said at the same time.

Jim shoved his tray to one side. "It was a very formal little murder. He was bound first, hands and feet, no possibility of a struggle when the time came, and then shot. They wanted that bullet to go right where it did."

"An execution," Kate said. "Part of the message."

"Hi, you all," a voice said.

They looked up to see Candi standing next to their table, tray in hand and a bright smile on her freshly made-up face.

It took Jim a second to remember her name. But only a second. "Candi," he said, and flashed out his broadest, most welcoming smile. He scooted over in the booth. "Have a seat."

Candi didn't even look at Kate, who stood up and said, "I'll just check on Mutt."

Jim didn't need to see her meaningful look to know what he was supposed to do. He put his arm along the back of the booth and smiled down at little Candi. "How nice to see you again."

Little Candi's blush was so powerful it caused her pancake makeup to glow like pale pink neon.

"Well?" Kate said. She was sitting in the crew-cab she had borrowed from the clerk at Stoddard's Aircraft Parts, and since it was coming up on Jeannie's quitting time she was getting a little restive.

"She didn't know anything, either," he said, slamming into the passenger seat. Mutt poked her nose into the front seat and rested a consoling chin on his shoulder.

"Did she know Paul, at least?"

"Yes, she knew Paul, enough to give him his paycheck every two weeks. Oh, and to forward his calls to the shop."

"What calls?"

He gave an irritable shrug. Mutt gave him a wounded look and withdrew her support. "Seems like his sister called a lot."

"Sonia?"

He nodded. "Yeah."

Kate, in the act of starting the engine, paused with her hand on the key. "Define 'a lot.' "

"Often enough for Candi to recognize her voice. Maybe once a day, sometimes more."

Kate stared out the windshield at the unprepossessing city winterscape. There was a lot of slush on the road, a lot of snow on the sides of the road, and the hum of studded tires on pavement as vehicles so dirty you couldn't make out their color, never mind their make, splattered by. "Why at work, I wonder?"

"I don't know. Maybe when he was at work was he only time she could get to a phone. She lives in he Park, right?"

"Yes, outside Niniltna. And no, I don't think she as a phone. She'd have to go into town to make he call."

"Maybe he couldn't afford one."

"If he was a Teamster, he could afford a phone. Sut then why call so often? Every day, twice a day, vhat's that about?" She started bouncing her knee, a sure sign of intense Shugak rumination. "Their parents are okay, last time I checked. There aren't any ther brothers or sisters. Why's she calling him so nuch?" She looked at the clock on the dash and tarted the truck. "We've got to get this truck back efore Jeannie thinks we've taken it and headed for California."

The three of them were back in the Cessna and alfway home, crossing the silver ribbon of the ransAlaska Pipeline five thousand feet below when ne spoke again. "Jim, do you have a list of dates of hen semis have skidded off of Hell Hill?"

"No," he said in surprise. "Hazen probably does, nce he's the one who responds to them most of ne time."

"Let's go to Ahtna," she said.

He changed course without asking why. It was ng after dark when they landed. He taxied up to ne Frontier Air terminal, where the Ahtna police nief was waiting. "I hope you've got something to ll me more interesting than my dinner," the police nief said, "which I was about to sit down to."

Kate brightened. "We going to Tony's?"

Tony's was the Ahtna Lodge, a hotel on the edge of the river. What it lacked for in the way of rooms, which were converted Atco trailers, it more than made up for in its chef, Tony's partner in life and in the business.

Hazen sighed. "I guess we are."

Both men knew there was no point in asking Kate Shugak any questions until she was on the safe side of her exquisitely charred sixteen-ounce New York, not to mention the green salad with blue cheese on the side, a baked potato with all the trimmings, and pumpkin pie to follow. The Ahtna police chief, who was a big man with a bigger beer belly, said, "Where the hell does she put it all?"

"Maybe she diets," Jim said, who was thinking of the cheeseburger and wondering the same thing.

Kate surfaced for long enough to say "Diet?" like it was a bad word.

When the plates had been cleared they all sat back with similar satisfied expressions on their faces. A high-pressure system had moved in from the northwest, and outside the window the river's icy surface began to glow, a reflection of the light of the rising moon. The snow-covered peaks of the Quilaks stood out in bold relief against a black, starry sky. Mutt, recipient of her own steak, served rare, gave a satisfied sigh and lay down on Jim's feet.

Jim stirred. Admiring the view was all well and good. He had been known to pause in his duty on more than one occasion to do so, or why live in Alaska? But a man had been murdered. "You have that list?" he said to Hazen.

"Sure. Although I'm still waiting to find out why you want it." Hazen handed it across.

Jim put it on the table between him and Kate. He was aware with every breath that he took that she was mere inches away from him. It felt like the right side of his body was being cooked over a slow fire. He wondered if she knew.

She met his eyes and smiled at him, a rich, almost languid smile. Oh yeah, she knew.

"Why did you want this list?" Jim said.

Her smile widened at the brusque tone of his voice.

"Like me to get the two of you a room?" Hazen said, his voice heavy with sarcasm, and if you listened for it, a trace of envy.

"Thanks for the offer," Kate said lazily, not taking her eyes from Jim, "but we can always get our own."

Jim could feel the color rising up into his neck and could do nothing to stop it. He tapped the printout on the table between them. "The list, Shugak."

She actually pouted. He hadn't known she could do that. But she picked up the piece of paper and studied the columns. "Hell Hill's body count is up this year," she said.

"Yeah," Hazen said, "I noticed that, too, when I was putting the list together. We'll get one, at most two semis jackknifing on that curve in a year. This year there have been four."

"What accounts for four, do you think?" Kate said. "Weather, maybe?"

Hazen frowned and shook his head. "This winter's been no worse than normal."

"Maintenance?"

Hazen shook his head again. "Far as I know, it's been business as usual. The guys up at the state highway-maintenance station are always griping about their equipment, always wanting the next new

John Deere one-hundred-fifty-five-horsepower road grader, but they're all still employed. I imagine the governor knows well enough to leave Pete Heiman's district alone when it comes to budget cuts."

Kate handed the list to him. "Did you notice anything else on that list of yours?"

Jim had, but he remained silent.

Hazen looked at the printout. "Okay," he said after a moment. "Three of the four semis were owned by Masterson Hauling and Storage."

"You don't have the cargo on the list."

Hazen stared at her. "Probably groceries for the AC store in Tok. Not a lot of construction supplies being hauled up the highway in the winter. Okay, Kate, what's going on?"

The waiter brought them coffee all around, with a small aluminum pitcher of half-and-half just for Kate. She rewarded him with a warm smile. Blinded, he turned away and ran into a customer sitting at the next table, who knocked over his wineglass.

When the resulting disturbance died down, Kate said, "Have you guys ever heard of wreckers?"

" 'Wreckers'?" Jim looked at Hazen. They both shrugged. "Guess not. Who or what is a wrecker?"

"Wrecking, as it was defined in England, particularly on the coast of Cornwall, was the deliberate luring of a cargo-laden ship onto an offshore reef, usually by means of false signal lights, or by extinguishing the lights of lighthouses built to warn ships away from dangerous waters. The ship would run aground, break apart, and the cargo would float to shore, where the wreckers were standing by to pick it up."

Hazen looked at her. "Where the hell do you get this stuff?"

She shrugged. "I read a lot."

Jim was thinking back to that drizzly morning below the curve coming off of Hell Hill. "Are you saying—"

"One, Paul Kameroff went to work for Masterson Hauling and Storage last fall, leaving a perfectly good job on the North Slope for no good reason. Two, his sister, Sonia, called him at work once or twice a day from November on. Three, Bert O'Shaugnnessy said she braked because she saw a woman run in front of her semi. Four, all the Masterson trucks were hauling groceries bound for AC in Tok."

"Jesus Christ," Hazen said.

"You're saying that the grocery loads Masterson Hauling was running to Tok were deliberately targeted?" Jim said.

"By this Sonia? Who's what, the sister of the dead man?" Hazen said.

"By Sonia and whoever's in it with her," Kate said. "There were a lot of people on the hillside that day, you told me. She was just one of them." She drank coffee. "You should talk to the drivers of the other trucks that went over. See how many of them saw someone run in front of their semi."

"And Masterson found out," Jim said.

Kate nodded. "He'd lost at most one truck per year in previous years, and there are other trucking outfits that make that run. He must have wondered why he was being picked on."

"So," Hazen said, "Paul Kameroff was fingering loads for his sister, Sonia?"

"There was a big dry board in Masterson's office," Kate said. "It had all the trips on it, all the trucks, where they were going and what they were carrying, when they were leaving, and when they were scheduled to arrive. I think Sonia called Paul a couple of times every day just to see what was heading our way."

"I don't get it," Jim said. "The trucking firms lose a semi of stuff a year, maybe, and they don't make a fuss about who picks it up after. The Park rats are onto a good thing here. Why get greedy? Why ruin it? Is the Park having a rough year?"

"I don't think they were picking up stuff for subsistence purposes," Kate said.

"You think they were reselling it?" Jim said.

She nodded. "Otherwise, why so many? It was bound to attract notice. Which, of course, it did."

There was a brief silence. "So—" Hazen said.

"I think Masterson figured it out, killed Kameroff, and tossed the body in the back of Bert's trailer, knowing it was going to be run off the road like the others had been," Kate said. "Knowing that the body would send a message to the people at the other end."

"Jesus Christ," Hazen said again. "The driver could have been killed."

"She sure could," Kate said. She looked at Jim. "I told you. That's a tough crowd."

Jim found a friendly judge and got a warrant to toss the premises of Masterson Hauling and Storage. He didn't find anything. The three drivers of the previous three wrecks had taken early retirement long before he ever got there and had moved Outside.

Candi was genuinely distressed when she couldn't find their personnel files. The union local knew a different judge and Jim never did get a look at the union's membership files.

During her interrogation Sonia Kameroff cried a lot and said very little. Jim talked to a few of the others he had seen at the wreck that day, only to be greeted with blank stares. "Trucks always go off that hill," one man told him. "Always will. It's a bad hill. Shit, Jim, we're doing a public service by cleaning up the mess. That trucking outfit sure ain't gonna do nothing. And no point in letting all that food go to waste."

"I can't prove a damn thing," Jim said to Kate.

"No," Kate said, face turned up to the sun. They were in back of her cabin, sitting on the boulder perched at the edge of the cliff overlooking the stream. March had come in like the proverbial lion and the snow cover was melting almost as they watched.

"They could have killed someone, Kate."

"Someone did get killed," she said.

Jim hated to let any case go, especially murder. "Got any thoughts about the gun?"

She opened her eyes and looked at him, not without sympathy. "Sure. They probably tossed it off Point Woronzof, let the tide take it out. That's what I would have done."

Nettled, he said, "You're taking this awfully calmly. You went to school with the guy. Don't you care?"

She was silent for a moment. "Those wreckers I told you about?"

"Yeah?"

"Sometimes they drowned. Sometimes they got caught, and sometimes they got hanged. Sometimes people off the ships drowned. But most of the wreckers were peasants living way below the poverty line, no jobs to speak of, no homes, no way of feeding their kids. They thought the risk was worth it."

He was silenced.

"Wreck rights," she said after a while. "We call it salvage rights now, but it was wreck rights then. If it washes up on shore and you find it, it's yours."

"And if it falls off the highway and you find it—"

"Then that's yours, too," she said.

Mutt came back with a ptarmigan and sat down to lunch. The three of them sat in the sun for a while longer, and then Kate went back to her cabin, and Jim went back to town.

MY HEART WENT BOOM

John Straley

That this story ends with sirens and police cars coming to the elementary school just as the fifth-grade production of *A Midsummer-Night's Dream* was ending, you will know soon enough. Anyway, it's not the ending that matters much in these kinds of stories: the ones about love and treachery. The endings are almost always known ahead of time. They're known by the reader, and sadly, they're known by almost all of the characters themselves.

I say almost all the characters because as I sat outside on the steps with blood running down my fingers and people pushing all around me. I still had no idea what had happened, or what was about to happen next for that matter. The whole scene was brand-new to me. The flashing blue and red lights sweeping through the alder trees lit up the woods around the elementary school like a deserted arcade. The mountains looming above Sitka, Alaska, were covered in new snow so that they seemed to float in the darkness behind town. Someone gave me a blue towel, which I pressed against the wound to stop the flow of blood, and I remembered where I was. I remembered that it was early spring and the herring were coming in to spawn, the gulls were singing their spring song above the harbor, and it hadn't rained in days.

There had been a few dark clouds that morning when Gloria called to tell me that her husband was about to go crazy because his girlfriend planned to dump him, but it never rained. I didn't ask her how she knew this piece of information about her husband because Gloria had a life so complex that it bordered on the Byzantine. Max was going to pieces, she said.

"How do you know this, that he's going to pieces?" I asked.

"Listen, Cecil, I know. You can't be married to a guy for as long as I have and not know the signs. He tries to watch TV but gets up and goes for a walk, then he comes back in a few minutes and watches more TV. When the phone rings he snaps at anybody who tries to pick it up before he does. Poor baby, he's losing it."

"Well, what do you want me do about it?"

"You're a private investigator, right? I want you to follow him." On the other end of the line I heard her taking a whistling teapot off the stove. In the background, the radio was playing a Beatles song, "I Saw Her Standing There," I think.

"What for?" I asked.

"Listen, when Lori dumps him, and trust me, she's going to dump him as soon as Alex gets back to town, he's going to lose it big-time. I don't want him to do anything stupid." She stopped talking and we both listened to the chorus in the background.

"You mean something stupid like falling in love with a younger woman who has a rich and handsome boyfriend?" I asked her.

"Don't be a smart aleck, Cecil. Are you going to help me or not?"

I was going to help her. I liked Gloria. To tell the truth, I had a strange kind of crush on her that stemmed from only one occurrence some ten summers ago. I had known her vaguely all that summer. I had once helped her dig for clams out at Brent's Beach, but that was about the extent of our interaction. Gloria had been working on a fish tender for the summer. She had spent three months off-loading fish and shoveling ice and then decided to quit. She walked into the Pioneer Bar wearing a blue velvet dress. Her red hair was down and her eyes glittered as she walked around the pool table, slipped her arm around my waist, and kissed me briefly. "Let's go out in the woods and make out," she said to me without a trace of the sarcasm I was expecting.

"All right," I said gallantly, and she kissed me again.

"I'll be right back," she said, and I put up my cue stick.

The Pioneer is a fisherman's bar with deep booths and big windows facing the parking lot of the commercial harbor. Up behind the back door is a muddy little pathway that ends in a tangle of salmonberry bushes. Bar patrons often smoked pot there, and sometimes settled old disputes. I walked out the bar to see if anyone was there and found myself alone. Drops of rain hung from the thorny vines and glittered in the lights from the houses in the old Indian village up the hill. A song sparrow flitted in the bramble, and I could hear a neighbor's dog barking above the low clatter of the slow night in the bar. I stood there and imagined kissing Gloria there in the underbrush. I imagined running my hand up the back of her velvet dress and kissing her until we both could stop and laugh and go back inside for a drink.

But of course she never came, and I waited out there until some drunk came out to take a piss; than I went back inside where Gloria was talking to one of the deck hands off the fish tender and she never mentioned kissing me again.

I didn't know Gloria all that well, only that she had a deep laugh, liked digging clams, and loved drinking beer. I wasn't then, and am not now, in love with her. I just wanted to go to that wild place out behind the bar, where no one but the song sparrows would watch us kiss. I wanted to go there, and she, at least for a moment, wanted to go there with me, and for a person with an active imagination that was enough information to form a long-lasting crush.

"I'll do it," I said lamely. "I'll keep an eye on your wayward husband."

"You are a total doll," she said.

"Why do you guys stay married?" I asked as an afterthought.

"Aw, Cecil," she said, "he's a good guy. He's a great father, and we're too damn close to getting these kids out of the house to screw around with a divorce. Maybe later, but this works good for now."

"All right," I said, and I hung up the phone because I didn't really feel like pursuing the subject any further.

I walked down the ramp of the harbor on my way to Max's boat. Max had been a commercial fisherman back in the late seventies. Gloria was working as a barmaid by then, and they had met one late fall after fishing was done. Max had taught her to play pool that winter. Now Max had a bad back, a big gut, and he worked as a teacher's aid, helping kids with special needs. Max still had his boat and commercial fished during the summer. If Max was in a bad mood, he would hole up on his boat.

The herring fleet was in town, and the harbor was stacked with seine boats. The outer floats were three boats deep, one fishing boat tying up to the next. Walking along the float there were several knots of fishermen standing around conferring about something. In each group there was usually one man talking into a cell phone. These fishermen owned expensive boats and they fished multiple fisheries up and down the West Coast. Some would fish for different species from halibut in the Bering Sea to squid off the coast of California. They were prosperous businessmen with international concerns. They had satellite phones and hired spotter planes to locate fish. They owned interests in their own processing companies and would be as likely to get stock quotes on their laptops as they would be the latest storm reports. These fishermen wore the most expensive fleece clothes and wintered in France.

Max was more of a smelly wool coat fisherman, and he had generally wintered in the Pioneer Bar. On my way to Max's boat I shouldered myself through a group of herring fishermen, one of whom held a tiny phone to his ear saying, "So, is there going to be an announcement at two o'clock or not?" as he rolled his eyes to the guys he was standing with.

Max wasn't in his boat, but the door was unlocked. I knocked and called out, but no one was there. Max's boat was an old wooden troller, probably forty feet long. The back deck was clean and the gear was stowed neatly. I swung up on the deck and walked into the house. The bedding was thrown on the floor near the forward berth. There was half a pot of chili sitting on the diesel stove. The chili was baking into red asphalt at the bottom of the pan. The iron stove was warm, but the fire was out. There was an empty bottle of bourbon on the shelf near the steering station, and a cardboard box was on the floor with the contents strewn about: old tide books, fuel bills, some rusty circle hooks, and a couple of plastic boxes of stainless-steel screws.

All of this looked pretty normal for a fisherman's hidey-hole. Max had turned off the stove before he left, so he wasn't too drunk or self-destructive. I was feeling pretty optimistic about him until I saw the box of nine-millimeter ammunition under the table. The outer cardboard of the box was ripped away, and six holes for shells were empty.

I walked back down the dock and was thinking about whether I should call Gloria to give her a heads up that her husband could be drunk, heartbroken, and now armed, but I decided against it. She wasn't going to call the police. Besides I doubted Max intended to shoot her, anyway.

Sitka is on Baranof Island. There are five thousand brown bears on Baranof, some eight thousand people, and only fifteen miles of road. It isn't that hard for the bears to avoid the humans because the roads take up so little of the eighty-mile-long island. But it's incredibly hard for the human beings to avoid each other. On some days I know too much information about virtually everyone I see, and sometimes it's only the unpleasant events I remember when someone first comes into view: the miscarriages, the drunken rages, the sloppy midwinter infidelities. It's like looking around at everyone in your therapist's waiting room and knowing their secrets. And if that weren't bad enough, people feel compelled to tell me about themselves because they figure I'm going to hear about it sooner or later so they'll just get it out of the way with a preemptive gossip strike.

So it was with a mixture of dread and relief that I saw Weasel at the end of the harbor ramp. Relief because I knew that Weasel would know where Max was and dread because I knew he would make me jump through several dozen hoops before he gave me the whole story.

"Yo, Cecil, what's up, man?"

"Nothing much, Wease. Hey, you seen Max around?"

Weasel stroked his chin as if he were a wine connoisseur and looked straight up into the sky, squinting. He held that pose for several moments.

Finally I looked up into the sky myself. Weasel was a good old-fashioned pot smoker from a village up the coast called Cold Storage. I thought maybe this staring into the sky was some sort of arcane Cold Storage custom.

Finally he spoke. "Whoa, man, Max is really kind of fucked up. You know what I'm saying? He was charging around like a pit bull. I gave him a quaalude and let him kick back in my boat for a while."

"You're a great American, Weaze," I said, still staring up at a ragged-looking raven flying overhead. It looked like the big black bird had something tied around one of its legs: a red thread maybe. I tried to figure it out, but the bird disappeared up over the Alaska Native Brotherhood Hall.

"He called in sick, Cecil. No way that guy was going to show up at school as cranked off as he was." Now Weasel was following my gaze up over the building.

We were both staring off into the distance. When footsteps came rattling down the ramp to the harbor, both Weasel and I looked up as Lori came barreling toward us.

"Hey, have you guys seen the *Alice May* come in?" Lori asked, not looking at either of us. The *Alice May* was Alex's boat: Alex, the new boyfriend, one of the potential recipients of one of Max's nine-millimeter slugs.

Both Weasel and I shook our heads "no" as if we were a couple of stars in the silent movies.

"You seen Max?" I finally asked Lori.

"No," Lori said with a hint of irritation in her voice. "Haven't seen him in a while." Then she looked at me as if daring me to ask the next question.

I was almost about to say something about the

weather when Lori spotted the *Alice May* over at the fuel dock and turned on her heels and walked back up the ramp.

When she was about a hundred feet away, Weasel turned to me and asked, "You ever sleep with her?"

"Not to my certain knowledge, Wease. You?"

"Brrrrrrr," was all he said, and he shrugged his shoulders.

Twenty years ago Lori came to Sitka to fish for the season. She was young and athletic. She wore tight jeans, tank tops, and wraparound shades. She had been the kind of beautiful woman who looked like she was ready for anything, and now, of course, most of the things she had been ready for had happened. Now she had no husband, a daughter in the fifth grade, and the weather had taken its toll on her face. She was still a good hand, smart and strong, and if she was going to end up with an interest in a good boat with a skipper who had the permits and the capital, she was going to have to make a move pretty soon. Weasel and I would not even register on her radar as men. We needed better clothes and bigger boats.

"Listen, Weasel, I want you to keep Max on your boat. If he has a gun with him I want you to take it away. Make him sleep. Keep him on the boat. Can you do that?"

"He said he had to go to the fifth-grade play tonight." Weasel was still looking up toward Lori.

"Under no circumstances can he go to the play. You stay with him, all right? Here . . ." I reached into my pocket and gave him two twenty-dollar bills. "Get some movies. Get a pizza. Whatever. Don't let him go to the play at the elementary school."

"Cool," Weasel said as he took the money and walked back to the boat.

I walked home just as a cloud rolled over the town. It was a single dark cloud and a few flakes of fine snow zigzagged down between the old wooden buildings. Then it passed and the world glittered again with the hope of springtime.

Each year the fifth grade produced a Shakespeare play, and it was one of the big cultural events of spring, like the herring coming in to spawn or the first day of Little League practice. It was something to look forward to. The teachers spent many extra hours with the kids, helping them through their lines, and each year the parents put in weeks of time on the costumes and the sets. This year Lori's daughter was playing Titania, Queen of the Fairies, and one of Max's special-needs kids named Finn was playing Snout the tinker, who also played the wall in the rustic play within the play. Finn had poor hearing and even though he wore hearing aids he was learning American sign language. The fifth grader's speaking voice was loud, and his intonation was uncertain, so that even if the kids didn't tease him Finn could tell from their expressions they thought he was weird. Max worked many hours after school with Finn. The boy struggled to understand and speak his lines properly. He sat and squinted at his rumpled script and manfully recited the lines, slowly and clearly, as if he were mouthing the words in a foreign language. So when he said, "In this same interlude it doth befall, That I, one Snout by name, present a wall," his face stayed screwed up in anxiety and his voice boomed the words like bricks falling from the sky. Yet Max worked with him each day, and finally the teacher allowed Finn to read from his script for the performance, and this allowed him to relax a bit. But he would still be expecting Max to be in the audience.

Lori would certainly be there. Her daughter was perfectly cast as the fairy queen, and she would be a beautiful sight. Lori's daughter had in fact enjoyed the fifth-grade play so much that somehow she had found a way to repeat the entire fifth grade, so she was in fact the only second-year veteran in the cast. Max had met Lori during the rehearsals for last year's play. He had first talked to Lori while helping her daughter get ready for her role as Kate in *Taming of the Shrew*. They had both stayed late to help put the props away and had struck up a conversation, which had led them several weeks later to spending the night together down on Max's boat.

No one was home at my house. Toddy was working in the kitchen of the Pioneer Home and Jane Marie had taken Blossom to see her grandma in Juneau. The house was as quiet as a bower in the woods. Sun shown on the water in the harbor, and sunlight rippled up the walls of our living room. I lay down on the couch to read a short magazine article and fell asleep in the sunshine where I dreamed of fairies flitting through the woods.

I woke up with a start and checked my watch. It was six thirty, and I decided to walk down to the Chinese restaurant and get some hot-and-sour soup. The wind was blowing from the southwest, and a paper cup rattled down the pavement like a cartoon mouse. I was still kind of groggy when I walked past the big windows of the Pioneer Bar. I would have missed him sitting there if it hadn't been for someone breaking a glass on the floor inside. I turned to look and there was Weasel—without Max.

"What'd you do with him?" I asked, once I pushed my way through the herring fishermen crowded around the bar.

"He's cool," Weasel said, smiling up at me as if I were coming in for a drink. "He said he's just going to kick back and watch *Reservoir Dogs* on the boat. He's cool, Cecil."

"So you left him there. Where's the gun?"

"Don't have to snap at me, dude. I took it from him like you said."

"What did you do with the gun, Wease?" I was squinting my eyes shut, hoping, I suppose, to change the answer I knew was coming.

"I put it under my pillow, dude. It's cool anyway. He said he's not going to the play."

"Yeah, and I bet he'd never think of looking under your pillow for the gun. Christ!" I turned and walked out. Once I was outside, I started running. The school was about a quarter mile away, and I had about ten minutes before the play started.

When I got there, Robby Ellis as Ageus was standing on stage with his arms spread wide as if he were measuring a fish, saying, "Full of vexation come I, with complaint against my child, My daughter Hermia . . ." so I knew I hadn't missed much.

Max was sitting in the middle of the audience on the aisle. He looked to be a bit wobbly on his chair, but he was holding it together. His hands were in

his jacket pockets. Two rows ahead of him sat Lori
and Alex. Lori had both her hands in Alex's lap, and
if she pushed a bit closer to him she could have given
up her seat to one of us who had to stand in the back.

I settled into the back of the crowded lunchroom-
turned-theater to watch the play and keep my eye
on my principal players. I have to admit, if it weren't
so messy I might have enjoyed seeing Alex get shot.
He was an easy person to dislike from a distance.
He was thin and dark with one of those wispy goa-
tees. He had made good choices by buying all the
fishing permits he could before the prices went
through the roof, so now he was a millionaire and
could earn money by leasing his permits if he didn't
feel like fishing. Alex had a palapa in Puerto Villarta
and a ski lodge in Jackson Hole. He liked to lord
his Spanish accent over you while eating at the local
Mexican restaurant. He was wearing a beret, for
chrissake. I would have shot him myself given half
a chance.

But it would have been messy at the elementary
school.

The scenes changed, and Lori's daughter came onstage. The bare trees were strung with crepe paper
and tiny Christmas lights creating a believable fairy
land. Lori saw her daughter and almost wiggled
right up into Alex's lap. She gave a little wave
toward the stage, which the Queen of the Fairies hau-
tily ignored. Now Bottom has been turned into an
ass, and she rises up magically in love with him.
Here the queen says, "What angels wake me from
my flow'ry bed?" but unfortunately the actress
sounded mildly pissed off, as if she were going to

throw a shoe at Bottom. For there are many things that the magic of theater can transform, but the ability of a fifth-grade girl to announce her love for a boy wearing his brother's donkey head from Halloween is not one of them.

But of course everyone loved the play. Parents clapped and elbowed each other out of the way with their camcorders. Max never applauded, even when Finn read his lines perfectly in the first act. Max kept twitching in his seat, nervously watching Lori and Alex snuggling a couple of rows ahead.

But finally the rustics came out to put on *Pyramus and Thisbe* for the duke. Finn was there in his cumbersome wall costume. He looked mortified at first and clearly was aware that he was the only one in the cast who was reading his lines. He was red in the face when he read the first part of the speech, and then he stopped because it looked as if he were going to cry. The lunchroom was quiet. Everyone could smell the spilled milk and the boiled vegetables in the air. We leaned forward and waited while Finn lowered his paper and spoke from memory, gesturing with one hand to his clumsy costume of a wall, and with the other making a plausible chink.

"This loam, this roughcast, and this stone doth show, that I am that same wall; the truth is so. And this the cranny is, right and sinister, through which the fearful lovers are to whisper."

Max was openly crying now, and in his right hand I could see that he was pulling back the hammer of the gun. I started walking down the middle aisle crouched low so I wouldn't block the parents' view.

I came up to his side, and Max looked at me through his tears. "Didn't he do great?" he said.

"Yeah," I said. "Come on, Max. Let's go outside for a minute."

"But it's not over," he said. I reached my hand up and I could feel the muscles in his arm tighten.

"You know, Cecil, the rustics are always the best in these plays. Bottom, Quince, Snout . . . You know . . ." He pointed with his chin toward the stage, where Alex Carlton as Flute was dressed as a girl holding Jason Keebles's head in his lap. "Asleep, my love? What, dead, my dove?"

For some reason I found myself crying then. I don't really know why, but I felt some unexpected empathy for all the kids who were awkwardly saying their lines in a play they didn't quite understand.

Maybe Max was right. The rustics are always the best.

Then Robin Goodfellow bid us all good night, and suddenly there was clapping. The entire cast was onstage, bowing and mugging for the audience. Lori and Alex were the first on their feet for the standing ovation. Her daughter barely acknowledged the cheers of the crowd. Max stood up but kept his hand in his pocket. Then Finn came onstage to loud applause and whistling. Some of the whistling came from Max, but he kept his hands in his pockets. Lori was not clapping anymore, but was whispering something in Alex's ear.

Max started to take the gun out of his pocket, but I jammed my hand toward him to stop it. As I did, it went off.

The sound of a gunshot in a school auditorium may be one of the loudest noises in creation. People screamed and ducked. No one knew where the shot had come from. Max looked at me with a strange mixture of sadness and surprise. He looked at the ragged hole in the chair in front of him where the bullet had passed without harm. He started to take the gun out again, and again I reached for it.

"No, Max. This is a comedy," I said.

Then I reached into his pocket, and as he pulled the trigger, the hammer fell on the fleshy part of my hand between thumb and forefinger. Blood started to spurt even before I could jerk my hand out of his pocket.

In pain I jerked my hand back. "This really, really hurts," I said cleverly.

"I'm sorry, Cecil," Max said, as people began to stick their heads above their seats to see me standing in the middle of the lunchroom with Max's gun dangling from my hand like an angry rat.

So, when the one kind person in the place gave me the blue towel to stop the bleeding, I was in handcuffs. The lights of the police cars were dazzling my eyes, and I was watching the mountains floating above town, wishing I could rise up out of the parking lot and fly to one of their summits. There would be lawyers and charges filed. Eventually it would all sort itself out when Max explained what had happened. But that night, as I sat there on the curb in handcuffs looking around my wild little town, I was almost blinded by the loveliness of it all.

About the Authors

Michael Armstrong was born in Virginia in 1956, grew up in Tampa, Florida, and moved to Anchorage, Alaska, in 1979. He has lived in Homer since 1994. Michael attended the Clarion Science Fiction Writers Workshop and received a BA from New College of Florida. His first novel, *After the Zap*, was his MFA thesis at the University of Alaska Anchorage. Michael's short fiction has been published in *Asimov's*, *F & SF*, *Fiction Quarterly*, and various anthologies. His other novels include *Aqvig* and *The Hidden War*. He's taught creative writing, English, and dog mushing at UAA. He is a reporter for the *Homer News*, where his beats include crime, politics, science, and religion. Michael and his wife, Jenny Stroyeck, live in a cabin on Diamond Ridge above Homer, which they share with a large cat and an even larger dog.

Margaret Coel is the award-winning author of both fiction and nonfiction on the American West. Her

Wind River mystery novels set among the Arapahos have received the Willa Award for Best Novel of the West, the Colorado Book Award, and have been on the *New York Times* bestseller list. *Killing Raven,* published in 2003, is the latest novel in the series. Margaret's short stories and articles have appeared in numerous anthologies and in national publications. A lifelong Westerner, Margaret lives in Boulder, Colorado.

Mike Doogan is a third-generation Alaskan who lives in Anchorage with his wife, Kathy. Doogan is the author of two books of nonsense about Alaska and the editor of a collection of essays about life in the far north. His first mystery story, "War Can Be Murder," won the 2003 Robert L. Fish Award from the Mystery Writers of America.

Loren D. Estleman has published more than fifty novels in the mystery, historical Western, and mainstream genres. His Amos Walker detective series has earned four Notable Book of the Year mentions from the *New York Times Book Review,* and *The Master Executioner* was featured by *Publishers Weekly* in "The Year in Books" (2001). The recipient of sixteen national writing awards, Estleman has been nominated for the Edgar Allan Poe Award, England's Silver Dagger Award, the National Book Award, and the Pulitzer Prize. His latest Amos Walker novel, *Poison Blonde,* is currently available. In 2002, Estleman was presented with the honorary degree of Doctor of Humane Letters by his alma mater, Eastern Michigan

University. He lives in Michigan with his wife, author Deborah Morgan.

Laurie R. King's first novel, *The Beekeeper's Apprentice* was written in 1987, although it was not published until 1994. Laurie has averaged a book a year since she began writing. In 1997, as recognition of her application of her master's degree in divinity studies to fiction, she was granted an honorary doctorate from the Church Divinity School of the Pacific, her Berkeley seminary. The award sits proudly on a shelf with the 1993 Edgar for Best First Novel (for *A Grave Talent*, 1993), the 2002 Macavity for *Folly*, the Creasey dagger from England's Crime Writer's Association (also for *A Grave Talent*), and the 1995 Nero award (*A Monstrous Regiment of Women*). She has also received the Nevermore and the Gail Rich awards, and has been nominated for two other Edgars (for *With Child* and the short story "Paleta Man"), an Anthony, an Agatha, a Macavity, and England's Orange Prize. Her novels are published in eighteen languages, and are edging up toward their second million in sales worldwide.

Writer, photographer, and former East Africa bush guide, **Skye K. Moody**'s latest mystery/thriller, *Medusa*, is called "a page turner" by *Booklist*. Moody's first novel in her Venus Diamond mystery series, *Rain Dance*, was nominated for the Friends of Mystery Spotted Owl award. Her third novel in the series, *Wildcrafters*, received a *Kirkus* starred review. Her first book of nonfiction, *Hillbilly Women*, was adapted for the stage in New York City and received a *Mademoiselle* magazine "Woman of the Year" award. Her work as a journalist and photojournalist has taken her around the world numerous times. Skye's second book of nonfiction, *Fruits of Our Labor: Soviet & American Workers Talk About Making a Living*, received a National Endowment for the Humanities president's award. Her seventh novel, *The Good Diamond*, is scheduled for release in summer 2004.

Father Brad Reynolds, S.J., is the author of the Mark Townsend mystery novels. His work as a writer and photographer has appeared in magazines and newspapers all over the nation, including *National Geographic*, *America* magazine, *American Scholar*, the *Seattle Times*, and the *Anchorage Daily News*. He resides in Portland, Oregon, and in Toksook Bay whenever he can.

S. J. Rozan is the author of nine crime novels, one of which, *Winter and Night*, won the Edgar, Macavity, and Nero awards for Best Novel. Her work has also won the Shamus and Anthony for Best Novel and the Shamus for Best Short Story. S. J. has served on the National Board of Mystery Writers of America and is currently on the National Board of Sisters in Crime, and has just been elected to a two-year term as President of Private Eye Writers of America. Her new book, *Absent Friends*, has just been published by Delacorte.

James Sarafin is a lawyer who lives in Anchorage and visits the rest of Alaska whenever he can. His previous fiction, "The Word for Breaking August

Sky," won a ghost story contest sponsored by Doubleday and the Robert L. Fish award for best first mystery story from the Mystery Writers of America.

Dana Stabenow is the author of twenty-one novels and the Alaska Traveler column in *Alaska* magazine, as well as various short stories, essays, and the occasional vitriolic guest editorial in the *Anchorage Daily News*. The first Kate Shugak novel won an Edgar award, and the fourteenth, *A Taint in the Blood,* comes out from Minotaur in September, 2004. Dana edits anthologies, she cohosts the radio book club Book Talk Alaska, is the co-chair of Bouchercon 2007, and obviously has no life.

John Straley is a private investigator and the author of the Cecil Younger series of Alaskan mysteries. His first book, *The Woman Who Married a Bear,* won the Shamus award for best first mystery in 1993. He has lived in Sitka, Alaska, for the past twenty-five years.

The Mysterious North

12 COLD CRIMES IN ALASKA FROM THE HOTTEST NAMES IN MYSTERY

Sue Henry
Anne Perry
S.J. Rozan
Dana Stabenow
John Straley
Kate Grilley
Michael Armstrong
Donna Andrews
Mike Doogan
Brad Reynolds
Kim Rich
James Sarafin

Edited by Dana Stabenow

0-451-20742-4

Available wherever books are sold or at
www.penguin.com

s012